FROM THE PAGES OF
THE SOULS OF BLACK FOLK

The problem of the Twentieth Century is the problem of the color-line. (page 3)

To be a poor man is hard, but to be a poor race in a land of dollars is the very bottom of hardships. (page 12)

We the darker ones come even now not altogether empty-handed: there are to-day no truer exponents of the pure human spirit of the Declaration of Independence than the American Negroes. (page 15)

The opposition to Negro education in the South was at first bitter, and showed itself in ashes, insult, and blood; for the South believed an educated Negro to be a dangerous Negro. (page 29)

I have called my tiny community a world, and so its isolation made it; and yet there was among us but a half-awakened common consciousness, sprung from common joy and grief, at burial, birth, or wedding; from a common hardship in poverty, poor land, and low wages; and above all, from the sight of the Veil that hung between us and Opportunity. (page 53)

In the midst, then, of the larger problem of Negro education sprang up the more practical question of work, the inevitable economic quandary that faces a people in the transition from slavery to freedom, and especially those who make that change amid hate and prejudice, lawlessness and ruthless competition. (page 70)

There stand in the South two separate worlds; and separate not simply in the higher realms of social intercourse, but also in church and school, on railway and street-car, in hotels and theatres, in streets and city sections, in books and newspapers, in asylums and jails, in hospitals and graveyards. (page 72)

We seldom study the condition of the Negro to-day honestly and carefully. It is so much easier to assume that we know it all. Or perhaps, having already reached conclusions in our own minds, we are loth to have them disturbed by facts. (page 99)

America is not another word for Opportunity to *all* her sons.
(page 104)

It is, then, the strife of all honorable men of the twentieth century to see that in the future competition of races the survival of the fittest shall mean the triumph of the good, the beautiful, and the true; that we may be able to preserve for future civilization all that is really fine and noble and strong, and not continue to put a premium on greed and impudence and cruelty. (page 117)

Some day the Awakening will come, when the pent-up vigor of ten million souls shall sweep irresistibly toward the Goal, out of the Valley of the Shadow of Death, where all that makes life worth living—Liberty, Justice, and Right—is marked "For White People Only." (page 146)

Herein lies the tragedy of the age: not that men are poor,—all men know something of poverty; not that men are wicked,—who is good? not that men are ignorant,—what is Truth? Nay, but that men know so little of men. (page 161)

Little of beauty has America given the world save the rude grandeur God himself stamped on her bosom; the human spirit in this new world has expressed itself in vigor and ingenuity rather than in beauty. And so by fateful chance the Negro folk-song—the rhythmic cry of the slave—stands to-day not simply as the sole American music, but as the most beautiful expression of human experience born this side the seas. (page 178)

W. E. B. DU BOIS

THE SOULS OF BLACK FOLK

With an Introduction and Notes by
Farah Jasmine Griffin

GEORGE STADE
CONSULTING EDITORIAL DIRECTOR

JB

BARNES & NOBLE CLASSICS
NEW YORK

ℬ

BARNES & NOBLE CLASSICS
NEW YORK

Published by Barnes & Noble Books
122 Fifth Avenue
New York, NY 10011

www.barnesandnoble.com/classics

The Souls of Black Folk was first published in 1903.

Originally published in trade paperback format in 2003 by Barnes & Noble Classics
with new Introduction, Notes, Biography, Chronology, Inspired By,
Comments & Questions, and For Further Reading.
This hardcover edition published in 2005.

Introduction, Notes, and For Further Reading
Copyright © 2003 by Farah Jasmine Griffin.

Note on W. E. B. Du Bois, The World of W. E. B. Du Bois and *The Souls of Black Folk*,
Inspired by *The Souls of Black Folk*, and Comments & Questions
Copyright © 2003 by Barnes & Noble, Inc.

The Souls of Black Folk
ISBN-13: 978-1-59308-171-3
ISBN-10: 1-59308-171-5
LC Control Number 2004110473

Produced and published in conjunction with:
Fine Creative Media, Inc.
322 Eighth Avenue
New York, NY 10001

Michael J. Fine, President and Publisher

Printed in the United States of America

QM

5   7   9   10   8   6

W. E. B. DU BOIS

William Edward Burghardt Du Bois was born on February 23, 1868, in Great Barrington, Massachusetts. His father left shortly after his birth, and Du Bois was raised by his mother and grew up in New England. While in high school, he excelled in academics and reported for New York newspapers, and began to discover the social inequities that blacks were expected to accept. Under the guidance of his high school principal, Du Bois won a scholarship to Fisk University, the country's preeminent black university, where he developed an interest in African-American history. He earned a second bachelor's degree at Harvard University, then pursued graduate studies in African-American history at Harvard, devoting himself to the study of black culture in America.

Du Bois was the first African American to receive a Ph.D. from Harvard. His doctoral thesis, *The Suppression of the African Slave Trade*, was published as a book in 1896, and in 1899 he published *The Philadelphia Negro*, the first sociological study of African Americans. Du Bois's belief that social science could help us find answers to the question of race and the "problem of the color-line" led him to publish, between 1897 and 1903, a series of significant essays in a range of widely read periodicals. He taught sociology at the University of Pennsylvania and economics and history at Atlanta University in Georgia.

In the early years of the twentieth century, when the topic of civil rights for blacks was already part of the national discourse, Du Bois's view of what was best for the movement met with opposition from various groups, both white and black. Among his black ideological contenders was Booker T. Washington, founder of the Tuskegee Institute, whose gradualist policy clashed with Du Bois's demand for immediate equal rights, regardless of race or gender. Despite the differences of opinion within the movement, over the course of Du Bois's lifetime substantive change occurred. In 1909 Du Bois co-founded the National Association for the Advancement of Colored People; he served as its director of publicity and research and the editor of its magazine, *The Crisis*.

Du Bois realized that integration and social equity for blacks would not happen quickly in the United States, and he grew increasingly disenchanted with America. He joined the Communist Party in 1961 and subsequently renounced his U.S. citizenship. A chance to leave the country came when Ghana's President Kwame Nkrumah invited Du Bois to move to Ghana and edit the *Encyclopedia Africana*. Du Bois settled in the city of Accra, where he spent his final years. Six months after becoming a citizen of Ghana, he died, on August 27, 1963.

W. E. B. Du Bois is remembered as a leading civil rights leader of the first half of the twentieth century. With his groundbreaking treatise *The Souls of Black Folk*, published in 1903, he intended to reveal the "strange meaning of being black here in the dawning of the Twentieth Century." On the day after Du Bois's death, as the March on Washington began, Martin Luther King, Jr., eulogized him as a pioneer for civil rights. Du Bois left a political and social legacy that continues today, and his works are a vital part of American studies.

TABLE OF CONTENTS

THE WORLD OF W. E. B. DU BOIS
AND *THE SOULS OF BLACK FOLK*

1865 The Civil War ends, and the Thirteenth Amendment to the U.S. Constitution abolishes slavery. In the South, implementation of racial segregation, or "Jim Crow" laws, begins. The Freedmen's Bureau is established to protect the economic interests of the freed slaves.

1866 The first branch of the Ku Klux Klan is established in Pulaski, Tennessee. The American Missionary Association establishes Fisk University in Nashville, Tennessee, for former slaves.

1867 When most southern states refuse to ratify the proposed Fourteenth Amendment, designed to protect the rights of black citizens, Congress passes the Reconstruction Acts, which divide the South into five jurisdictions and require new state constitutions to include universal manhood suffrage.

1868 William Edward Burghardt Du Bois is born on February 23 in Great Barrington, Massachusetts, to Alfred Du Bois and Mary Silvina Burghardt. Soon after his birth, Alfred leaves home, and William is raised mostly by his mother. The Fourteenth Amendment to the Constitution grants the freed slaves citizenship and guarantees their civil rights.

1870 The Fifteenth Amendment gives black men the right to vote.

1880 While attending Great Barrington High School, Du Bois works as the western Massachusetts correspondent for the *New York Age*, the *New York Globe*, and the *Springfield Republican*.

1881 Booker T. Washington founds the Tuskegee Institute in Alabama; the school emphasizes industrial training as a way for blacks to gain economic independence.

1884 Du Bois graduates as valedictorian of his class and wins a scholarship to Fisk University.

1885 He enrolls at Fisk and serves as editor of the *Fisk Herald*, the college newspaper. His summer job teaching in the school districts of rural Tennessee exposes him to the reality of the Jim Crow laws and sparks in him an interest in civil rights. He receives his Bachelor of Arts degree in 1888.

1888 Du Bois enters Harvard University as a junior.

1890 He graduates with honors from Harvard in the spring and begins his graduate studies in African-American history at Harvard in the fall.

1892 Du Bois receives a Slater Fund fellowship and travels to Germany to study at the University of Berlin for the next two years.

1894 He teaches Latin and Greek at Wilberforce University in Ohio.

1895 In a speech delivered in Atlanta, Georgia, Booker T. Washington urges blacks to place economic independence before social equality, a position that many black leaders, including Du Bois, oppose. Harvard awards Du Bois a Ph.D., making him the first African American to earn the degree. Harvard University Press publishes his dissertation, *The Suppression of the African Slave Trade*.

1896 The U.S. Supreme Court rules in favor of "separate but equal" segregation laws in *Plessey v. Ferguson*. The National Association of Colored Women is established in Washington, D.C. Du Bois marries Nina Gomer and moves to Philadelphia to teach sociology at the University of Pennsylvania.

1897 Du Bois moves to Georgia to teach economics and history at Atlanta University.

1899 He publishes *The Philadelphia Negro*, the first sociological study of African Americans.

1900 Booker T. Washington organizes the National Negro Business League to promote black economic independence.

1903 Du Bois publishes *The Souls of Black Folk*, a treatise that includes an attack on Booker T. Washington's "accommodating" policy and Du Bois's solution to the "race problem."

1905 Du Bois founds the Niagara Movement and serves as its general secretary. The group, made up of black leaders, promotes racial equality.

1909 Du Bois's *John Brown* is published. The 1908 lynching of two blacks in Springfield, Illinois, leads to the formation of the National Association for the Advancement of Colored People (NAACP). Du Bois is appointed the NAACP's director of publicity and research and is elected, the only black, to the board of directors. He founds and edits *The Crisis*, the NAACP's monthly journal, in which he criticizes segregation and gender inequality, stating that "every argument for Negro suffrage is an argument for women's suffrage."

1914 Marcus Garvey founds the Universal Negro Improvement Association to promote "the spirit of race pride" and encourage African Americans to participate in a mass exodus back to Africa.

1915 Du Bois's *The Negro* is published. The NAACP leads a boycott of D. W. Griffith's film *The Birth of a Nation*, which stereotypes blacks.

1919 Du Bois organizes the Pan-African Congress in Paris.

1920 The NAACP awards Du Bois its Spingarn Medal for achievement. The Nineteenth Amendment gives women the right to vote. Du Bois publishes *Darkwater: Voices from Within the Veil*.

1923 Du Bois visits Africa for the first time.

1924 Du Bois's book *The Gift of Black Folk: The Negroes in the Making of America* is published.

1934 Du Bois begins to subscribe to Marxist ideology and its interpretation of race relations. He resigns from the NAACP over the issue of voluntary segregation, which he favors over integration. He returns to Atlanta University as chairman of the department of sociology.

1935 Du Bois publishes *Black Reconstruction in America: An Essay Toward a History of the Part Which Black Folk*

Played in the Attempt to Reconstruct Democracy in Amer-ica, 1860–1880.

1941 Philip Randolph and Baynard Rustin's March on Washington for Jobs and Equal Participation in National Defense is called off when President Franklin D. Roosevelt issues the Fair Employment Act to prohibit racial discrimination by private employers.

1944 Du Bois returns to the NAACP as director of publicity and research.

1945 On behalf of the NAACP, Du Bois attends the founding conference of the United Nations in San Francisco. At the Fifth Pan-African Congress in Manchester, England, he meets with the African leaders Kwame Nkrumah, president of Ghana, and Jomo Kenyatta, the first president of Kenya.

1948 Du Bois is dismissed from the NAACP. He is appointed co-chairman of the Council on African Affairs, which monitors political events in Africa and supports African liberation movements.

1950 Du Bois is appointed chairman of the Peace Information Center in New York City and is nominated by the New York Progressive Party for the U.S. Senate. His wife, Nina, dies.

1951 At the height of McCarthyism, Du Bois is indicted as a spy for the Soviet Union and is put on trial. Although he was acquitted of "subversive activities" charges brought against him by the Justice Department, he is denied a passport until 1958. Du Bois marries Shirley Graham.

1952 He publishes *In Battle for Peace: The Story of My 83rd Birthday*.

1954 The Supreme Court's ruling in *Brown v. Board of Education* prohibits segregation in public schools.

1955 On December 1, Rosa Parks is arrested in Montgomery, Alabama, for refusing to give up her seat on a public bus to a white man. As a result, Martin Luther King, Jr., leads a boycott.

1957 Martin Luther King helps found the Southern Christian Leadership Conference, an organization that promotes a nonviolent struggle for civil rights.

1958 Du Bois is awarded the Lenin Peace Prize.

1961 He joins the Communist Party. When he is invited by Ghana's President Nkrumah to move to Ghana and edit the *Encyclopedia Africana*, Du Bois leaves the United States for good.

1962 He renounces his American citizenship.

1963 Du Bois becomes a citizen of Ghana. He dies on August 27 and is buried in Accra, Ghana. On August 28, on the eve of the March on Washington, Martin Luther King leads a eulogy to Du Bois.

1964 The Civil Rights Act is passed to make voting easier for African Americans but is thwarted by the power of the states to impose registration restrictions.

1965 With much opposition from politicians in the South, the Voting Rights Act is passed, empowering the national government to override state-imposed limitations on the right of African Americans to vote.

INTRODUCTION

The task of "introducing" *The Souls of Black Folk* is an awesome one for at least two reasons. First, there is the historical and literary significance of the text itself. As the distinguished scholar Arnold Rampersad notes: "If all of a nation's literature may stem from one book, as Hemingway implied about *The Adventures of Huckleberry Finn*, then it can as accurately be said that all of Afro-American literature of a creative nature has proceeded from Du Bois's comprehensive statement on the nature of people in *The Souls of Black Folk*" (Rampersad, p. 89). Second, a number of brilliant minds have already written about *The Souls of Black Folk*, among them Rampersad, Nathan Huggins, Herbert Aptheker, Cornel West, Eric Sundquist, Hazel Carby, Manning Marable, Houston Baker, Robert Stepto, and Henry Louis Gates. That so many distinguished writers have focused attention on *The Souls of Black Folk* is only one measure of the continuing importance of this collection of fourteen essays by one of the major thinkers of the twentieth century. Clearly, a book of such complexity and magnitude demands and can withstand a number of diverse readings.

Since its publication in the spring of 1903, *The Souls of Black Folk* has become a founding text of African-American studies: Its insistence on an interdisciplinary understanding of black life, on historically grounded and philosophically sound analysis, on the scholar's role as advocate and activist, and on close study of the cultural products of the objects of examination—all became tenets of the study of black life in the United States. In its insistence that any understanding of the United States has to be attentive to the contributions and struggles of black Americans, *Souls* has also contributed to a revision of American history and culture. Furthermore, in recent years the book has spoken to students of postcolonial and critical race studies as well. However, the text was never meant for a purely academic audience. And perhaps here lies its greatest contribution: It is a brilliant, multifaceted, learned book addressed to an intelligent lay audience as a means of informing social and political action.

Du Bois's best-known intellectual contributions are introduced here: "double consciousness," "the Talented Tenth," "the Veil," and the Du Bois versus Washington debate (see "Comments and Questions," p. 205) that has characterized our understandings of black leadership throughout the twentieth century continue to be the major contributions of the text, and they have been explored and written about at length. With these concepts, Du Bois provided a basic vocabulary and foundational language for scholars and students of African-American history and culture. Double consciousness defines a psychological sense experienced by African Americans whereby they possess a national identity, "an American," within a nation that despises their racial identity, "a Negro." It also refers to the ability of black Americans to see themselves only through the eyes of white Americans, to measure their intelligence, beauty, and sense of self-worth by standards set by others. Du Bois defined the Talented Tenth as "leadership of the Negro race in America by a trained few." In *The Souls of Black Folk*, he envisions this educated elite at the vanguard of racial uplift. Later in his life he disavowed this theory.

Du Bois's ideas have been explored in detail, but only recently, through the efforts of black feminist writers such as Hazel Carby, Joy James, Beverly Guy-Sheftall, and Nellie McKay, has his notion of black leadership as fundamentally masculine received scholarly attention. These writers have opened up new ways of reading *The Souls of Black Folk*.

Another distinctive feature of the book is Du Bois's consistent use of the first person, his insertion of himself as a subjective student of and participant in black life and culture. In the opening pages, he introduces himself to his reader in the following manner: "And, finally, need I add that I who speak here am bone of the bone and flesh of the flesh of them that live within the Veil." With this Old Testament allusion Du Bois establishes his relationship to the people about whom he writes as one of sacred matrimony: of man to woman, of husband to wife. In Genesis 2:23 Adam says of Eve: "This is now bone of my bones, and flesh of my flesh: she shall be called Woman, because she was taken out of Man." Du Bois's use of the Veil, the enduring metaphor of the book, not only refers to that which separates black from white, to that through which black folk peer at the world, but it might also be the veil that covers women's faces in many religious traditions. So those who live beneath the Veil, the black folk, might be gendered as female—ever mysterious, unknowing, and unknowable—while the black elite, intellectuals and leaders, are gendered male. Du Bois promises readers that he has "stepped within the veil" and raised it to expose "deeper recesses." While he elsewhere claims to have lived behind the Veil throughout his life, here he positions himself as someone who dwells both within and just outside its cover—and, most important, as the investigator, the communicator, the native informant who can render the mysteries behind the Veil known.

The fourteen chapters that follow this promise represent Du Bois's best efforts to make known the strivings and yearnings of black folk in the United States of America. In the first nine chapters, all of which were revised from previously published essays, Du Bois turns to academic fields of knowledge such as history, sociology, and philosophy to assist in his interpretation of the complexity of black lives. While these fields help to provide the framework for his analysis, his prose is shaped by biblical and mythological narrative, metaphor and allusion. In the last five chapters, only one of which had been published previously, though they are still informed by philosophy, sociology, and history, Du Bois turns to elegy, poetry, religion, and song. In doing so, he attempts to better understand and express the longings of those who live beneath the Veil; consequently, he turns his critical eye to black people and their culture in an effort to comprehend how they have made sense of the absurdity of their situation.

And yet, there is something that remains as alien to him as the lyrics he recalls hearing as a child, lyrics passed down from a West African female ancestor,

Do bana coba, gene me, gene me!
Do bana coba, gene me, gene me!
Bend' nuli, nuli, nuli, nuli, bend'le.

As Du Bois renders these lyrics and transcribes the melody they appear as a modified blues form, with the repetition of the first two lines before the resolution of the third. Furthermore, he transcribes the song in the complex, dark key of D-flat, a key that is favored by African-American improvisers and that is quite distinct from the paradigmatic key of C. Of the song he writes: "Two hundred years it has travelled down to us and we sing it to our children, knowing as little as our fathers what its words may mean, but knowing well the meaning of its music" (p. 180). Later he names it "the voice of exile." David Levering Lewis, Du Bois's biographer, notes that the song's lyrics have stumped linguists, but his own research suggests that it may be a "Wolof song from Senegambia about captivity and confinement: 'gene me, gene me' . . . Get me out, get me out!' " (Lewis, pp. 14, 585).

One gets the sense that the connection to the ancestor's music is similar to the New Englander Du Bois's relationship to those rural southern black folk he discovers for the first time in the summer of his eighteenth year when, as a rising junior at Fisk University, he seeks summer employment as a teacher in the hills of Tennessee. This is documented in the book's fourth chapter, "Of the Meaning of Progress."

The young Du Bois who first encounters the rural blacks he has deemed bone of his bone and flesh of his flesh had had little if any contact with the culture of more than 90 percent of African Americans prior to his first trips South. Born in Great Barrington, Massachusetts, on February 23, 1868, three years after the end of the Civil War, and reared in that predominantly white New England town (which could boast but thirty black families) during a period when the American South was going through Reconstruction and its aftermath, the young Du Bois experienced little of this national drama during his childhood. A descendant of Tom Burghardt (an enslaved African who likely won his freedom after fighting in the Battle of Yorktown during the War of Independence) and of generations of free, property-owning blacks, the precocious Du Bois's intellectual talents were early recognized and nurtured by his maternal family as well as by black and white members of his community. Though the color line did exist in Great Barrington, and though his family experienced economic instability after the death of his grandfather and his father's mysterious desertion, the young Du Bois's life was distinctly different from the lives of those southern blacks he would encounter as a young adult. Fisk University, the most prestigious black institution of higher education, gave him his first opportunity to meet a large number of young blacks, many of whom constituted a mulatto elite. The institution served as a threshold to the complex and foreign culture he would attempt to render in *The Souls of Black Folk*.

In 1888 Du Bois earned his bachelor's degree from Fisk, and in 1890 he earned a second bachelor's from Harvard. He studied for two years in Berlin at Friedrich Wilhelm University; during his time there he traveled throughout Europe and for the first time in his life experienced life free of American racial politics. In 1895 he became the first African American to receive a Ph.D. from Harvard; his dissertation in history was published a year later as *The Supression of the African Slave Trade to the United States of America, 1638–1870*, the first volume of the prestigious Harvard Historical Monograph Series.

Du Bois's first teaching position took him to another black institution, Wilberforce College, in Ohio, where he met and married his wife, Nina Gormer. In 1896 he moved to Philadelphia to complete the research for a book that would become one of the first American sociological studies, *The Philadelphia Negro: A Social Study* (1899). Unable to gain employment in elite white institutions such as the University of Pennsylvania, in 1897 Du Bois headed south again to begin his tenure at yet another school for African Americans, Atlanta University. While at Atlanta he oversaw the production of sixteen reports on the economic, political, and cultural conditions of black life. During this period, he wrote most of the essays that would become *The Souls of Black Folk*.

The Souls of Black Folk introduced a unique and singularly eloquent voice to contemporary discourse on race in the United States. It appeared at a time when "separate but equal" had been ruled to be the law of the land in the infamous *Plessy v. Ferguson* decision of 1896. Black southerners had been successfully disenfranchised and were suppressed economically, socially, and politically through Jim Crow segregation, sharecropping, tenant farming, debt-peonage, and the rise of the chain gang. If this were not enough, they were systematically terrorized by white su-

premacist organizations such as the Ku Klux Klan. Thousands of
blacks were lynched between 1880 and 1920. In the midst of all of
this, their supposed racial inferiority was taken for granted in popular culture and academic discourse. Thomas Dixon's white supremacist play *The Leopard's Spots* appeared on Broadway to
large audiences in 1903, and in 1905 Dixon published the best-
selling *The Clansmen*, the basis for D. W. Griffith's film *The Birth
of a Nation* and a praise song to the Ku Klux Klan. This is the context that gave birth to *Souls*.

By the time he published *The Souls of Black Folk*, Du Bois had
established himself as a major scholar and social scientist with an
international reputation. He was widely recognized as one of the
nation's most highly educated citizens and as the leading scholar
of black life in the United States. Throughout his early academic
career, Du Bois remained convinced of the role reason, the social
sciences, and academic research might play in the eradication of
racial ignorance and prejudice. In 1898 he wrote, "At such a time
true lovers of humanity can only hold higher the pure ideals of
science, and continue to insist that if we would solve a problem we
must study it, and that there is but one coward on earth, and that
is the coward that dare not know" (Du Bois, "The Study of Negro
Problems," p. 27).

Living in the American South—where his young son died in
1899 of nasopharyngeal diphtheria, having been denied the med-
ical attention of white doctors, where the black farm worker Sam
Hose was brutally lynched, burned, and mutilated in the same
year, and where the Atlanta riots of 1906 destroyed a middle-class
black community and killed both blacks and whites—Du Bois
came to question the sufficiency of academic knowledge alone to
address the problems facing those who lived within the Veil.

Within the pages of *The Souls of Black Folk* we see a lingering
belief in the power of academic knowledge to invoke social change
and in the possibility offered by contact between "the best of the
black race and the best of whites." However, ultimately *Souls* is a
book about a people's thwarted yearnings for political freedom,
economic and educational opportunity, and the free expression of
their humanity. Misguided leadership, mob violence, racial ignorance, and governmental neglect frustrate these desires. African
Americans' frustrations are best expressed in the failure of Re-

construction, the rise of industrial education, and the tragic figures of Du Bois's deceased child and Alexander Crummell and the fictional John, but perhaps the greatest metaphor of thwarted desire lies in the text's women and their cries for freedom: the grandmother's captivity song, Josie's desire for higher education in "Of the Meaning of Progress," and Jennie's intellectual longings, to which even the author is incapable of giving full expression in "Of the Coming of John." These women are ultimately the black folk—not the exceptional intellectuals Crummell and John or the chosen and sacrificed golden boy child, and certainly not Du Bois himself. The women come closest to representing the longing for freedom, for intellectual and artistic expression, and for transcendence that Du Bois finds best expressed in black religion and song.

Du Bois introduces us to Josie in "Of the Meaning of Progress": "She was a thin, homely girl of twenty, with a dark-brown face and thick, hard hair." She enthusiastically tells Du Bois that "she herself longed to learn,—and thus she ran on, talking fast and loud, with much earnestness and energy." She is his introduction to the "folk" as well as the one who will facilitate Du Bois's navigation of this new landscape. Before long, he is boarding with her family. Josie

> *seemed to be the centre of the family: always busy at service,*
> *or at home, or berry-picking. . . . She had about her a certain*
> *fineness, the shadow of an unconscious moral heroism that*
> *would willingly give all of life to make life broader, deeper,*
> *and fuller for her and hers (p. 50).*

In other words, Josie, who emerges from the folk, has all of the qualities of a leader who emerges from her people. But she is prevented from realizing her ambitions, not for lack of desire or the willingness to work, but because she is the economic and spiritual backbone of her family. When Du Bois returns to visit the family a decade following his last summer with them, he learns of Josie's premature death. Du Bois's description of her death is not the elegiac prose that characterizes "Of the Passing of the First-Born" or "Of Alexander Crummell." Elegy is reserved for the extraordinary. Yet, somehow, Josie's death marks the truest tragedy of black

folk: the lack of opportunity to take advantage of the small possibilities that might exist; the potential for leadership and accomplishment that is never realized. "How shall man measure
Progress there where the dark-faced Josie lies?" asks Du Bois.

If Josie represents the thwarted aspirations of black folk, then
their religion bears the immensity of their hope. Wisely, Du Bois
recognizes the impossibility of truly knowing black southerners
without attempting to understand the power of their faith, even
while he is overwhelmed by its terrible, frightening beauty.

Chapter X, "Of the Faith of the Fathers," is the first systematic
discussion of the history of the black church and the power of religious faith in the lives of black Americans. Du Bois astutely argues that "It is . . . clear that the study of Negro religion is not only
a vital part of the history of the Negro in America, but no uninteresting part of American history" (p. 137).

Du Bois opens the chapter by positing his own cultural and
spiritual distance from rural black worshipers. It is worth quoting
at length:

> *It was out in the country, far from home, far from my foster
> home, on a dark Sunday night. The road wandered from our
> rambling log-house up the stony bed of a creek, past wheat
> and corn, until we could hear dimly across the fields a
> rhythmic cadence of song,—soft, thrilling, powerful, that
> swelled and died sorrowfully in our ears. I was a country
> school-teacher then, fresh from the East, and had never seen
> a Southern Negro revival. To be sure, we in Berkshire were
> not perhaps as stiff and formal as they in Suffolk of olden
> time; yet we were very quiet and subdued, and I know not
> what would have happened those clear Sabbath mornings
> had some one punctuated the sermon with a wild scream, or
> interrupted the long prayer with a loud Amen! And so most
> striking to me, as I approached the village and the little plain
> church perched aloft, was the air of intense excitement that
> possessed that mass of black folk. A sort of suppressed terror
> hung in the air and seemed to seize us,—a pythian madness,
> a demoniac possession, that lent terrible reality to song and
> word. The black and massive form of the preacher swayed
> and quivered as the words crowded to his lips and flew at us*

in singular eloquence. The people moaned and fluttered, and then the gaunt-cheeked brown woman beside me suddenly leaped straight into the air and shrieked like a lost soul, while round about came wail and groan and outcry, and a scene of human passion such as I had never conceived before (pp. 134–135).

The paragraph opens with a description of physical distance: "far," "from," "past." Soon this physical distance will give way to cultural, experiential distance not just of space but also time. Note the adjectives used to describe expressions of religious fervor: "wild," "loud," "madness," "demoniac possession," "terrible," "terror." Again, he closes with "such as I had never conceived before." Not only is this a scene he has never witnessed, it is even beyond his powers of imagination. When Du Bois writes, "so most striking to me, . . . was the air of intense excitement that possessed that mass of black folk," it is an excitement that will infect him, but he remains outside, apart and distant from it. In this way, he is not unlike the character Kabnis, in Jean Toomer's classic novel *Cane* (1923) or the historical figures Charlotte Forten and Rebecca Primus, northern black teachers working in the South. (Who all differ from Richard Wright and James Baldwin, both of whom describe such religious rituals as critical participants.) For Du Bois the scene is "awful." However, throughout the chapter he provides an eloquent and forceful history of the black church as a political and social institution capable of containing the strivings of the mass of black people, and he insists upon its importance in the development of a people and of the nation. He recognizes the power of this faith and its potential to sweep them "out of the Valley of the Shadow of Death," beyond the Veil.

Until that day, it seems that the only way to transcend a place where "all that makes life worth living—Liberty, Justice, and Right—is marked 'For White People Only'" (p. 146) is death itself, the subject of the two chapters that follow: "Of the Passing of the First-Born" and "Of Alexander Crummell." Both of these give us portraits of the lives and deaths of extraordinary individuals whose lives are crushed by the injustices of a racist society: one whose promise is thwarted before he has time to grow up, and the other who meets resistance at every turn. Crummell must confront three temptations as he tries to realize his potential: the temptation of Hate, the temptation of Despair, and the temptation of Doubt. The last one proves to be the most significant in that it is a doubt of his people's desire and ability to better themselves. As a young priest, "the dark young clergyman labored; he wrote his sermons carefully; he intoned his prayers with a soft, earnest voice; he haunted the streets and accosted the wayfarers; he visited the sick and knelt beside the dying," and yet in spite of his most sincere efforts, his "congregation dwindled." The best efforts of the learned young man are not enough for his own people to heed his leadership.

Du Bois follows the sketches of his deceased son and of Alexander Crummell with the only fictional piece in the book—"Of the Coming of John," a story of a young black intellectual who returns to his southern roots only to find himself unable to communicate with his own people and conceived of as a threat by the whites of his hometown. As with the child Burghardt and the adult Crummell, one here senses that Du Bois really knows this figure, identifies with him, and sees himself in the young man's strivings. Du Bois makes this connection between himself and John in a number of ways. First the young John experiences rapture in a northern theater:

> *He sat in a half-maze minding the scene about him; the delicate beauty of the hall, the faint perfume, the moving myriad of men, the rich clothing and low hum of talking seemed all a part of a world so different from his, so strangely more beautiful than anything he had known, that he sat in dreamland, and started when, after a hush, rose high and clear the music of Lohengrin's swan. The infinite beauty of the wail lingered and swept through every muscle of his frame, and put it all a-tune (p. 167).*

This description is not unlike Du Bois's own experiences during his two years in Berlin. Furthermore, when John returns South, he attempts to address a black church congregation:

> *[John] spoke slowly and methodically. . . . A painful hush seized that crowded mass. Little had they understood of*

what he said, for he spoke an unknown tongue. . . . Then at last a low suppressed snarl came from the Amen corner, and an old bent man arose, walked over the seats, and climbed straight up into the pulpit. He was wrinkled and black, with scant gray and tufted hair; his voice and hands shook as with palsy; but on his face lay the intense rapt look of the religious fanatic. He seized the Bible with his rough, huge hands; twice he raised it inarticulate, and then fairly burst into the words, with rude and awful eloquence. He quivered, swayed, and bent; then rose aloft in perfect majesty, till the people moaned and wept, wailed and shouted, and a wild shrieking arose from the corners where all the pent-up feeling of the hour gathered itself and rushed into the air; John never knew clearly what the old man said; he only felt himself held up to scorn and scathing denunciation for trampling on the true Religion, and he realized with amazement that all unknowingly he had put rough, rude hands on something this little world held sacred (pp. 170–171).

Compare this to Du Bois's description of his own first visit to a black southern church. Here the young black intellectual is challenged by the racism of the town's whites and the ignorance of its blacks. He is no longer able to communicate with them and he fails to respect all that they hold dear. Most important, the folk preacher is frustratingly eloquent and inarticulate. John does not understand him but the black congregants do.

As with "Of the Passing of the First-Born" and "Of Alexander Crummell," this chapter too ends with the death of the gifted black man, but not before John murders his former childhood playmate, the white John. An act of a black man protecting a black woman, in this case John's younger sister, from dishonor by a white man leads to the murder of both Johns. It is a trope that returns in later writings by black American artists, most notably Jean Toomer's story "Blood Burning Moon." Hazel Carby notes, "In this struggle over the control of female sexuality and sexual reproduction, John gains self-respect in his own black manhood. . . . The future of Du Bois's imagined black community is to be determined by the nature of the struggle among men over the bodies of women" (Carby, p. 25). For Carby "white and black male desires and hopes violently conflict and result in their mutual destruction" (p. 31).

Significantly, Du Bois knows and can give voice to John's desires and destruction. For John, like Crummell and like Du Bois, is an ambitious, learned young black man who at times feels an unknowing distance from the "flesh of his flesh." Part of the tragedy of John is that his acquisition of knowledge, his brief experience of a different, more intellectual way of life, makes him long for freedom beyond the Veil and creates a distance between himself and his community of origin. John leaves his home to attend a black college; he spends a year in the North to earn extra money, and while there he experiences life in an unsegregated society. He attends the theater and walks crowded urban streets; he is given the opportunity to taste, if briefly, just what that life might be like.

However, the truly thwarted desire of this story is that of John's younger sister, Jennie, who follows him from the church on that fateful night. John looks to her, "remembering with sudden pain how little thought he had given her." As she weeps quietly beside him they have the following exchange:

> *"John," she said, "does it make every one—unhappy when they study and learn lots of things?"*
> *. . . "I am afraid it does," he said.*
> *"And, John, are you glad you studied?"*
> *"Yes," came the answer, slowly but positively.*
> *. . . "I wish I was unhappy,—and—and," putting both arms about his neck, "I think I am, a little, John" (p. 171).*

The young girl is quietly representative of the yearnings of black folk for opportunity and self-expression. She too shares her brother's understanding of the despair of their lives but is not given the opportunity to articulate it. Unlike Crummell or Du Bois or John himself, she shares more with Josie, who embodies both a love of her people, a connection to them, a sense of responsibility for them, and the yearning to know, to live, which will be forever denied her. She remains inarticulate, unable to express her longings and her desires. When accosted by the white John she "stared at him in surprise and confusion,—faltered something inarticulate, and attempted to pass." If death awaits the baby Burghardt, Crummell, and John, the specter of rape forever haunts the young black woman, and even her protests are ineffective in their inarticulateness.

As if trying to address the absence of an articulate statement from the black folk of this book, Du Bois closes his famous volume with one of the most eloquent treatments of black song in all literature. The chapter "The Sorrow Songs" puts forward a highly important and influential theory of black music by paying close attention to both the lyrics and the "sound" of the spirituals. Du Bois writes, "I know that these songs are the articulate message of the slave to the world." And for Du Bois that message is one "of an unhappy people, of the children of disappointment; they tell of death and suffering and unvoiced longing toward a truer world, of misty wanderings and hidden ways" (p. 179). Later he will write that the slaves' message to the world "is naturally veiled and half articulate," but this is as much a consequence of language as it is an attempt of the slaves to keep their true longings for freedom and their communication about acquiring it away from their oppressors. In this instance they are agents of resistance. For the sorrow songs not only communicate a longing for freedom, but they also "breathe a hope—a faith in the ultimate justice of things." In an important discussion of the book, Anthony Monteiro writes, "Du Bois locates the Negro spirituals within the context of the striving for freedom and justice and the realization of a collective self—a peoplehood. He, however, defines the sorrow songs as the central historical narrative of black folk" (Monteiro, p. 231).

For the black folk who created the sorrow songs are not defeated by the temptation of despair, as was the learned priest Crummell. It is not insignificant that this book of the Talented Tenth, of the double consciousness of extraordinary Negroes, of leaders and the led, ends with the articulation of the folk it has claimed to represent. Even as Du Bois's distance from the black folk about whom he writes remains evident throughout this text, *The Souls of Black Folk* is nonetheless a document of an intellectual activist devoted to the black masses.

Farah Jasmine Griffin is Professor of English and Comparative Literature and African-American Studies at Columbia University. She is the author of *Who Set You Flowin'?: The African-American Migration Narrative* (New York: Oxford University Press, 1995) and *If You Can't Be Free, Be a Mystery: In Search of Billie Holiday* (New York: The Free Press, 2001). She is also the editor of *Beloved Sisters and Loving Friends: Letters from Rebecca Primus of Royal Oak, Maryland, and Addie Brown of Hartford, Connecticut, 1854–1868* (New York: Alfred A. Knopf, 1999) and *A Stranger in the Village: Two Centuries of African-American Travel Writing* (co-edited with Cheryl J. Fish; Boston: Beacon Press, 1998). She has written extensively on American literature, music, and politics.

THE SOULS OF
BLACK FOLK

THE FORETHOUGHT

HEREIN LIE BURIED MANY things which if read with patience may show the strange meaning of being black here in the dawning of the Twentieth Century. This meaning is not without interest to you, Gentle Reader; for the problem of the Twentieth Century[1] is the problem of the color-line.

I pray you, then, receive my little book in all charity, studying my words with me, forgiving mistake and foible for sake of the faith and passion that is in me, and seeking the grain of truth hidden there.

I have sought here to sketch, in vague, uncertain outline, the spiritual world in which ten thousand thousand Americans live and strive. First, in two chapters I have tried to show what Emancipation meant to them, and what was its aftermath. In a third chapter I have pointed out the slow rise of personal leadership, and criticised candidly the leader who bears the chief burden of his race to-day. Then, in two other chapters I have sketched in swift outline the two worlds within and without the Veil, and thus have come to the central problem of training men for life. Venturing now into deeper detail, I have in two chapters studied the struggles of the massed millions of the black peasantry, and in another have sought to make clear the present relations of the sons of master and man.

Leaving, then, the world of the white man, I have stepped within the Veil, raising it that you may view faintly its deeper recesses,—the meaning of its religion, the passion of its human sorrow, and the struggle of its greater souls. All this I have ended with a tale twice told but seldom written.

Some of these thoughts of mine have seen the light before in other guise. For kindly consenting to their republication here, in altered and extended form, I must thank the publishers of *The At-*

3

lantic Monthly, The World's Work, The Dial, The New World, and the *Annals of the American Academy of Political and Social Science.*

Before each chapter, as now printed, stands a bar of the Sorrow Songs,[2]—some echo of haunting melody from the only American music which welled up from black souls in the dark past. And, finally, need I add that I who speak here am bone of the bone and flesh of the flesh* of them that live within the Veil?

W. E. B. Du B.
Atlanta, Ga., Feb. 1, 1903.

---

*See the Bible, Genesis 2:23. Adam says, "This is now bone of my bones, and flesh of my flesh" (King James Version).

HEREIN IS WRITTEN

I

Of Our Spiritual Strivings[1]

O water, voice of my heart, crying in the sand,
All night long crying with a mournful cry,
As I lie and listen, and cannot understand
  The voice of my heart in my side or the voice of the sea,
O water, crying for rest, is it I, is it I?
  All night long the water is crying to me.

Unresting water, there shall never be rest
  Till the last moon droop and the last tide fail,
And the fire of the end begin to burn in the west;
    And the heart shall be weary and wonder and cry like
    the sea,
  All life long crying without avail,
    As the water all night long is crying to me.
                                        Arthur Symons.*

2†

BETWEEN ME AND THE other world there is ever an unasked question: unasked by some through feelings of delicacy; by others through the difficulty of rightly framing it. All, nevertheless, flutter round it. They approach me in a half-hesitant sort of way, eye me curiously or compassionately, and then, instead of saying directly, How does it feel to be a problem? they say, I know an excellent colored man in my town; or, I fought at Mechanicsville;† or, Do not these Southern outrages make your blood boil? At these I

---

*From "The Crying of Water" (1903), by Arthur Symons.
†From "Nobody Knows the Trouble I've Seen."
‡Site of a Civil War battle, fought in June 1862, outside Richmond, Virginia.

7

smile, or am interested, or reduce the boiling to a simmer, as the occasion may require. To the real question, How does it feel to be a problem? I answer seldom a word.

And yet, being a problem is a strange experience,—peculiar even for one who has never been anything else, save perhaps in babyhood and in Europe. It is in the early days of rollicking boyhood that the revelation first bursts upon one, all in a day, as it were. I remember well when the shadow swept across me. I was a little thing, away up in the hills of New England, where the dark Housatonic* winds between Hoosac and Taghkanic to the sea. In a wee wooden schoolhouse, something put it into the boys' and girls' heads to buy gorgeous visiting-cards—ten cents a package— and exchange. The exchange was merry, till one girl, a tall newcomer, refused my card,—refused it peremptorily, with a glance. Then it dawned upon me with a certain suddenness that I was different from the others; or like, mayhap, in heart and life and longing, but shut out from their world by a vast veil. I had thereafter no desire to tear down that veil, to creep through; I held all beyond it in common contempt, and lived above it in a region of blue sky and great wandering shadows. That sky was bluest when I could beat my mates at examination time, or beat them at a footrace, or even beat their stringy heads. Alas, with the years all this fine contempt began to fade; for the worlds I longed for, and all their dazzling opportunities, were theirs, not mine. But they should not keep these prizes, I said; some, all, I would wrest from them. Just how I would do it I could never decide: by reading law, by healing the sick, by telling the wonderful tales that swam in my head,—some way. With other black boys the strife was not so fiercely sunny: their youth shrunk into tasteless sycophancy, or into silent hatred of the pale world about them and mocking distrust of everything white; or wasted itself in a bitter cry, Why did God make me an outcast and a stranger in mine own house?† The shades of the prison-house closed round about us all: walls strait and stubborn to the whitest, but relentlessly narrow, tall, and unscalable to sons of night who must plod darkly on in resignation,

---

*River in Great Barrington, Massachusetts, Du Bois's birthplace.
†Reference to the Bible, Exodus 2:22. Moses states, "I have been a stranger in a strange land" (KJV).

or beat unavailing palms against the stone, or steadily, half hope-lessly, watch the streak of blue above.

After the Egyptian and Indian, the Greek and Roman, the Teu-ton and Mongolian, the Negro is a sort of seventh son, born with a veil, and gifted with second-sight[3] in this American world,—a world which yields him no true self-consciousness, but only lets him see himself through the revelation of the other world. It is a peculiar sensation, this double-consciousness, this sense of always looking at one's self through the eyes of others, of measuring one's soul by the tape of a world that looks on in amused contempt and pity. One ever feels his two-ness,—an American, a Negro; two souls, two thoughts, two unreconciled strivings; two warring ideals in one dark body, whose dogged strength alone keeps it from being torn asunder.

The history of the American Negro is the history of this strife,—this longing to attain self-conscious manhood, to merge his double self into a better and truer self. In this merging he wishes neither of the older selves to be lost. He would not African-ize America, for America has too much to teach the world and Africa. He would not bleach his Negro soul in a flood of white Americanism, for he knows that Negro blood has a message for the world. He simply wishes to make it possible for a man to be both a Negro and an American, without being cursed and spit upon by his fellows, without having the doors of Opportunity closed roughly in his face.

This, then, is the end of his striving: to be a co-worker in the kingdom of culture, to escape both death and isolation, to husband and use his best powers and his latent genius. These powers of body and mind have in the past been strangely wasted, dispersed, or forgotten. The shadow of a mighty Negro past flits through the tale of Ethiopia the Shadowy and of Egypt the Sphinx. Throughout history, the powers of single black men flash here and there like falling stars, and die sometimes before the world has rightly gauged their brightness. Here in America, in the few days since Emancipation, the black man's turning hither and thither in hesi-tant and doubtful striving has often made his very strength to lose effectiveness, to seem like absence of power, like weakness. And yet it is not weakness,—it is the contradiction of double aims. The double-aimed struggle of the black artisan—on the one hand to es-cape white contempt for a nation of mere hewers of wood and drawers of water, and on the other hand to plough and nail and dig for a poverty-stricken horde—could only result in making him a poor craftsman, for he had but half a heart in either cause. By the poverty and ignorance of his people, the Negro minister or doctor was tempted toward quackery and demagogy; and by the criticism of the other world, toward ideals that made him ashamed of his lowly tasks. The would-be black *savant* was confronted by the paradox that the knowledge his people needed was a twice-told tale to his white neighbors, while the knowledge which would teach the white world was Greek to his own flesh and blood. The innate love of harmony and beauty that set the ruder souls of his people a-dancing and a-singing raised but confusion and doubt in the soul of the black artist; for the beauty revealed to him was the soul-beauty of a race which his larger audience despised, and he could not articulate the message of another people. This waste of double aims, this seeking to satisfy two unreconciled ideals, has wrought sad havoc with the courage and faith and deeds of ten thousand thousand people,—has sent them often wooing false gods and invoking false means of salvation, and at times has even seemed about to make them ashamed of themselves.

Away back in the days of bondage they thought to see in one divine event the end of all doubt and disappointment; few men ever worshipped Freedom with half such unquestioning faith as did the American Negro for two centuries. To him, so far as he thought and dreamed, slavery was indeed the sum of all villainies, the cause of all sorrow, the root of all prejudice; Emancipation was the key to a promised land of sweeter beauty than ever stretched before the eyes of wearied Israelites. In song and exhortation swelled one refrain—Liberty; in his tears and curses the God he implored had Freedom in his right hand. At last it came,—suddenly, fearfully, like a dream. With one wild carnival of blood and passion came the message in his own plaintive cadences:—

> *"Shout, O children!*
> *Shout, you're free!*
> *For God has bought your liberty!"**

---

*From "Shout O Children."

Years have passed away since then,—ten, twenty, forty; forty years of national life, forty years of renewal and development, and yet the swarthy spectre sits in its accustomed seat at the Nation's feast. In vain do we cry to this our vastest social problem:—

> *"Take any shape but that, and my firm nerves*
> *Shall never tremble!"* °

The Nation has not yet found peace from its sins; the freedman has not yet found in freedom his promised land. Whatever of good may have come in these years of change, the shadow of a deep disappointment rests upon the Negro people,—a disappointment all the more bitter because the unattained ideal was unbounded save by the simple ignorance of a lowly people.

The first decade was merely a prolongation of the vain search for freedom, the boon that seemed ever barely to elude their grasp,—like a tantalizing will-o'-the-wisp, maddening and misleading the headless host. The holocaust of war, the terrors of the Ku-Klux Klan,[†] the lies of carpet-baggers,[‡] the disorganization of industry, and the contradictory advice of friends and foes, left the bewildered serf with no new watchword beyond the old cry for freedom. As the time flew, however, he began to grasp a new idea. The ideal of liberty demanded for its attainment powerful means, and these the Fifteenth Amendment gave him. The ballot, which before he had looked upon as a visible sign of freedom, he now regarded as the chief means of gaining and perfecting the liberty with which war had partially endowed him. And why not? Had not votes made war and emancipated millions? Had not votes enfranchised the freedmen? Was anything impossible to a power that had done all this? A million black men started with renewed zeal to vote themselves into the kingdom. So the decade flew away, the revolution of 1876[4] came, and left the half-free serf weary, wondering, but still inspired. Slowly but steadily, in the following

---

°From act 3, scene 4 of *Macbeth,* by William Shakespeare.
†White-supremacist terrorist organization founded in 1866.
‡Derogatory term for opportunistic northerners who came to the South following the Civil War; refers to the type of luggage they carried.

years, a new vision began gradually to replace the dream of political power,—a powerful movement, the rise of another ideal to
guide the unguided, another pillar of fire by night after a clouded
day. It was the ideal of "book-learning"; the curiosity, born of com-
pulsory ignorance, to know and test the power of the cabalistic letters of the white man, the longing to know. Here at last seemed to
have been discovered the mountain path to Canaan;° longer than
the highway of Emancipation and law, steep and rugged, but
straight, leading to heights high enough to overlook life.

Up the new path the advance guard toiled, slowly, heavily,
doggedly; only those who have watched and guided the faltering
feet, the misty minds, the dull understandings, of the dark pupils
of these schools know how faithfully, how piteously, this people
strove to learn. It was weary work. The cold statistician wrote
down the inches of progress here and there, noted also where
here and there a foot had slipped or some one had fallen. To the
tired climbers, the horizon was ever dark, the mists were often
cold, the Canaan was always dim and far away. If, however, the vistas disclosed as yet no goal, no resting-place, little but flattery and
criticism, the journey at least gave leisure for reflection and self-
examination; it changed the child of Emancipation to the youth
with dawning self-consciousness, self-realization, self-respect. In
those sombre forests of his striving his own soul rose before him,
and he saw himself,—darkly as through a veil;† and yet he saw in
himself some faint revelation of his power, of his mission. He
began to have a dim feeling that, to attain his place in the world,
he must be himself, and not another. For the first time he sought
to analyze the burden he bore upon his back, that dead-weight of
social degradation partially masked behind a half-named Negro
problem. He felt his poverty; without a cent, without a home,
without land, tools, or savings, he had entered into competition
with rich, landed, skilled neighbors. To be a poor man is hard, but
to be a poor race in a land of dollars is the very bottom of hardships. He felt the weight of his ignorance,—not simply of letters,

---

°The Promised Land.
†See the Bible, 1 Corinthians 13:12: "For now we see through a glass, darkly; but
then face to face: now I know in part; but then shall I know even as also I am
known" (KJV).

but of life, of business, of the humanities; the accumulated sloth and shirking and awkwardness of decades and centuries shackled his hands and feet. Nor was his burden all poverty and ignorance. The red stain of bastardy, which two centuries of systematic legal defilement of Negro women had stamped upon his race, meant not only the loss of ancient African chastity, but also the hereditary weight of a mass of corruption from white adulterers, threatening almost the obliteration of the Negro home.

A people thus handicapped ought not to be asked to race with the world, but rather allowed to give all its time and thought to its own social problems. But alas! while sociologists gleefully count his bastards and his prostitutes, the very soul of the toiling, sweating black man is darkened by the shadow of a vast despair. Men call the shadow prejudice, and learnedly explain it as the natural defence of culture against barbarism, learning against ignorance, purity against crime, the "higher" against the "lower" races. To which the Negro cries Amen! and swears that to so much of this strange prejudice as is founded on just homage to civilization, culture, righteousness, and progress, he humbly bows and meekly does obeisance. But before that nameless prejudice that leaps beyond all this he stands helpless, dismayed, and well-nigh speechless; before that personal disrespect and mockery, the ridicule and systematic humiliation, the distortion of fact and wanton license of fancy, the cynical ignoring of the better and the boisterous welcoming of the worse, the all-pervading desire to inculcate disdain for everything black, from Toussaint* to the devil,—before this there rises a sickening despair that would disarm and discourage any nation save that black host to whom "discouragement" is an unwritten word.

But the facing of so vast a prejudice could not but bring the inevitable self-questioning, self-disparagement, and lowering of ideals which ever accompany repression and breed in an atmosphere of contempt and hate. Whisperings and portents came borne upon the four winds: Lo! we are diseased and dying, cried the dark hosts; we cannot write, our voting is vain; what need of education, since we must always cook and serve? And the Nation

---

*The full names, birth and death dates (when available), and brief biographical notes for historical figures are provided in the Glossary of Names.

echoed and enforced this self-criticism, saying: Be content to be servants, and nothing more; what need of higher culture for half-men? Away with the black man's ballot, by force or fraud,—and behold the suicide of a race! Nevertheless, out of the evil came something of good,—the more careful adjustment of education to real life, the clearer perception of the Negroes' social responsibilities, and the sobering realization of the meaning of progress.

So dawned the time of *Sturm und Drang:*° storm and stress to-day rocks our little boat on the mad waters of the world-sea; there is within and without the sound of conflict, the burning of body and rending of soul; inspiration strives with doubt, and faith with vain questionings. The bright ideals of the past,—physical freedom, political power, the training of brains and the training of hands,—all these in turn have waxed and waned, until even the last grows dim and overcast. Are they all wrong,—all false? No, not that, but each alone was over-simple and incomplete,—the dreams of a credulous race-childhood, or the fond imaginings of the other world which does not know and does not want to know our power. To be really true, all these ideals must be melted and welded into one. The training of the schools we need to-day more than ever,—the training of deft hands, quick eyes and ears, and above all the broader, deeper, higher culture of gifted minds and pure hearts. The power of the ballot we need in sheer self-defence,—else what shall save us from a second slavery? Freedom, too, the long-sought, we still seek,—the freedom of life and limb, the freedom to work and think, the freedom to love and aspire. Work, culture, liberty,—all these we need, not singly but together, not successively but together, each growing and aiding each, and all striving toward that vaster ideal that swims before the Negro people, the ideal of human brotherhood, gained through the unifying ideal of Race; the ideal of fostering and developing the traits and talents of the Negro, not in opposition to or contempt for other races, but rather in large conformity to the greater ideals of the American Republic, in order that some day on American soil two world-races may give each to each those characteris-

---

°Storm and stress (German); the name given to a German literary movement whose authors Du Bois greatly admired.

tics both so sadly lack. We the darker ones come even now not al-together empty-handed: there are to-day no truer exponents of the pure human spirit of the Declaration of Independence than the American Negroes; there is no true American music but the wild sweet melodies of the Negro slave; the American fairy tales and folk-lore are Indian and African; and, all in all, we black men seem the sole oasis of simple faith and reverence in a dusty desert of dollars and smartness. Will America be poorer if she replace her brutal dyspeptic blundering with light-hearted but deter-mined Negro humility? or her coarse and cruel wit with loving jovial good-humor? or her vulgar music with the soul of the Sor-row Songs?

Merely a concrete test of the underlying principles of the great republic is the Negro Problem, and the spiritual striving of the freedmen's sons is the travail of souls whose burden is almost be-yond the measure of their strength, but who bear it in the name of an historic race, in the name of this the land of their fathers' fa-thers, and in the name of human opportunity.

And now what I have briefly sketched in large outline let me on coming pages tell again in many ways, with loving emphasis and deeper detail, that men may listen to the striving in the souls of black folk.

II

Of the Dawn of Freedom[1]

> *Careless seems the great Avenger;*
> *History's lessons but record*
> *One death-grapple in the darkness*
> *'Twixt old systems and the Word;*
> *Truth forever on the scaffold,*
> *Wrong forever on the throne;*
> *Yet that scaffold sways the future,*
> *And behind the dim unknown*
> *Standeth God within the shadow*
> *Keeping watch above His own.*
>
> Lowell. *

THE PROBLEM OF THE twentieth century is the problem of the color-line,—the relation of the darker to the lighter races of men in Asia and Africa, in America and the islands of the sea. It was a phase of this problem that caused the Civil War; and however much they who marched South and North in 1861 may have fixed on the technical points of union and local autonomy as a

---

*From "The Present Crisis" (1844), by James Russell Lowell.
†From "My Lord, What a Mourning."

16

shibboleth, all nevertheless knew, as we know, that the question of
Negro slavery was the real cause of the conflict. Curious it was,
too, how this deeper question ever forced itself to the surface
despite effort and disclaimer. No sooner had Northern armies
touched Southern soil than this old question, newly guised, sprang
from the earth,—What shall be done with Negroes? Peremptory
military commands, this way and that, could not answer the query;
the Emancipation Proclamation seemed but to broaden and intensify the difficulties; and the War Amendments[2] made the
Negro problems of to-day.

It is the aim of this essay to study the period of history from
1861 to 1872 so far as it relates to the American Negro. In effect,
this tale of the dawn of Freedom is an account of that government
of men called the Freedmen's Bureau,[3]—one of the most singular
and interesting of the attempts made by a great nation to grapple
with vast problems of race and social condition.

The war has naught to do with slaves, cried Congress, the President, and the Nation; and yet no sooner had the armies, East and
West, penetrated Virginia and Tennessee than fugitive slaves appeared within their lines. They came at night, when the flickering
camp-fires shone like vast unsteady stars along the black horizon:
old men and thin, with gray and tufted hair; women, with frightened eyes, dragging whimpering hungry children; men and girls,
stalwart and gaunt,—a horde of starving vagabonds, homeless,
helpless, and pitiable, in their dark distress. Two methods of treating these newcomers seemed equally logical to opposite sorts of
minds. Ben Butler, in Virginia, quickly declared slave property
contraband of war, and put the fugitives to work; while Fremont,
in Missouri, declared the slaves free under martial law. Butler's action was approved, but Fremont's was hastily countermanded, and
his successor, Halleck, saw things differently. "Hereafter," he commanded, "no slaves should be allowed to come into your lines at
all; if any come without your knowledge, when owners call for
them deliver them." Such a policy was difficult to enforce; some
of the black refugees declared themselves freemen, others
showed that their masters had deserted them, and still others
were captured with forts and plantations. Evidently, too, slaves
were a source of strength to the Confederacy, and were being
used as laborers and producers. "They constitute a military re-

source," wrote Secretary Cameron, late in 1861; "and being such, that they should not be turned over to the enemy is too plain to discuss." So gradually the tone of the army chiefs changed; Congress forbade the rendition of fugitives, and Butler's "contrabands" were welcomed as military laborers. This complicated rather than solved the problem, for now the scattering fugitives became a steady stream, which flowed faster as the armies marched.

Then the long-headed man with care-chiselled face who sat in the White House saw the inevitable, and emancipated the slaves of rebels on New Year's, 1863. A month later Congress called earnestly for the Negro soldiers whom the act of July, 1862, had half grudgingly allowed to enlist. Thus the barriers were levelled and the deed was done. The stream of fugitives swelled to a flood, and anxious army officers kept inquiring: "What must be done with slaves, arriving almost daily? Are we to find food and shelter for women and children?"

It was a Pierce of Boston who pointed out the way, and thus became in a sense the founder of the Freedmen's Bureau. He was a firm friend of Secretary Chase;[4] and when, in 1861, the care of slaves and abandoned lands devolved upon the Treasury officials, Pierce was specially detailed from the ranks to study the conditions. First, he cared for the refugees at Fortress Monroe; and then, after Sherman had captured Hilton Head, Pierce was sent there to found his Port Royal experiment of making free workingmen out of slaves. Before his experiment was barely started, however, the problem of the fugitives had assumed such proportions that it was taken from the hands of the over-burdened Treasury Department and given to the army officials. Already centres of massed freedmen were forming at Fortress Monroe, Washington, New Orleans, Vicksburg and Corinth, Columbus, Ky., and Cairo, Ill., as well as at Port Royal. Army chaplains found here new and fruitful fields; "superintendents of contrabands" multiplied, and some attempt at systematic work was made by enlisting the able-bodied men and giving work to the others.

Then came the Freedmen's Aid societies, born of the touching appeals from Pierce and from these other centres of distress. There was the American Missionary Association, sprung from the *Amistad*,[5] and now full-grown for work; the various church organizations, the National Freedmen's Relief Association, the American Freedmen's Union, the Western Freedmen's Aid Commission,—in all fifty or more active organizations, which sent clothes, money, school-books, and teachers southward. All they did was needed, for the destitution of the freedmen was often reported as "too appalling for belief," and the situation was daily growing worse rather than better.

And daily, too, it seemed more plain that this was no ordinary matter of temporary relief, but a national crisis; for here loomed a labor problem of vast dimensions. Masses of Negroes stood idle, or, if they worked spasmodically, were never sure of pay; and if perchance they received pay, squandered the new thing thoughtlessly. In these and other ways were camp-life and the new liberty demoralizing the freedmen. The broader economic organization thus clearly demanded sprang up here and there as accident and local conditions determined. Here it was that Pierce's Port Royal plan of leased plantations and guided workmen pointed out the rough way. In Washington the military governor, at the urgent appeal of the superintendent, opened confiscated estates to the cultivation of the fugitives, and there in the shadow of the dome gathered black farm villages. General Dix gave over estates to the freedmen of Fortress Monroe, and so on, South and West. The government and benevolent societies furnished the means of cultivation, and the Negro turned again slowly to work. The systems of control, thus started, rapidly grew, here and there, into strange little governments, like that of General Banks in Louisiana, with its ninety thousand black subjects, its fifty thousand guided laborers, and its annual budget of one hundred thousand dollars and more. It made out four thousand pay-rolls a year, registered all freedmen, inquired into grievances and redressed them, laid and collected taxes, and established a system of public schools. So, too, Colonel Eaton, the superintendent of Tennessee and Arkansas, ruled over one hundred thousand freedmen, leased and cultivated seven thousand acres of cotton land, and fed ten thousand paupers a year. In South Carolina was General Saxton, with his deep interest in black folk. He succeeded Pierce and the Treasury officials, and sold forfeited estates, leased abandoned plantations, encouraged schools, and received from Sherman, after that terribly

picturesque march to the sea, thousands of the wretched camp
followers.

Three characteristic things one might have seen in Sherman's
raid through Georgia, which threw the new situation in shadowy
relief: the Conqueror, the Conquered, and the Negro. Some see
all significance in the grim front of the destroyer, and some in the
bitter sufferers of the Lost Cause. But to me neither soldier nor
fugitive speaks with so deep a meaning as that dark human cloud
that clung like remorse on the rear of those swift columns,
swelling at times to half their size, almost engulfing and choking
them. In vain were they ordered back, in vain were bridges hewn
from beneath their feet; on they trudged and writhed and surged,
until they rolled into Savannah, a starved and naked horde of tens
of thousands. There too came the characteristic military remedy:
"The islands from Charleston south, the abandoned rice-fields
along the rivers for thirty miles back from the sea, and the country bordering the St. John's River, Florida, are reserved and set
apart for the settlement of Negroes now made free by act of war."
So read the celebrated "Field-order Number Fifteen."[6]

All these experiments, orders, and systems were bound to at-
tract and perplex the government and the nation. Directly after
the Emancipation Proclamation, Representative Eliot had introduced a bill creating a Bureau of Emancipation; but it was never
reported. The following June a committee of inquiry, appointed
by the Secretary of War, reported in favor of a temporary bureau
for the "improvement, protection, and employment of refugee
freedmen," on much the same lines as were afterwards followed.
Petitions came in to President Lincoln from distinguished citizens
and organizations, strongly urging a comprehensive and unified
plan of dealing with the freedmen, under a bureau which should
be "charged with the study of plans and execution of measures for
easily guiding, and in every way judiciously and humanely aiding,
the passage of our emancipated and yet to be emancipated blacks
from the old condition of forced labor to their new state of voluntary industry."

Some half-hearted steps were taken to accomplish this, in part,
by putting the whole matter again in charge of the special Treasury agents. Laws of 1863 and 1864 directed them to take charge
of and lease abandoned lands for periods not exceeding twelve

months, and to "provide in such leases, or otherwise, for the employment and general welfare" of the freedmen. Most of the army officers greeted this as a welcome relief from perplexing "Negro affairs," and Secretary Fessenden, July 29, 1864, issued an excellent system of regulations, which were afterward closely followed by General Howard. Under Treasury agents, large quantities of land were leased in the Mississippi Valley, and many Negroes were employed; but in August, 1864, the new regulations were suspended for reasons of "public policy," and the army was again in control.

Meanwhile Congress had turned its attention to the subject; and in March the House passed a bill by a majority of two establishing a Bureau for Freedmen in the War Department. Charles Sumner, who had charge of the bill in the Senate, argued that freedmen and abandoned lands ought to be under the same department, and reported a substitute for the House bill attaching the Bureau to the Treasury Department. This bill passed, but too late for action by the House. The debates wandered over the whole policy of the administration and the general question of slavery, without touching very closely the specific merits of the measure in hand. Then the national election took place; and the administration, with a vote of renewed confidence from the country, addressed itself to the matter more seriously. A conference between the two branches of Congress agreed upon a carefully drawn measure which contained the chief provisions of Sumner's bill, but made the proposed organization a department independent of both the War and the Treasury officials. The bill was conservative, giving the new department "general superintendence of all freedmen." Its purpose was to "establish regulations" for them, protect them, lease them lands, adjust their wages, and appear in civil and military courts as their "next friend." There were many limitations attached to the powers thus granted, and the organization was made permanent. Nevertheless, the Senate defeated the bill, and a new conference committee was appointed. This committee reported a new bill, February 28, which was whirled through just as the session closed, and became the act of 1865 establishing in the War Department a "Bureau of Refugees, Freedmen, and Abandoned Lands."

This last compromise was a hasty bit of legislation, vague and uncertain in outline. A Bureau was created, "to continue during the present War of Rebellion, and for one year thereafter," to which was given "the supervision and management of all abandoned lands and the control of all subjects relating to refugees and freedmen," under "such rules and regulations as may be presented by the head of the Bureau and approved by the President." A Commissioner, appointed by the President and Senate, was to control the Bureau, with an office force not exceeding ten clerks. The President might also appoint assistant commissioners in the seceded States, and to all these offices military officials might be detailed at regular pay. The Secretary of War could issue rations, clothing, and fuel to the destitute, and all abandoned property was placed in the hands of the Bureau for eventual lease and sale to ex-slaves in forty-acre parcels.

Thus did the United States government definitely assume charge of the emancipated Negro as the ward of the nation. It was a tremendous undertaking. Here at a stroke of the pen was erected a government of millions of men,—and not ordinary men either, but black men emasculated by a peculiarly complete system of slavery, centuries old; and now, suddenly, violently, they come into a new birthright, at a time of war and passion, in the midst of the stricken and embittered population of their former masters. Any man might well have hesitated to assume charge of such a work, with vast responsibilities, indefinite powers, and limited resources. Probably no one but a soldier would have answered such a call promptly; and, indeed, no one but a soldier could be called, for Congress had appropriated no money for salaries and expenses.

Less than a month after the weary Emancipator passed to his rest, his successor assigned Major-Gen. Oliver O. Howard to duty as Commissioner of the new Bureau. He was a Maine man, then only thirty-five years of age. He had marched with Sherman to the sea, had fought well at Gettysburg, and but the year before had been assigned to the command of the Department of Tennessee. An honest man, with too much faith in human nature, little aptitude for business and intricate detail, he had had large opportunity of becoming acquainted at first hand with much of the work before him. And of that work it has been truly said that "no approximately correct history of civilization can ever be written which does not throw out in bold relief, as one of the great landmarks of political and social progress, the organization and administration of the Freedmen's Bureau."

On May 12, 1865, Howard was appointed; and he assumed the duties of his office promptly on the 15th, and began examining the field of work. A curious mess he looked upon: little despotisms, communistic experiments, slavery, peonage, business speculations, organized charity, unorganized alms-giving,—all reeling on under the guise of helping the freedmen, and all enshrined in the smoke and blood of war and the cursing and silence of angry men. On May 19 the new government—for a government it really was—issued its constitution; commissioners were to be appointed in each of the seceded States, who were to take charge of "all subjects relating to refugees and freedmen," and all relief and rations were to be given by their consent alone. The Bureau invited continued cooperation with benevolent societies, and declared: "It will be the object of all commissioners to introduce practicable systems of compensated labor," and to establish schools. Forthwith nine assistant commissioners were appointed. They were to hasten to their fields of work; seek gradually to close relief establishments, and make the destitute self-supporting; act as courts of law where there were no courts, or where Negroes were not recognized in them as free; establish the institution of marriage among ex-slaves, and keep records; see that freedmen were free to choose their employers, and help in making fair contracts for them; and finally, the circular said: "Simple good faith, for which we hope on all hands for those concerned in the passing away of slavery, will especially relieve the assistant commissioners in the discharge of their duties toward the freedmen, as well as promote the general welfare."

No sooner was the work thus started, and the general system and local organization in some measure begun, than two grave difficulties appeared which changed largely the theory and outcome of Bureau work. First, there were the abandoned lands of the South. It had long been the more or less definitely expressed theory of the North that all the chief problems of Emancipation might be settled by establishing the slaves on the forfeited lands of their masters,—a sort of poetic justice, said some. But this poetry done into solemn prose meant either wholesale confiscation of private property in the South, or vast appropriations. Now Congress had not appropriated a cent, and no sooner did the proclamations of general amnesty appear than the eight hundred thousand acres of abandoned lands in the hands of the Freedmen's Bureau melted quickly away. The second difficulty lay in perfecting the local organization of the Bureau throughout the wide field of work. Making a new machine and sending out officials of duly ascertained fitness for a great work of social reform is no child's task; but this task was even harder, for a new central organization had to be fitted on a heterogeneous and confused but already existing system of relief and control of ex-slaves; and the agents available for this work must be sought for in an army still busy with war operations,—men in the very nature of the case ill fitted for delicate social work,—or among the questionable camp followers of an invading host. Thus, after a year's work, vigorously as it was pushed, the problem looked even more difficult to grasp and solve than at the beginning. Nevertheless, three things that year's work did, well worth the doing: it relieved a vast amount of physical suffering; it transported seven thousand fugitives from congested centres back to the farm; and, best of all, it inaugurated the crusade of the New England school-ma'am.

The annals of this Ninth Crusade are yet to be written,—the tale of a mission that seemed to our age far more quixotic than the quest of St. Louis seemed to his. Behind the mists of ruin and rapine waved the calico dresses of women who dared, and after the hoarse mouthings of the field guns rang the rhythm of the alphabet.[7] Rich and poor they were, serious and curious. Bereaved now of a father, now of a brother, now of more than these, they came seeking a life work in planting New England schoolhouses among the white and black of the South. They did their work well. In that first year they taught one hundred thousand souls, and more.

Evidently, Congress must soon legislate again on the hastily organized Bureau, which had so quickly grown into wide significance and vast possibilities. An institution such as that was well-nigh as difficult to end as to begin. Early in 1866 Congress took up the matter, when Senator Trumbull, of Illinois, introduced a bill to extend the Bureau and enlarge its powers. This measure received, at the hands of Congress, far more thorough discussion and attention than its predecessor. The war cloud had thinned enough to allow a clearer conception of the work of Emancipation. The champions of the bill argued that the strengthening of the Freedmen's Bureau was still a military necessity; that it was needed for the proper carrying out of the Thirteenth Amendment, and was a work of sheer justice to the ex-slave, at a trifling cost to the government. The opponents of the measure declared that the war was over, and the necessity for war measures past; that the Bureau, by reason of its extraordinary powers, was clearly unconstitutional in time of peace, and was destined to irritate the South and pauperize the freedmen, at a final cost of possibly hundreds of millions. These two arguments were unanswered, and indeed unanswerable: the one that the extraordinary powers of the Bureau threatened the civil rights of all citizens; and the other that the government must have power to do what manifestly must be done, and that present abandonment of the freedmen meant their practical re-enslavement. The bill which finally passed enlarged and made permanent the Freedmen's Bureau. It was promptly vetoed by President Johnson as "unconstitutional," "unnecessary," and "extrajudicial," and failed of passage over the veto. Meantime, however, the breach between Congress and the President began to broaden, and a modified form of the lost bill was finally passed over the President's second veto, July 16.

The act of 1866 gave the Freedmen's Bureau its final form,— the form by which it will be known to posterity and judged of men. It extended the existence of the Bureau to July, 1868; it authorized additional assistant commissioners, the retention of army officers mustered out of regular service, the sale of certain forfeited lands to freedmen on nominal terms, the sale of Confederate public property for Negro schools, and a wider field of judicial interpretation and cognizance. The government of the unreconstructed South was thus put very largely in the hands of the Freedmen's Bureau, especially as in many cases the departmental military commander was now made also assistant commissioner. It was thus that the Freedmen's Bureau became a full-fledged government of men. It made laws, executed them and interpreted them; it laid and collected taxes, defined and punished crime, maintained and used military force, and dictated such measures as it thought necessary and proper for the accomplishment of its var-

ied ends. Naturally, all these powers were not exercised continuously nor to their fullest extent; and yet, as General Howard has
said, "scarcely any subject that has to be legislated upon in civil society failed, at one time or another, to demand the action of this
singular Bureau."

To understand and criticise intelligently so vast a work, one
must not forget an instant the drift of things in the later sixties.
Lee had surrendered, Lincoln was dead, and Johnson and Congress were at loggerheads; the Thirteenth Amendment was
adopted, the Fourteenth pending, and the Fifteenth declared in
force in 1870. Guerrilla raiding, the ever-present flickering after-
flame of war, was spending its force against the Negroes, and all
the Southern land was awakening as from some wild dream to
poverty and social revolution. In a time of perfect calm, amid willing neighbors and streaming wealth, the social uplifting of four
million slaves to an assured and self-sustaining place in the body
politic and economic would have been a herculean task; but when
to the inherent difficulties of so delicate and nice a social operation were added the spite and hate of conflict, the hell of war;
when suspicion and cruelty were rife, and gaunt Hunger wept beside Bereavement,—in such a case, the work of any instrument of
social regeneration was in large part foredoomed to failure. The
very name of the Bureau stood for a thing in the South which for
two centuries and better men had refused even to argue,—that
life amid free Negroes was simply unthinkable, the maddest of experiments.

The agents that the Bureau could command varied all the way
from unselfish philanthropists to narrow-minded busybodies and
thieves; and even though it be true that the average was far better
than the worst, it was the occasional fly that helped spoil the oint-
ment.

Then amid all crouched the freed slave, bewildered between
friend and foe. He had emerged from slavery,—not the worst
slavery in the world, not a slavery that made all life unbearable,
rather a slavery that had here and there something of kindliness,
fidelity, and happiness,—but withal slavery, which, so far as
human aspiration and desert were concerned, classed the black
man and the ox together. And the Negro knew full well that, whatever their deeper convictions may have been, Southern men had

fought with desperate energy to perpetuate this slavery under which the black masses, with half-articulate thought, had writhed and shivered. They welcomed freedom with a cry. They shrank from the master who still strove for their chains; they fled to the friends that had freed them, even though those friends stood ready to use them as a club for driving the recalcitrant South back into loyalty. So the cleft between the white and black South grew. Idle to say it never should have been; it was as inevitable as its results were pitiable. Curiously incongruous elements were left arrayed against each other,—the North, the government, the carpet-bagger, and the slave, here; and there, all the South that was white, whether gentleman or vagabond, honest man or rascal, lawless murderer or martyr to duty.

Thus it is doubly difficult to write of this period calmly, so intense was the feeling, so mighty the human passions that swayed and blinded men. Amid it all, two figures ever stand to typify that day to coming ages,—the one, a gray-haired gentleman, whose fathers had quit themselves like men, whose sons lay in nameless graves; who bowed to the evil of slavery because its abolition threatened untold ill to all; who stood at last, in the evening of life, a blighted, ruined form, with hate in his eyes;—and the other, a form hovering dark and mother-like, her awful face black with the mists of centuries, had aforetime quailed at that white master's command, had bent in love over the cradles of his sons and daughters, and closed in death the sunken eyes of his wife,—aye, too, at his behest had laid herself low to his lust, and borne a tawny manchild to the world, only to see her dark boy's limbs scattered to the winds by midnight marauders riding after "cursed Niggers." These were the saddest sights of that woful day; and no man clasped the hands of these two passing figures of the present-past; but, hating, they went to their long home, and, hating, their children's children live to-day.

Here, then, was the field of work for the Freedmen's Bureau; and since, with some hesitation, it was continued by the act of 1868 until 1869, let us look upon four years of its work as a whole. There were, in 1868, nine hundred Bureau officials scattered from Washington to Texas, ruling, directly and indirectly, many millions of men. The deeds of these rulers fall mainly under seven heads: the relief of physical suffering, the overseeing of the be-

ginnings of free labor, the buying and selling of land, the establishment of schools, the paying of bounties, the administration of
justice, and the financiering of all these activities.

Up to June, 1869, over half a million patients had been treated
by Bureau physicians and surgeons, and sixty hospitals and asylums had been in operation. In fifty months twenty-one million
free rations were distributed at a cost of over four million dollars.
Next came the difficult question of labor. First, thirty thousand
black men were transported from the refuges and relief stations
back to the farms, back to the critical trial of a new way of working. Plain instructions went out from Washington: the laborers
must be free to choose their employers, no fixed rate of wages was
prescribed, and there was to be no peonage or forced labor. So far,
so good; but where local agents differed *toto cælo** in capacity and
character, where the *personnel* was continually changing, the outcome was necessarily varied. The largest element of success lay in
the fact that the majority of the freedmen were willing, even
eager, to work. So labor contracts were written,—fifty thousand in
a single State,—laborers advised, wages guaranteed, and employers supplied. In truth, the organization became a vast labor bureau,—not perfect, indeed, notably defective here and there, but
on the whole successful beyond the dreams of thoughtful men.
The two great obstacles which confronted the officials were the
tyrant and the idler,—the slaveholder who was determined to perpetuate slavery under another name; and the freedman who regarded freedom as perpetual rest,—the Devil and the Deep Sea.

In the work of establishing the Negroes as peasant proprietors,
the Bureau was from the first handicapped and at last absolutely
checked. Something was done, and larger things were planned;
abandoned lands were leased so long as they remained in the
hands of the Bureau, and a total revenue of nearly half a million
dollars derived from black tenants. Some other lands to which the
nation had gained title were sold on easy terms, and public lands
were opened for settlement to the very few freedmen who had
tools and capital. But the vision of "forty acres and a mule"—the
righteous and reasonable ambition to become a landholder, which

---

*By the whole extent of the heavens; in other words entirely, absolutely (Latin).

the nation had all but categorically promised the freedmen—was destined in most cases to bitter disappointment. And those men of marvellous hindsight who are to-day seeking to preach the Negro back to the present peonage of the soil know well, or ought to know, that the opportunity of binding the Negro peasant willingly to the soil was lost on that day when the Commissioner of the Freedmen's Bureau had to go to South Carolina and tell the weeping freedmen, after their years of toil, that their land was not theirs, that there was a mistake—somewhere. If by 1874 the Georgia Negro alone owned three hundred and fifty thousand acres of land, it was by grace of his thrift rather than by bounty of the government.

The greatest success of the Freedmen's Bureau lay in the planting of the free school among Negroes, and the idea of free elementary education among all classes in the South. It not only called the schoolmistresses through the benevolent agencies and built them schoolhouses, but it helped discover and support such apostles of human culture as Edmund Ware, Samuel Armstrong, and Erastus Cravath. The opposition to Negro education in the South was at first bitter, and showed itself in ashes, insult, and blood; for the South believed an educated Negro to be a dangerous Negro. And the South was not wholly wrong; for education among all kinds of men always has had, and always will have, an element of danger and revolution, of dissatisfaction and discontent. Nevertheless, men strive to know. Perhaps some inkling of this paradox, even in the unquiet days of the Bureau, helped the bayonets allay an opposition to human training which still to-day lies smouldering in the South, but not flaming. Fisk, Atlanta, Howard, and Hampton were founded in these days, and six million dollars were expended for educational work, seven hundred and fifty thousand dollars of which the freedmen themselves gave of their poverty.

Such contributions, together with the buying of land and various other enterprises, showed that the ex-slave was handling some free capital already. The chief initial source of this was labor in the army, and his pay and bounty as a soldier. Payments to Negro soldiers were at first complicated by the ignorance of the recipients, and the fact that the quotas of colored regiments from Northern States were largely filled by recruits from the South, unknown to their fellow soldiers. Consequently, payments were accompanied by such frauds that Congress, by joint resolution in 1867, put the whole matter in the hands of the Freedmen's Bureau. In two years six million dollars was thus distributed to five thousand claimants, and in the end the sum exceeded eight million dollars. Even in this system fraud was frequent; but still the work put needed capital in the hands of practical paupers, and some, at least, was well spent.

The most perplexing and least successful part of the Bureau's work lay in the exercise of its judicial functions. The regular Bureau court consisted of one representative of the employer, one of the Negro, and one of the Bureau. If the Bureau could have maintained a perfectly judicial attitude, this arrangement would have been ideal, and must in time have gained confidence; but the nature of its other activities and the character of its *personnel* prejudiced the Bureau in favor of the black litigants, and led without doubt to much injustice and annoyance. On the other hand, to leave the Negro in the hands of Southern courts was impossible. In a distracted land where slavery had hardly fallen, to keep the strong from wanton abuse of the weak, and the weak from gloating insolently over the half-shorn strength of the strong, was a thankless, hopeless task. The former masters of the land were peremptorily ordered about, seized, and imprisoned, and punished over and again, with scant courtesy from army officers. The former slaves were intimidated, beaten, raped, and butchered by angry and revengeful men. Bureau courts tended to become centres simply for punishing whites, while the regular civil courts tended to become solely institutions for perpetuating the slavery of blacks. Almost every law and method ingenuity could devise was employed by the legislatures to reduce the Negroes to serfdom,—to make them the slaves of the State, if not of individual owners; while the Bureau officials too often were found striving to put the "bottom rail on top," and give the freedmen a power and independence which they could not yet use. It is all well enough for us of another generation to wax wise with advice to those who bore the burden in the heat of the day. It is full easy now to see that the man who lost home, fortune, and family at a stroke, and saw his land ruled by "mules and niggers," was really benefited by the passing of slavery. It is not difficult now to say to the young freedman, cheated and cuffed about, who has seen his father's head beaten to a jelly and his own mother namelessly assaulted, that the meek shall inherit the earth. Above all, nothing is more convenient than to heap on the Freedmen's Bureau all the evils of that evil day, and damn it utterly for every mistake and blunder that was made.

All this is easy, but it is neither sensible nor just. Some one had blundered, but that was long before Oliver Howard was born; there was criminal aggression and heedless neglect, but without some system of control there would have been far more than there was. Had that control been from within, the Negro would have been re-enslaved, to all intents and purposes. Coming as the control did from without, perfect men and methods would have bettered all things; and even with imperfect agents and questionable methods, the work accomplished was not undeserving of commendation.

Such was the dawn of Freedom; such was the work of the Freedmen's Bureau, which, summed up in brief, may be epitomized thus: For some fifteen million dollars, beside the sums spent before 1865, and the dole of benevolent societies, this Bureau set going a system of free labor, established a beginning of peasant proprietorship, secured the recognition of black freedmen before courts of law, and founded the free common school in the South. On the other hand, it failed to begin the establishment of good-will between ex-masters and freedmen, to guard its work wholly from paternalistic methods which discouraged self-reliance, and to carry out to any considerable extent its implied promises to furnish the freedmen with land. Its successes were the result of hard work, supplemented by the aid of philanthropists and the eager striving of black men. Its failures were the result of bad local agents, the inherent difficulties of the work, and national neglect.

Such an institution, from its wide powers, great responsibilities, large control of moneys, and generally conspicuous position, was naturally open to repeated and bitter attack. It sustained a searching Congressional investigation at the instance of Fernando Wood in 1870. Its archives and few remaining functions were with blunt discourtesy transferred from Howard's control, in his absence, to the supervision of Secretary of War Belknap in 1872, on the Secretary's recommendation. Finally, in consequence of grave intimations of wrong-doing made by the Secretary and his subordinates,

General Howard was court-martialed in 1874. In both of these trials the Commissioner of the Freedmen's Bureau was officially exonerated from any wilful misdoing, and his work commended. Nevertheless, many unpleasant things were brought to light,—the methods of transacting the business of the Bureau were faulty; several cases of defalcation were proved, and other frauds strongly suspected; there were some business transactions which savored of dangerous speculation, if not dishonesty; and around it all lay the smirch of the Freedmen's Bank.*

Morally and practically, the Freedmen's Bank was part of the Freedmen's Bureau, although it had no legal connection with it. With the prestige of the government back of it, and a directing board of unusual respectability and national reputation, this banking institution had made a remarkable start in the development of that thrift among black folk which slavery had kept them from knowing. Then in one sad day came the crash,—all the hard-earned dollars of the freedmen disappeared; but that was the least of the loss,—all the faith in saving went too, and much of the faith in men; and that was a loss that a Nation which to-day sneers at Negro shiftlessness has never yet made good. Not even ten additional years of slavery could have done so much to throttle the thrift of the freedmen as the mismanagement and bankruptcy of the series of savings banks chartered by the Nation for their especial aid. Where all the blame should rest, it is hard to say; whether the Bureau and the Bank died chiefly by reason of the blows of its selfish friends or the dark machinations of its foes, perhaps even time will never reveal, for here lies unwritten history.

Of the foes without the Bureau, the bitterest were those who attacked not so much its conduct or policy under the law as the necessity for any such institution at all. Such attacks came primarily from the Border States and the South; and they were summed up by Senator Davis, of Kentucky, when he moved to entitle the act of 1866 a bill "to promote strife and conflict between the white and black races . . . by a grant of unconstitutional power." The argument gathered tremendous strength South and North; but its very strength was its weakness. For, argued the plain common-sense of the nation, if it is unconstitutional, unpractical, and futile for the

---

*Established by Congress in 1865; failed in 1874.

nation to stand guardian over its helpless wards, then there is left but one alternative,—to make those wards their own guardians by arming them with the ballot. Moreover, the path of the practical politician pointed the same way; for, argued this opportunist, if we cannot peacefully reconstruct the South with white votes, we certainly can with black votes. So justice and force joined hands.

The alternative thus offered the nation was not between full and restricted Negro suffrage; else every sensible man, black and white, would easily have chosen the latter. It was rather a choice between suffrage and slavery, after endless blood and gold had flowed to sweep human bondage away. Not a single Southern legislature stood ready to admit a Negro, under any conditions, to the polls; not a single Southern legislature believed free Negro labor was possible without a system of restrictions that took all its freedom away; there was scarcely a white man in the South who did not honestly regard Emancipation as a crime, and its practical nullification as a duty. In such a situation, the granting of the ballot to the black man was a necessity, the very least a guilty nation could grant a wronged race, and the only method of compelling the South to accept the results of the war. Thus Negro suffrage ended a civil war by beginning a race feud. And some felt gratitude toward the race thus sacrificed in its swaddling clothes on the altar of national integrity; and some felt and feel only indifference and contempt.

Had political exigencies been less pressing, the opposition to government guardianship of Negroes less bitter, and the attachment to the slave system less strong, the social seer can well imagine a far better policy,—a permanent Freedmen's Bureau, with a national system of Negro schools; a carefully supervised employment and labor office; a system of impartial protection before the regular courts; and such institutions for social betterment as savings-banks, land and building associations, and social settlements. All this vast expenditure of money and brains might have formed a great school of prospective citizenship, and solved in a way we have not yet solved the most perplexing and persistent of the Negro problems.

That such an institution was unthinkable in 1870 was due in part to certain acts of the Freedmen's Bureau itself. It came to regard its work as merely temporary, and Negro suffrage as a final answer to all present perplexities. The political ambition of many of its agents and *protégés* led it far afield into questionable activi-

ties, until the South, nursing its own deep prejudices, came easily
to ignore all the good deeds of the Bureau and hate its very name
with perfect hatred. So the Freedmen's Bureau died, and its child
was the Fifteenth Amendment.

The passing of a great human institution before its work is
done, like the untimely passing of a single soul, but leaves a
legacy of striving for other men. The legacy of the Freedmen's
Bureau is the heavy heritage of this generation. To-day, when
new and vaster problems are destined to strain every fibre of the
national mind and soul, would it not be well to count this legacy
honestly and carefully? For this much all men know: despite
compromise, war, and struggle, the Negro is not free. In the
backwoods of the Gulf States, for miles and miles, he may not
leave the plantation of his birth; in well-nigh the whole rural
South the black farmers are peons, bound by law and custom to
an economic slavery, from which the only escape is death or the
penitentiary. In the most cultured sections and cities of the South
the Negroes are a segregated servile caste, with restricted rights
and privileges. Before the courts, both in law and custom, they
stand on a different and peculiar basis. Taxation without representation is the rule of their political life. And the result of all this
is, and in nature must have been, lawlessness and crime. That is
the large legacy of the Freedmen's Bureau, the work it did not do
because it could not.

I have seen a land right merry with the sun, where children sing,
and rolling hills lie like passioned women wanton with harvest.
And there in the King's Highway° sat and sits a figure veiled and
bowed, by which the traveller's footsteps hasten as they go. On the
tainted air broods fear. Three centuries' thought has been the raising and unveiling of that bowed human heart, and now behold a
century new for the duty and the deed. The problem of the Twentieth Century is the problem of the color-line.

°See the Bible, Numbers 20:17 and 21:22. The Hebrews are prohibited from
using the road called the King's Highway and therefore are forced to wander in
the desert.

III

Of Mr. Booker T. Washington and Others[1]

From birth till death enslaved; in word, in deed, unmanned!

Hereditary bondsmen! Know ye not
Who would be free themselves must strike the blow?

Byron.*

EASILY THE MOST STRIKING thing in the history of the American Negro since 1876 is the ascendancy of Mr. Booker T. Washington. It began at the time when war memories and ideals were rapidly passing; a day of astonishing commercial development was dawning; a sense of doubt and hesitation overtook the freedmen's sons,—then it was that his leading began. Mr. Washington came, with a simple definite programme, at the psychological moment when the nation was a little ashamed of having bestowed so much sentiment on Negroes, and was concentrating its energies on Dollars. His programme of industrial education, conciliation of the South, and submission and silence as to civil and political rights, was not wholly original; the Free Negroes from 1830 up to wartime had striven to build industrial schools, and the American Missionary Association had from the first taught various trades; and Price and others had sought a way of honorable alliance with the best of the Southerners. But Mr. Washington first indissolubly linked these things; he put enthusiasm, unlimited energy, and perfect

---

*From *Childe Harold's Pilgrimage* (1812), by George Gordon, Lord Byron.
† From "A Great Camp-Meeting in the Promised Land."

35

faith into this programme, and changed it from a by-path into a veritable Way of Life. And the tale of the methods by which he did this is a fascinating study of human life.

It startled the nation to hear a Negro advocating such a programme after many decades of bitter complaint; it startled and won the applause of the South, it interested and won the admiration of the North; and after a confused murmur of protest, it silenced if it did not convert the Negroes themselves.

To gain the sympathy and coöperation of the various elements comprising the white South was Mr. Washington's first task; and this, at the time Tuskegee was founded, seemed, for a black man, well-nigh impossible. And yet ten years later it was done in the word spoken at Atlanta: "In all things purely social we can be as separate as the five fingers, and yet one as the hand in all things essential to mutual progress." This "Atlanta Compromise"[2] is by all odds the most notable thing in Mr. Washington's career. The South interpreted it in different ways: the radicals received it as a complete surrender of the demand for civil and political equality; the conservatives, as a generously conceived working basis for mutual understanding. So both approved it, and to-day its author is certainly the most distinguished Southerner since Jefferson Davis, and the one with the largest personal following.

Next to this achievement comes Mr. Washington's work in gaining place and consideration in the North. Others less shrewd and tactful had formerly essayed to sit on these two stools and had fallen between them; but as Mr. Washington knew the heart of the South from birth and training, so by singular insight he intuitively grasped the spirit of the age which was dominating the North. And so thoroughly did he learn the speech and thought of triumphant commercialism, and the ideals of material prosperity, that the picture of a lone black boy poring over a French grammar[3] amid the weeds and dirt of a neglected home soon seemed to him the acme of absurdities. One wonders what Socrates and St. Francis of Assisi would say to this.

And yet this very singleness of vision and thorough oneness with his age is a mark of the successful man. It is as though Nature must needs make men narrow in order to give them force. So Mr. Washington's cult has gained unquestioning followers, his work has wonderfully prospered, his friends are legion, and his en-

emies are confounded. To-day he stands as the one recognized
spokesman of his ten million fellows, and one of the most notable
figures in a nation of seventy millions. One hesitates, therefore, to
criticise a life which, beginning with so little, has done so much.
And yet the time is come when one may speak in all sincerity and
utter courtesy of the mistakes and shortcomings of Mr. Washington's career, as well as of his triumphs, without being thought cap-
tious or envious, and without forgetting that it is easier to do ill
than well in the world.

The criticism that has hitherto met Mr. Washington has not always been of this broad character. In the South especially has he
had to walk warily to avoid the harshest judgments,—and naturally so, for he is dealing with the one subject of deepest sensitiveness to that section. Twice—once when at the Chicago
celebration of the Spanish-American War he alluded to the color-
prejudice that is "eating away the vitals of the South," and once
when he dined with President Roosevelt—has the resulting
Southern criticism been violent enough to threaten seriously his
popularity. In the North the feeling has several times forced itself
into words, that Mr. Washington's counsels of submission overlooked certain elements of true manhood, and that his educational
programme was unnecessarily narrow. Usually, however, such criticism has not found open expression, although, too, the spiritual
sons of the Abolitionists have not been prepared to acknowledge
that the schools founded before Tuskegee, by men of broad ideals
and self-sacrificing spirit, were wholly failures or worthy of ridicule. While, then, criticism has not failed to follow Mr. Washington, yet the prevailing public opinion of the land has been but too
willing to deliver the solution of a wearisome problem into his
hands, and say, "If that is all you and your race ask, take it."

Among his own people, however, Mr. Washington has encoun-
tered the strongest and most lasting opposition, amounting at
times to bitterness, and even to-day continuing strong and insistent even though largely silenced in outward expression by the
public opinion of the nation. Some of this opposition is, of course,
mere envy; the disappointment of displaced demagogues and the
spite of narrow minds. But aside from this, there is among educated and thoughtful colored men in all parts of the land a feeling
of deep regret, sorrow, and apprehension at the wide currency and

ascendancy which some of Mr. Washington's theories have gained. These same men admire his sincerity of purpose, and are willing to forgive much to honest endeavor which is doing something worth the doing. They coöperate with Mr. Washington as far as they conscientiously can; and, indeed, it is no ordinary tribute to this man's tact and power that, steering as he must between so many diverse interests and opinions, he so largely retains the respect of all.

But the hushing of the criticism of honest opponents is a dangerous thing. It leads some of the best of the critics to unfortunate silence and paralysis of effort, and others to burst into speech so passionately and intemperately as to lose listeners. Honest and earnest criticism from those whose interests are most nearly touched,—criticism of writers by readers, of government by those governed, of leaders by those led,—this is the soul of democracy and the safeguard of modern society. If the best of the American Negroes receive by outer pressure a leader whom they had not recognized before, manifestly there is here a certain palpable gain. Yet there is also irreparable loss,—a loss of that peculiarly valuable education which a group receives when by search and criticism it finds and commissions its own leaders. The way in which this is done is at once the most elementary and the nicest problem of social growth. History is but the record of such group-leadership; and yet how infinitely changeful is its type and character! And of all types and kinds, what can be more instructive than the leadership of a group within a group?—that curious double movement where real progress may be negative and actual advance be relative retrogression. All this is the social student's inspiration and despair.

Now in the past the American Negro has had instructive experience in the choosing of group leaders, founding thus a peculiar dynasty which in the light of present conditions is worth while studying. When sticks and stones and beasts form the sole environment of a people, their attitude is largely one of determined opposition to and conquest of natural forces. But when to earth and brute is added an environment of men and ideas, then the attitude of the imprisoned group may take three main forms,—a feeling of revolt and revenge; an attempt to adjust all thought and action to the will of the greater group; or, finally, a determined effort at self-realization and self-development despite environing opinion. The influence of all of these attitudes at various times can be traced in the history of the American Negro, and in the evolution of his successive leaders.

Before 1750, while the fire of African freedom still burned in the veins of the slaves, there was in all leadership or attempted leadership but the one motive of revolt and revenge,—typified in the terrible Maroons, the Danish blacks, and Cato of Stono,[4] and veiling all the Americas in fear of insurrection. The liberalizing tendencies of the latter half of the eighteenth century brought, along with kindlier relations between black and white, thoughts of ultimate adjustment and assimilation. Such aspiration was especially voiced in the earnest songs of Phyllis, in the martyrdom of Attucks, the fighting of Salem and Poor, the intellectual accomplishments of Banneker and Derham, and the political demands of the Cuffes.

Stern financial and social stress after the war cooled much of the previous humanitarian ardor. The disappointment and impatience of the Negroes at the persistence of slavery and serfdom voiced itself in two movements. The slaves in the South, aroused undoubtedly by vague rumors of the Haytian revolt, made three fierce attempts at insurrection,—in 1800 under Gabriel[*] in Virginia, in 1822 under Vesey in Carolina, and in 1831 again in Virginia under the terrible Nat Turner. In the Free States, on the other hand, a new and curious attempt at self-development was made. In Philadelphia and New York color-prescription led to a withdrawal of Negro communicants from white churches and the formation of a peculiar socio-religious institution among the Negroes known as the African Church,[†]—an organization still living and controlling in its various branches over a million of men.

Walker's wild appeal against the trend of the times showed how the world was changing after the coming of the cotton-gin. By 1830 slavery seemed hopelessly fastened on the South, and the slaves thoroughly cowed into submission. The free Negroes of the North, inspired by the mulatto immigrants from the West Indies,

---

[*]Gabriel Prosser (see Appendix).
[†]The African Methodist Episcopal Church.

began to change the basis of their demands; they recognized the slavery of slaves, but insisted that they themselves were freemen, and sought assimilation and amalgamation with the nation on the same terms with other men. Thus, Forten and Purvis of Philadelphia, Shad of Wilmington, Du Bois of New Haven, Barbadoes of Boston, and others, strove singly and together as men, they said, not as slaves; as "people of color," not as "Negroes." The trend of the times, however, refused them recognition save in individual and exceptional cases, considered them as one with all the despised blacks, and they soon found themselves striving to keep even the rights they formerly had of voting and working and moving as freemen. Schemes of migration and colonization arose among them; but these they refused to entertain, and they eventually turned to the Abolition movement as a final refuge.

Here, led by Remond, Nell, Wells-Brown, and Douglass, a new period of self-assertion and self-development dawned. To be sure, ultimate freedom and assimilation was the ideal before the leaders, but the assertion of the manhood rights of the Negro by himself was the main reliance, and John Brown's raid was the extreme of its logic. After the war and emancipation, the great form of Frederick Douglass, the greatest of American Negro leaders, still led the host. Self-assertion, especially in political lines, was the main programme, and behind Douglass came Elliot, Bruce, and Langston, and the Reconstruction politicians, and, less conspicuous but of greater social significance Alexander Crummell and Bishop Daniel Payne.

Then came the Revolution of 1876, the suppression of the Negro votes, the changing and shifting of ideals, and the seeking of new lights in the great night. Douglass, in his old age, still bravely stood for the ideals of his early manhood,—ultimate assimilation *through* self-assertion, and on no other terms. For a time Price arose as a new leader, destined, it seemed, not to give up, but to re-state the old ideals in a form less repugnant to the white South. But he passed away in his prime. Then came the new leader. Nearly all the former ones had become leaders by the silent suffrage of their fellows, had sought to lead their own people alone, and were usually, save Douglass, little known outside their race. But Booker T. Washington arose as essentially the leader not of one race but of two,—a compromiser between the

South, the North, and the Negro. Naturally the Negroes resented, at first bitterly, signs of compromise which surrendered their civil and political rights, even though this was to be exchanged for larger chances of economic development. The rich and dominating North, however, was not only weary of the race problem, but was investing largely in Southern enterprises, and welcomed any method of peaceful coöperation. Thus, by national opinion, the Negroes began to recognize Mr. Washington's leadership; and the voice of criticism was hushed.

Mr. Washington represents in Negro thought the old attitude of adjustment and submission; but adjustment at such a peculiar time as to make his programme unique. This is an age of unusual economic development, and Mr. Washington's programme naturally takes an economic cast, becoming a gospel of Work and Money to such an extent as apparently almost completely to overshadow the higher aims of life. Moreover, this is an age when the more advanced races are coming in closer contact with the less developed races, and the race-feeling is therefore intensified; and Mr. Washington's programme practically accepts the alleged inferiority of the Negro races. Again, in our own land, the reaction from the sentiment of war time has given impetus to race-prejudice against Negroes, and Mr. Washington withdraws many of the high demands of Negroes as men and American citizens. In other periods of intensified prejudice all the Negro's tendency to self-assertion has been called forth; at this period a policy of submission is advocated. In the history of nearly all other races and peoples the doctrine preached at such crises has been that manly self-respect is worth more than lands and houses, and that a people who voluntarily surrender such respect, or cease striving for it, are not worth civilizing.

In answer to this, it has been claimed that the Negro can survive only through submission. Mr. Washington distinctly asks that black people give up, at least for the present, three things,—

First, political power,

Second, insistence on civil rights,

Third, higher education of Negro youth,—

and concentrate all their energies on industrial education, the accumulation of wealth, and the conciliation of the South. This policy has been courageously and insistently advocated for over fifteen years, and has been triumphant for perhaps ten years. As a result of this tender of the palm-branch, what has been the return? In these years there have occurred:

1. The disfranchisement of the Negro.
2. The legal creation of a distinct status of civil inferiority for the Negro.
3. The steady withdrawal of aid from institutions for the higher training of the Negro.

These movements are not, to be sure, direct results of Mr. Washington's teachings; but his propaganda has, without a shadow of doubt, helped their speedier accomplishment. The question then comes: Is it possible, and probable, that nine millions of men can make effective progress in economic lines if they are deprived of political rights, made a servile caste, and allowed only the most meagre chance for developing their exceptional men? If history and reason give any distinct answer to these questions, it is an emphatic *No*. And Mr. Washington thus faces the triple paradox of his career:

1. He is striving nobly to make Negro artisans business men and property-owners; but it is utterly impossible, under modern competitive methods, for workingmen and property-owners to defend their rights and exist without the right of suffrage.
2. He insists on thrift and self-respect, but at the same time counsels a silent submission to civic inferiority such as is bound to sap the manhood of any race in the long run.
3. He advocates common-school and industrial training, and depreciates institutions of higher learning; but neither the Negro common-schools, nor Tuskegee itself, could remain open a day were it not for teachers trained in Negro colleges, or trained by their graduates.

This triple paradox in Mr. Washington's position is the object of criticism by two classes of colored Americans. One class is spiritually descended from Toussaint the Savior, through Gabriel, Vesey, and Turner, and they represent the attitude of revolt and revenge;

they hate the white South blindly and distrust the white race generally, and so far as they agree on definite action, think that the Negro's only hope lies in emigration beyond the borders of the United States. And yet, by the irony of fate, nothing has more effectually made this programme seem hopeless than the recent course of the United States toward weaker and darker peoples in the West Indies, Hawaii, and the Philippines,—for where in the world may we go and be safe from lying and brute force?

The other class of Negroes who cannot agree with Mr. Washington has hitherto said little aloud. They deprecate the sight of scattered counsels, of internal disagreement; and especially they dislike making their just criticism of a useful and earnest man an excuse for a general discharge of venom from small-minded opponents. Nevertheless, the questions involved are so fundamental and serious that it is difficult to see how men like the Grimkes, Kelly Miller, J. W. E. Bowen, and other representatives of this group, can much longer be silent. Such men feel in conscience bound to ask of this nation three things:

1. The right to vote.
2. Civic equality.
3. The education of youth according to ability.

They acknowledge Mr. Washington's invaluable service in counselling patience and courtesy in such demands; they do not ask that ignorant black men vote when ignorant whites are debarred, or that any reasonable restrictions in the suffrage should not be applied; they know that the low social level of the mass of the race is responsible for much discrimination against it, but they also know, and the nation knows, that relentless color-prejudice is more often a cause than a result of the Negro's degradation; they seek the abatement of this relic of barbarism, and not its systematic encouragement and pampering by all agencies of social power from the Associated Press to the Church of Christ. They advocate, with Mr. Washington, a broad system of Negro common schools supplemented by thorough industrial training; but they are surprised that a man of Mr. Washington's insight cannot see that no such educational system ever has rested or can rest on any other basis than that of the well-equipped college and university, and they insist that there is a demand for a few such institutions throughout the South to train the best of the Negro youth as teachers, professional men, and leaders.

This group of men honor Mr. Washington for his attitude of conciliation toward the white South; they accept the "Atlanta Compromise" in its broadest interpretation; they recognize, with him, many signs of promise, many men of high purpose and fair judgment, in this section; they know that no easy task has been laid upon a region already tottering under heavy burdens. But, nevertheless, they insist that the way to truth and right lies in straightforward honesty, not in indiscriminate flattery; in praising those of the South who do well and criticising uncompromisingly those who do ill; in taking advantage of the opportunities at hand and urging their fellows to do the same, but at the same time in remembering that only a firm adherence to their higher ideals and aspirations will ever keep those ideals within the realm of possibility. They do not expect that the free right to vote, to enjoy civic rights, and to be educated, will come in a moment; they do not expect to see the bias and prejudices of years disappear at the blast of a trumpet; but they are absolutely certain that the way for a people to gain their reasonable rights is not by voluntarily throwing them away and insisting that they do not want them; that the way for a people to gain respect is not by continually belittling and ridiculing themselves; that, on the contrary, Negroes must insist continually, in season and out of season, that voting is necessary to modern manhood, that color discrimination is barbarism, and that black boys need education as well as white boys.

In failing thus to state plainly and unequivocally the legitimate demands of their people, even at the cost of opposing an honored leader, the thinking classes of American Negroes would shirk a heavy responsibility,—a responsibility to themselves, a responsibility to the struggling masses, a responsibility to the darker races of men whose future depends so largely on this American experiment, but especially a responsibility to this nation,—this common Fatherland. It is wrong to encourage a man or a people in evil-doing; it is wrong to aid and abet a national crime simply because it is unpopular not to do so. The growing spirit of kindliness and reconciliation between the North and South after the frightful differences of a generation ago ought to be a source of deep congratulation to all, and especially to those whose mistreatment caused the war; but if that reconciliation is to be marked by the industrial slavery and civic death of those same black men, with permanent legislation into a position of inferiority, then those black men, if they are really men, are called upon by every consideration of patriotism and loyalty to oppose such a course by all civilized methods, even though such opposition involves disagreement with Mr. Booker T. Washington. We have no right to sit silently by while the inevitable seeds are sown for a harvest of disaster to our children, black and white.

First, it is the duty of black men to judge the South discriminatingly. The present generation of Southerners are not responsible for the past, and they should not be blindly hated or blamed for it. Furthermore, to no class is the indiscriminate endorsement of the recent course of the South toward Negroes more nauseating than to the best thought of the South. The South is not "solid"; it is a land in the ferment of social change, wherein forces of all kinds are fighting for supremacy; and to praise the ill the South is to-day perpetrating is just as wrong as to condemn the good. Discriminating and broad-minded criticism is what the South needs,—needs it for the sake of her own white sons and daughters, and for the insurance of robust, healthy mental and moral development.

To-day even the attitude of the Southern whites toward the blacks is not, as so many assume, in all cases the same; the ignorant Southerner hates the Negro, the workingmen fear his competition, the money-makers wish to use him as a laborer, some of the educated see a menace in his upward development, while others—usually the sons of the masters—wish to help him to rise. National opinion has enabled this last class to maintain the Negro common schools, and to protect the Negro partially in property, life, and limb. Through the pressure of the money-makers, the Negro is in danger of being reduced to semi-slavery, especially in the country districts; the workingmen, and those of the educated who fear the Negro, have united to disfranchise him, and some have urged his deportation; while the passions of the ignorant are easily aroused to lynch and abuse any black man. To praise this intricate whirl of thought and prejudice is nonsense; to inveigh indiscriminately against "the South" is unjust; but to use the same breath in praising Governor Aycock, exposing Senator Morgan, arguing with Mr. Thomas Nelson Page, and denouncing Senator Ben Tillman, is not only sane, but the imperative duty of thinking black men.

It would be unjust to Mr. Washington not to acknowledge that in several instances he has opposed movements in the South which were unjust to the Negro; he sent memorials to the Louisiana and Alabama constitutional conventions, he has spoken against lynching, and in other ways has openly or silently set his influence against sinister schemes and unfortunate happenings. Notwithstanding this, it is equally true to assert that on the whole the distinct impression left by Mr. Washington's propaganda is, first, that the South is justified in its present attitude toward the Negro because of the Negro's degradation; secondly, that the prime cause of the Negro's failure to rise more quickly is his wrong education in the past; and, thirdly, that his future rise depends primarily on his own efforts. Each of these propositions is a dangerous half-truth. The supplementary truths must never be lost sight of: first, slavery and race-prejudice are potent if not sufficient causes of the Negro's position; second, industrial and common-school training were necessarily slow in planting because they had to await the black teachers trained by higher institutions,—it being extremely doubtful if any essentially different development was possible, and certainly a Tuskegee was unthinkable before 1880; and, third, while it is a great truth to say that the Negro must strive and strive mightily to help himself, it is equally true that unless his striving be not simply seconded, but rather aroused and encouraged, by the initiative of the richer and wiser environing group, he cannot hope for great success.

In his failure to realize and impress this last point, Mr. Washington is especially to be criticised. His doctrine has tended to make the whites, North and South, shift the burden of the Negro problem to the Negro's shoulders and stand aside as critical and rather pessimistic spectators; when in fact the burden belongs to the nation, and the hands of none of us are clean if we bend not our energies to righting these great wrongs.

The South ought to be led, by candid and honest criticism, to assert her better self and do her full duty to the race she has cruelly wronged and is still wronging. The North—her co-partner in guilt—cannot salve her conscience by plastering it with gold. We cannot settle this problem by diplomacy and suaveness, by "policy" alone. If worse come to worst, can the moral fibre of this country survive the slow throttling and murder of nine millions of men?

The black men of America have a duty to perform, a duty stern and delicate,—a forward movement to oppose a part of the work of their greatest leader. So far as Mr. Washington preaches Thrift, Patience, and Industrial Training for the masses, we must hold up his hands and strive with him, rejoicing in his honors and glorying in the strength of this Joshua called of God and of man to lead the headless host. But so far as Mr. Washington apologizes for injustice, North or South, does not rightly value the privilege and duty of voting, belittles the emasculating effects of caste distinctions, and opposes the higher training and ambition of our brighter minds,—so far as he, the South, or the Nation, does this,—we must unceasingly and firmly oppose them. By every civilized and peaceful method we must strive for the rights which the world accords to men, clinging unwaveringly to those great words which the sons of the Fathers would fain forget: "We hold these truths to be self-evident: That all men are created equal; that they are endowed by their Creator with certain unalienable rights; that among these are life, liberty, and the pursuit of happiness."*

---

*The Preamble to the Declaration of Independence.

IV

Of the Meaning of Progress[1]

Willst Du Deine Macht verkünden,
Wähle sie, die frei von Sünden
Steh'n in Deinem ew'gen Haus!
Deine Geister sende aus!
Die Unsterblichen, die Reinen,
Die nicht fühlen, die nicht weinen!
Nicht die zarte Jungfrau wähle,
Nicht der Hirtin weiche Seele![*]

Schiller.[†]

ONCE UPON A TIME I taught school in the hills of Tennessee, where the broad dark vale of the Mississippi begins to roll and crumple to greet the Alleghanies. I was a Fisk student then, and all Fisk men thought that Tennessee—beyond the Veil—was theirs alone, and in vacation time they sallied forth in lusty bands to meet the county school-commissioners. Young and happy, I too went, and I shall not soon forget that summer, seventeen years ago.

---

[*]When thou wouldst manifest thy might / Choose instruments beyond desire! / Celestial spirits robed in light, / The leaders of the angel choir! / Obedient children of the spheres / They know no longing, know no tears. / Choose not to wear God's coat of mail / A shepherd maiden, mild and frail. From a speech by Joan of Arc in act 4, scene 1 of *The Maid of Orleans*, by Johann Christoph Friedrich von Schiller, translated by George Sylvester Viereck, Girard, KS: Haldeman-Julius Co., 1925.

[†]From *The Maid of Orleans* (1801), by Johann Christoph Friedrich von Schiller.

[‡]From "My Way's Cloudy."

First, there was a Teachers' Institute at the county-seat; and there distinguished guests of the superintendent taught the teachers fractions and spelling and other mysteries,—white teachers in the morning, Negroes at night. A picnic now and then, and a supper, and the rough world was softened by laughter and song. I remember how—But I wander.

There came a day when all the teachers left the Institute and began the hunt for schools. I learn from hearsay (for my mother was mortally afraid of fire-arms) that the hunting of ducks and bears and men is wonderfully interesting, but I am sure that the man who has never hunted a country school has something to learn of the pleasures of the chase. I see now the white, hot roads lazily rise and fall and wind before me under the burning July sun; I feel the deep weariness of heart and limb as ten, eight, six miles stretch relentlessly ahead; I feel my heart sink heavily as I hear again and again, "Got a teacher? Yes." So I walked on and on— horses were too expensive—until I had wandered beyond railways, beyond stage lines, to a land of "varmints" and rattlesnakes, where the coming of a stranger was an event, and men lived and died in the shadow of one blue hill.

Sprinkled over hill and dale lay cabins and farmhouses, shut out from the world by the forests and the rolling hills toward the east. There I found at last a little school. Josie told me of it; she was a thin, homely girl of twenty, with a dark-brown face and thick, hard hair. I had crossed the stream at Watertown, and rested under the great willows; then I had gone to the little cabin in the lot where Josie was resting on her way to town. The gaunt farmer made me welcome, and Josie, hearing my errand, told me anxiously that they wanted a school over the hill; that but once since the war had a teacher been there; that she herself longed to learn,—and thus she ran on, talking fast and loud, with much earnestness and energy.

Next morning I crossed the tall round hill, lingered to look at the blue and yellow mountains stretching toward the Carolinas, then plunged into the wood, and came out at Josie's home. It was a dull frame cottage with four rooms, perched just below the brow of the hill, amid peach-trees. The father was a quiet, simple soul, calmly ignorant, with no touch of vulgarity. The mother was different,—strong, bustling, and energetic, with a quick, restless

tongue, and an ambition to live "like folks." There was a crowd of
children. Two boys had gone away. There remained two growing
girls; a shy midget of eight; John, tall, awkward, and eighteen; Jim,
younger, quicker, and better looking; and two babies of indefinite
age. Then there was Josie herself. She seemed to be the centre of
the family: always busy at service, or at home, or berry-picking; a
little nervous and inclined to scold, like her mother, yet faithful,
too, like her father. She had about her a certain fineness, the
shadow of an unconscious moral heroism that would willingly give
all of life to make life broader, deeper, and fuller for her and hers.
I saw much of this family afterwards, and grew to love them for
their honest efforts to be decent and comfortable, and for their
knowledge of their own ignorance. There was with them no affec-
tation. The mother would scold the father for being so "easy";
Josie would roundly berate the boys for carelessness; and all knew
that it was a hard thing to dig a living out of a rocky side-hill.

I secured the school. I remember the day I rode horseback out
to the commissioner's house with a pleasant young white fellow
who wanted the white school. The road ran down the bed of a
stream; the sun laughed and the water jingled, and we rode on.
"Come in," said the commissioner,—"come in. Have a seat. Yes,
that certificate will do. Stay to dinner. What do you want a
month?" "Oh," thought I, "this is lucky"; but even then fell the
awful shadow of the Veil, for they ate first, then I—alone.

The schoolhouse was a log hut, where Colonel Wheeler used to
shelter his corn. It sat in a lot behind a rail fence and thorn bushes,
near the sweetest of springs. There was an entrance where a door
once was, and within, a massive rickety fireplace; great chinks between the logs served as windows. Furniture was scarce. A pale
blackboard crouched in the corner. My desk was made of three
boards, reinforced at critical points, and my chair, borrowed from
the landlady, had to be returned every night. Seats for the children—these puzzled me much. I was haunted by a New England
vision of neat little desks and chairs, but, alas! the reality was
rough plank benches without backs, and at times without legs.
They had the one virtue of making naps dangerous,—possibly
fatal, for the floor was not to be trusted.

It was a hot morning late in July when the school opened. I
trembled when I heard the patter of little feet down the dusty

road, and saw the growing row of dark solemn faces and bright eager eyes facing me. First came Josie and her brothers and sisters. The longing to know, to be a student in the great school at Nashville, hovered like a star above this child-woman amid her work and worry, and she studied doggedly. There were the Dowells from their farm over toward Alexandria,—Fanny, with her smooth black face and wondering eyes; Martha, brown and dull; the pretty girl-wife of a brother, and the younger brood.

There were the Burkes,—two brown and yellow lads, and a tiny haughty-eyed girl. Fat Reuben's little chubby girl came, with golden face and old-gold hair, faithful and solemn. 'Thenie was on hand early,—a jolly, ugly, good-hearted girl, who slyly dipped snuff and looked after her little bow-legged brother. When her mother could spare her, 'Tildy came,—a midnight beauty, with starry eyes and tapering limbs; and her brother, correspondingly homely. And then the big boys,—the hulking Lawrences; the lazy Neills, unfathered sons of mother and daughter; Hickman, with a stoop in his shoulders; and the rest.

There they sat, nearly thirty of them, on the rough benches, their faces shading from a pale cream to a deep brown, the little feet bare and swinging, the eyes full of expectation, with here and there a twinkle of mischief, and the hands grasping Webster's blue-back spelling-book. I loved my school, and the fine faith the children had in the wisdom of their teacher was truly marvellous. We read and spelled together, wrote a little, picked flowers, sang, and listened to stories of the world beyond the hill. At times the school would dwindle away, and I would start out. I would visit Mun Eddings, who lived in two very dirty rooms, and ask why little Lugene, whose flaming face seemed ever ablaze with the dark-red hair uncombed, was absent all last week, or why I missed so often the inimitable rags of Mack and Ed. Then the father, who worked Colonel Wheeler's farm on shares,[2] would tell me how the crops needed the boys; and the thin, slovenly mother, whose face was pretty when washed, assured me that Lugene must mind the baby. "But we'll start them again next week." When the Lawrences stopped, I knew that the doubts of the old folks about book-learning had conquered again, and so, toiling up the hill, and getting as far into the cabin as possible, I put Cicero "pro Archia

Poeta"* into the simplest English with local applications, and usually convinced them—for a week or so.

On Friday nights I often went home with some of the children,—sometimes to Doc Burke's farm. He was a great, loud, thin Black, ever working, and trying to buy the seventy-five acres of hill and dale where he lived; but people said that he would surely fail, and the "white folks would get it all." His wife was a magnificent Amazon, with saffron face and shining hair, uncorseted and barefooted, and the children were strong and beautiful. They lived in a one-and-a-half-room cabin in the hollow of the farm, near the spring. The front room was full of great fat white beds, scrupulously neat; and there were bad chromos on the walls, and a tired centre-table. In the tiny back kitchen I was often invited to "take out and help" myself to fried chicken and wheat biscuit, "meat" and corn pone, string-beans and berries. At first I used to be a little alarmed at the approach of bedtime in the one lone bedroom, but embarrassment was very deftly avoided. First, all the children nodded and slept, and were stowed away in one great pile of goose feathers; next, the mother and the father discreetly slipped away to the kitchen while I went to bed; then, blowing out the dim light, they retired in the dark. In the morning all were up and away before I thought of awaking. Across the road, where fat Reuben lived, they all went outdoors while the teacher retired, because they did not boast the luxury of a kitchen.

I liked to stay with the Dowells, for they had four rooms and plenty of good country fare. Uncle Bird had a small, rough farm, all woods and hills, miles from the big road; but he was full of tales,—he preached now and then,—and with his children, berries, horses, and wheat he was happy and prosperous. Often, to keep the peace, I must go where life was less lovely; for instance, 'Tildy's mother was incorrigibly dirty, Reuben's larder was limited seriously, and herds of untamed insects wandered over the Eddingses' beds. Best of all I loved to go to Josie's, and sit on the porch, eating peaches, while the mother bustled and talked: how Josie had bought the sewing-machine; how Josie worked at service in winter, but that four dollars a month was "mighty little"

---

*Cicero's speech defending the poet Archias.

wages; how Josie longed to go away to school, but that it "looked like" they never could get far enough ahead to let her; how the crops failed and the well was yet unfinished; and, finally, how "mean" some of the white folks were.

For two summers I lived in this little world; it was dull and humdrum. The girls looked at the hill in wistful longing, and the boys fretted and haunted Alexandria. Alexandria was "town,"—a straggling, lazy village of houses, churches, and shops, and an aristocracy of Toms, Dicks, and Captains. Cuddled on the hill to the north was the village of the colored folks, who lived in three- or four-room unpainted cottages, some neat and homelike, and some dirty. The dwellings were scattered rather aimlessly, but they centred about the twin temples of the hamlet, the Methodist, and the Hard-Shell Baptist churches.° These, in turn, leaned gingerly on a sad-colored schoolhouse. Hither my little world wended its crooked way on Sunday to meet other worlds, and gossip, and wonder, and make the weekly sacrifice with frenzied priest at the altar of the "old-time religion." Then the soft melody and mighty cadences of Negro song fluttered and thundered.

I have called my tiny community a world, and so its isolation made it; and yet there was among us but a half-awakened common consciousness, sprung from common joy and grief, at burial, birth, or wedding; from a common hardship in poverty, poor land, and low wages; and, above all, from the sight of the Veil that hung between us and Opportunity. All this caused us to think some thoughts together; but these, when ripe for speech, were spoken in various languages. Those whose eyes twenty-five and more years before had seen "the glory of the coming of the Lord," saw in every present hindrance or help a dark fatalism bound to bring all things right in His own good time. The mass of those to whom slavery was a dim recollection of childhood found the world a puzzling thing: it asked little of them, and they answered with little, and yet it ridiculed their offering. Such a paradox they could not understand, and therefore sank into listless indifference, or shiftlessness, or reckless bravado. There were, however, some—such as Josie, Jim, and Ben—to whom War, Hell, and Slavery were but

---

°Fundamentalist sects of these denominations.

childhood tales, whose young appetites had been whetted to an edge by school and story and half-awakened thought. Ill could they be content, born without and beyond the World. And their weak wings beat against their barriers,—barriers of caste, of youth, of life; at last, in dangerous moments, against everything that opposed even a whim.

The ten years that follow youth, the years when first the realization comes that life is leading somewhere,—these were the years that passed after I left my little school. When they were past, I came by chance once more to the walls of Fisk University, to the halls of the chapel of melody.* As I lingered there in the joy and pain of meeting old school-friends, there swept over me a sudden longing to pass again beyond the blue hill, and to see the homes and the school of other days, and to learn how life had gone with my school-children; and I went.

Josie was dead, and the gray-haired mother said simply, "We've had a heap of trouble since you've been away." I had feared for Jim. With a cultured parentage and a social caste to uphold him, he might have made a venturesome merchant or a West Point cadet. But here he was, angry with life and reckless; and when Farmer Durham charged him with stealing wheat, the old man had to ride fast to escape the stones which the furious fool hurled after him. They told Jim to run away; but he would not run, and the constable came that afternoon. It grieved Josie, and great awkward John walked nine miles every day to see his little brother through the bars of Lebanon jail. At last the two came back together in the dark night. The mother cooked supper, and Josie emptied her purse, and the boys stole away. Josie grew thin and silent, yet worked the more. The hill became steep for the quiet old father, and with the boys away there was little to do in the valley. Josie helped them to sell the old farm, and they moved nearer town. Brother Dennis, the carpenter, built a new house with six rooms; Josie toiled a year in Nashville, and brought back ninety dollars to furnish the house and change it to a home.

---

*Fisk Jubilee Hall, built in 1875 with funds raised by the Fisk Jubilee Singers.

When the spring came, and the birds twittered, and the stream ran proud and full, little sister Lizzie, bold and thoughtless, flushed with the passion of youth, bestowed herself on the tempter, and brought home a nameless child. Josie shivered and worked on, with the vision of school-days all fled, with a face wan and tired,—worked until, on a summer's day, some one married another; then Josie crept to her mother like a hurt child, and slept—and sleeps.

I paused to scent the breeze as I entered the valley. The Lawrences have gone,—father and son forever,—and the other son lazily digs in the earth to live. A new young widow rents out their cabin to fat Reuben. Reuben is a Baptist preacher now, but I fear as lazy as ever, though his cabin has three rooms; and little Ella has grown into a bouncing woman, and is ploughing corn on the hot hillside. There are babies a-plenty, and one half-witted girl. Across the valley is a house I did not know before, and there I found, rocking one baby and expecting another, one of my schoolgirls, a daughter of Uncle Bird Dowell. She looked somewhat worried with her new duties, but soon bristled into pride over her neat cabin and the tale of her thrifty husband, the horse and cow, and the farm they were planning to buy.

My log schoolhouse was gone. In its place stood Progress; and Progress, I understand, is necessarily ugly. The crazy foundation stones still marked the former site of my poor little cabin, and not far away, on six weary boulders, perched a jaunty board house, perhaps twenty by thirty feet, with three windows and a door that locked. Some of the window-glass was broken, and part of an old iron stove lay mournfully under the house. I peeped through the window half reverently, and found things that were more familiar. The blackboard had grown by about two feet, and the seats were still without backs. The county owns the lot now, I hear, and every year there is a session of school. As I sat by the spring and looked on the Old and the New I felt glad, very glad, and yet—

After two long drinks I started on. There was the great double log-house on the corner. I remembered the broken, blighted family that used to live there. The strong, hard face of the mother, with its wilderness of hair, rose before me. She had driven her husband away, and while I taught school a strange man lived there, big and jovial, and people talked. I felt sure that Ben and

'Tildy would come to naught from such a home. But this is an odd world; for Ben is a busy farmer in Smith County, "doing well, too," they say, and he had cared for little 'Tildy until last spring, when a lover married her. A hard life the lad had led, toiling for meat, and laughed at because he was homely and crooked. There was Sam Carlon, an impudent old skinflint, who had definite notions about "niggers," and hired Ben a summer and would not pay him. Then the hungry boy gathered his sacks together, and in broad daylight went into Carlon's corn; and when the hard-fisted farmer set upon him, the angry boy flew at him like a beast. Doc Burke saved a murder and a lynching that day.

The story reminded me again of the Burkes, and an impatience seized me to know who won in the battle, Doc or the seventy-five acres. For it is a hard thing to make a farm out of nothing, even in fifteen years. So I hurried on, thinking of the Burkes. They used to have a certain magnificent barbarism about them that I liked. They were never vulgar, never immoral, but rather rough and primitive, with an unconventionality that spent itself in loud guffaws, slaps on the back, and naps in the corner. I hurried by the cottage of the misborn Neill boys. It was empty, and they were grown into fat, lazy farm-hands. I saw the home of the Hickmans, but Albert, with his stooping shoulders, had passed from the world. Then I came to the Burkes' gate and peered through; the inclosure looked rough and untrimmed, and yet there were the same fences around the old farm save to the left, where lay twenty-five other acres. And lo! the cabin in the hollow had climbed the hill and swollen to a half-finished six-room cottage.

The Burkes held a hundred acres, but they were still in debt. Indeed, the gaunt father who toiled night and day would scarcely be happy out of debt, being so used to it. Some day he must stop, for his massive frame is showing decline. The mother wore shoes, but the lion-like physique of other days was broken. The children had grown up. Rob, the image of his father, was loud and rough with laughter. Birdie, my school baby of six, had grown to a picture of maiden beauty, tall and tawny. "Edgar is gone," said the mother, with head half bowed,—"gone to work in Nashville; he and his father couldn't agree."

Little Doc, the boy born since the time of my school, took me horseback down the creek next morning toward Farmer Dowell's.

The road and the stream were battling for mastery, and the stream had the better of it. We splashed and waded, and the merry boy, perched behind me, chattered and laughed. He showed me where Simon Thompson had bought a bit of ground and a home; but his daughter Lana, a plump, brown, slow girl, was not there. She had married a man and a farm twenty miles away. We wound on down the stream till we came to a gate that I did not recognize, but the boy insisted that it was "Uncle Bird's." The farm was fat with the growing crop. In that little valley was a strange stillness as I rode up; for death and marriage had stolen youth and left age and childhood there. We sat and talked that night after the chores were done. Uncle Bird was grayer, and his eyes did not see so well, but he was still jovial. We talked of the acres bought,—one hundred and twenty-five,—of the new guest-chamber added, of Martha's marrying. Then we talked of death: Fanny and Fred were gone; a shadow hung over the other daughter, and when it lifted she was to go to Nashville to school. At last we spoke of the neighbors, and as night fell, Uncle Bird told me how, on a night like that, 'Thenie came wandering back to her home over yonder, to escape the blows of her husband. And next morning she died in the home that her little bow-legged brother, working and saving, had bought for their widowed mother.

My journey was done, and behind me lay hill and dale, and Life and Death. How shall man measure Progress there where the dark-faced Josie lies? How many heartfuls of sorrow shall balance a bushel of wheat? How hard a thing is life to the lowly, and yet how human and real! And all this life and love and strife and failure,—is it the twilight of nightfall or the flush of some faint-dawning day?

Thus sadly musing, I rode to Nashville in the Jim Crow car.°

° Refers to segregated seating on trains.

V

Of the Wings of Atalanta *

O black boy of Atlanta!
  But half was spoken;
The slave's chains and the master's
  Alike are broken;
The one curse of the races
  Held both in tether;
They are rising—all are rising—
  The black and white together.
                              Whittier.[†]

SOUTH OF THE NORTH, yet north of the South, lies the City of a Hundred Hills, peering out from the shadows of the past into the promise of the future. I have seen her in the morning, when the first flush of day had half-roused her; she lay gray and still on the crimson soil of Georgia; then the blue smoke began to curl from her chimneys, the tinkle of bell and scream of whistle broke the silence, the rattle and roar of busy life slowly gathered and swelled, until the seething whirl of the city seemed a strange thing in a sleepy land.

Once, they say, even Atlanta slept dull and drowsy at the foot-hills of the Alleghanies, until the iron baptism of war awakened her with its sullen waters, aroused and maddened her, and left her listening to the sea. And the sea cried to the hills and the hills answered the sea, till the city rose like a widow and cast away her weeds, and toiled for her daily bread; toiled steadily, toiled cun-

---

ningly,—perhaps with some bitterness, with a touch of *réclame,*—and yet with real earnestness, and real sweat.

It is a hard thing to live haunted by the ghost of an untrue dream; to see the wide vision of empire fade into real ashes and dirt; to feel the pang of the conquered, and yet know that with all the Bad that fell on one black day, something was vanquished that deserved to live, something killed that in justice had not dared to die; to know that with the Right that triumphed, triumphed something of Wrong, something sordid and mean, something less than the broadest and best. All this is bitter hard; and many a man and city and people have found in it excuse for sulking, and brooding, and listless waiting.

Such are not men of the sturdier make; they of Atlanta turned resolutely toward the future; and that future held aloft vistas of purple and gold:—Atlanta, Queen of the cotton kingdom; Atlanta, Gateway to the Land of the Sun; Atlanta, the new Lachesis,* spinner of web and woof for the world. So the city crowned her hundred hills with factories, and stored her shops with cunning handiwork, and stretched long iron ways to greet the busy Mercury[†] in his coming. And the Nation talked of her striving.

Perhaps Atlanta was not christened for the winged maiden of dull Bœotia;[‡] you know the tale,—how swarthy Atalanta, tall and wild, would marry only him who out-raced her; and how the wily Hippomenes laid three apples of gold in the way. She fled like a shadow, paused, startled over the first apple, but even as he stretched his hand, fled again; hovered over the second, then, slipping from his hot grasp, flew over river, vale, and hill; but as she lingered over the third, his arms fell round her, and looking on each other, the blazing passion of their love profaned the sanctuary of Love, and they were cursed. If Atlanta be not named for Atalanta, she ought to have been.

Atalanta is not the first or the last maiden whom greed of gold has led to defile the temple of Love; and not maids alone, but men in the race of life, sink from the high and generous ideals of youth

---

*One of the Three Fates of Greek mythology.
[†] Roman god of commerce, travelers, and thieves; also messenger of the gods.
[‡] Location of Thebes in Greece.

to the gambler's code of the Bourse;* and in all our Nation's striving is not the Gospel of Work befouled by the Gospel of Pay? So
common is this that one-half think it normal; so unquestioned,
that we almost fear to question if the end of racing is not gold, if
the aim of man is not rightly to be rich. And if this is the fault of
America, how dire a danger lies before a new land and a new city,
lest Atlanta, stooping for mere gold, shall find that gold accursed!

It was no maiden's idle whim that started this hard racing; a fear-
ful wilderness lay about the feet of that city after the War,—feudalism, poverty, the rise of the Third Estate, serfdom, the re-birth of
Law and Order, and above and between all, the Veil of Race. How
heavy a journey for weary feet! what wings must Atalanta have to flit
over all this hollow and hill, through sour wood and sullen water,
and by the red waste of sun-baked clay! How fleet must Atalanta be
if she will not be tempted by gold to profane the Sanctuary!

The Sanctuary of our fathers has, to be sure, few Gods,—some
sneer, "all too few." There is the thrifty Mercury of New England,
Pluto of the North, and Ceres of the West; and there, too, is the
half-forgotten Apollo of the South, under whose ægis the maiden
ran,—and as she ran she forgot him, even as there in Bœotia
Venus was forgot. She forgot the old ideal of the Southern gentleman,—that new-world heir of the grace and courtliness of patri-
cian, knight, and noble; forgot his honor with his foibles, his
kindliness with his carelessness, and stooped to apples of gold,—
to men busier and sharper, thriftier and more unscrupulous.
Golden apples are beautiful—I remember the lawless days of boyhood, when orchards in crimson and gold tempted me over fence
and field—and, too, the merchant who has dethroned the planter
is no despicable *parvenu*. Work and wealth are the mighty levers
to lift this old new land; thrift and toil and saving are the highways
to new hopes and new possibilities; and yet the warning is needed
lest the wily Hippomenes tempt Atalanta to thinking that golden
apples are the goal of racing, and not mere incidents by the way.

Atlanta must not lead the South to dream of material prosperity
as the touchstone of all success; already the fatal might of this idea
is beginning to spread; it is replacing the finer type of Southerner

---

*Stock exchange.

with vulgar money-getters; it is burying the sweeter beauties of Southern life beneath pretence and ostentation. For every social ill the panacea of Wealth has been urged,—wealth to overthrow the remains of the slave feudalism; wealth to raise the "cracker" Third Estate; wealth to employ the black serfs, and the prospect of wealth to keep them working; wealth as the end and aim of politics, and as the legal tender for Law and Order; and, finally, instead of Truth, Beauty, and Goodness, wealth as the ideal of the Public School.

Not only is this true in the world which Atlanta typifies, but it is threatening to be true of a world beneath and beyond that world,—the Black World beyond the Veil. To-day it makes little difference to Atlanta, to the South, what the Negro thinks or dreams or wills. In the soul-life of the land he is to-day, and naturally will long remain, unthought of, half forgotten; and yet when he does come to think and will and do for himself,—and let no man dream that day will never come,—then the part he plays will not be one of sudden learning, but words and thoughts he has been taught to lisp in his race-childhood. To-day the ferment of his striving toward self-realization is to the strife of the white world like a wheel within a wheel: beyond the Veil are smaller but like problems of ideals, of leaders and the led, of serfdom, of poverty, of order and subordination, and, through all, the Veil of Race. Few know of these problems, few who know notice them; and yet there they are, awaiting student, artist, and seer,—a field for somebody sometime to discover. Hither has the temptation of Hippomenes penetrated; already in this smaller world, which now indirectly and anon directly must influence the larger for good or ill, the habit is forming of interpreting the world in dollars. The old leaders of Negro opinion, in the little groups where there is a Negro social consciousness, are being replaced by new; neither the black preacher nor the black teacher leads as he did two decades ago. Into their places are pushing the farmers and gardeners, the well-paid porters and artisans, the businessmen,—all those with property and money. And with all this change, so curiously parallel to that of the Other-world, goes too the same inevitable change in ideals. The South laments to-day the slow, steady disappearance of a certain type of Negro,—the faithful, courteous slave of other days, with his incorruptible honesty and dignified humility. He is passing away just as surely as the old type of Southern gentleman is passing, and from not dissimilar causes,—the sudden transformation of a fair far-off ideal of Freedom into the hard reality of bread-winning and the consequent deification of Bread.

In the Black World, the Preacher and Teacher embodied once the ideals of this people,—the strife for another and a juster world, the vague dream of righteousness, the mystery of knowing; but to-day the danger is that these ideals, with their simple beauty and weird inspiration, will suddenly sink to a question of cash and a lust for gold. Here stands this black young Atalanta, girding herself for the race that must be run; and if her eyes be still toward the hills and sky as in the days of old, then we may look for noble running; but what if some ruthless or wily or even thoughtless Hippomenes lay golden apples before her? What if the Negro people be wooed from a strife for righteousness, from a love of knowing, to regard dollars as the be-all and end-all of life? What if to the Mammonism° of America be added the rising Mammonism of the reborn South, and the Mammonism of this South be reinforced by the budding Mammonism of its half-awakened black millions? Whither, then, is the new-world quest of Goodness and Beauty and Truth gone glimmering? Must this, and that fair flower of Freedom which, despite the jeers of latter-day striplings, sprung from our fathers' blood, must that too degenerate into a dusty quest of gold,—into lawless lust with Hippomenes?

The hundred hills of Atlanta are not all crowned with factories. On one, toward the west, the setting sun throws three buildings in bold relief against the sky. The beauty of the group lies in its simple unity:—a broad lawn of green rising from the red street with mingled roses and peaches; north and south, two plain and stately halls; and in the midst, half hidden in ivy, a larger building, boldly graceful, sparingly decorated, and with one low spire. It is a restful group,—one never looks for more; it is all here, all intelligible. There I live, and there I hear from day to day the low hum of restful life. In winter's twilight, when the red sun glows, I can see the dark figures pass between the halls to the music of the night-bell. In the morning, when the sun is golden, the clang of the day-bell brings the hurry and laughter of three hundred young hearts from

---

°The immoral pursuit of wealth.

hall and street, and from the busy city below,—children all dark and heavy-haired,—to join their clear young voices in the music of the morning sacrifice. In a half-dozen class-rooms they gather then,—here to follow the love song of Dido, here to listen to the tale of Troy divine; there to wander among the stars, there to wander among men and nations,—and elsewhere other well-worn ways of knowing this queer world. Nothing new, no time-saving devices,—simply old time-glorified methods of delving for Truth, and searching out the hidden beauties of life, and learning the good of living. The riddle of existence is the college curriculum that was laid before the Pharaohs, that was taught in the groves by Plato, that formed the *trivium* and *quadrivium*,° and is to-day laid before the freedmen's sons by Atlanta University. And this course of study will not change; its methods will grow more deft and effectual, its content richer by toil of scholar and sight of seer; but the true college will ever have one goal,—not to earn meat, but to know the end and aim of that life which meat nourishes.

The vision of life that rises before these dark eyes has in it nothing mean or selfish. Not at Oxford or at Leipsic, not at Yale or Columbia, is there an air of higher resolve or more unfettered striving; the determination to realize for men, both black and white, the broadest possibilities of life, to seek the better and the best, to spread with their own hands the Gospel of Sacrifice,—all this is the burden of their talk and dream. Here, amid a wide desert of caste and proscription, amid the heart-hurting slights and jars and vagaries of a deep race-dislike, lies this green oasis, where hot anger cools, and the bitterness of disappointment is sweetened by the springs and breezes of Parnassus; and here men may lie and listen, and learn of a future fuller than the past, and hear the voice of Time:

"Entbehren sollst du, sollst entbehren."†

°In medieval universities, the seven liberal arts were studied in two divisions. The *trivium*, the lower division, comprised grammar, rhetoric, and logic; the *quadrivium*, the upper division, comprised arithmetic, music, geometry, and astronomy.
†"Deny yourself, you must deny yourself" (German); from *Faust* (1808–1832), by Johann Wolfgang von Goethe.

They made their mistakes, those who planted Fisk and Howard and Atlanta before the smoke of battle had lifted; they made their mistakes, but those mistakes were not the things at which we lately laughed somewhat uproariously. They were right when they sought to found a new educational system upon the University: where, forsooth, shall we ground knowledge save on the broadest and deepest knowledge? The roots of the tree, rather than the leaves, are the sources of its life; and from the dawn of history, from Academus to Cambridge, the culture of the University has been the broad foundation-stone on which is built the kindergarten's A B C.

But these builders did make a mistake in minimizing the gravity of the problem before them; in thinking it a matter of years and decades; in therefore building quickly and laying their foundation carelessly, and lowering the standard of knowing, until they had scattered haphazard through the South some dozen poorly equipped high schools and miscalled them universities. They forgot, too, just as their successors are forgetting, the rule of inequality:—that of the million black youth, some were fitted to know and some to dig; that some had the talent and capacity of university men, and some the talent and capacity of blacksmiths; and that true training meant neither that all should be college men nor all artisans, but that the one should be made a missionary of culture to an untaught people, and the other a free workman among serfs. And to seek to make the blacksmith a scholar is almost as silly as the more modern scheme of making the scholar a blacksmith; almost, but not quite.

The function of the university is not simply to teach breadwinning, or to furnish teachers for the public schools, or to be a centre of polite society; it is, above all, to be the organ of that fine adjustment between real life and the growing knowledge of life, an adjustment which forms the secret of civilization. Such an institution the South of to-day sorely needs. She has religion, earnest, bigoted:—religion that on both sides of the Veil often omits the sixth, seventh, and eighth commandments,° but substitutes a dozen supplementary

---

°See the Bible, Deuteronomy 5:17–19: "Thou shalt not kill. Neither shalt thou commit adultery. Neither shalt thou steal" (KJV).

ones. She has, as Atlanta shows, growing thrift and love of toil; but she lacks that broad knowledge of what the world knows and knew of human living and doing, which she may apply to the thousand problems of real life to-day confronting her. The need of the South is knowledge and culture,—not in dainty limited quantity, as before the war, but in broad busy abundance in the world of work; and until she has this, not all the Apples of Hesperides, be they golden and bejewelled, can save her from the curse of the Bœotian lovers.

The Wings of Atalanta are the coming universities of the South. They alone can bear the maiden past the temptation of golden fruit. They will not guide her flying feet away from the cotton and gold; for—ah, thoughtful Hippomenes!—do not the apples lie in the very Way of Life? But they will guide her over and beyond them, and leave her kneeling in the Sanctuary of Truth and Freedom and broad Humanity, virgin and undefiled. Sadly did the Old South err in human education, despising the education of the masses, and niggardly in the support of colleges. Her ancient university foundations dwindled and withered under the foul breath of slavery; and even since the war they have fought a failing fight for life in the tainted air of social unrest and commercial selfishness, stunted by the death of criticism, and starving for lack of broadly cultured men. And if this is the white South's need and danger, how much heavier the danger and need of the freedmen's sons! how pressing here the need of broad ideals and true culture, the conservation of soul from sordid aims and petty passions! Let us build the Southern university—William and Mary, Trinity, Georgia, Texas, Tulane, Vanderbilt, and the others—fit to live; let us build, too, the Negro universities:—Fisk, whose foundation was ever broad; Howard, at the heart of the Nation; Atlanta at Atlanta, whose ideal of scholarship has been held above the temptation of numbers. Why not here, and perhaps elsewhere, plant deeply and for all time centres of learning and living, colleges that yearly would send into the life of the South a few white men and a few black men of broad culture, catholic tolerance, and trained ability, joining their hands to other hands, and giving to this squabble of the Races a decent and dignified peace?

Patience, Humility, Manners, and Taste, common schools and kindergartens, industrial and technical schools, literature and tolerance,—all these spring from knowledge and culture, the children of the university. So must men and nations build, not otherwise, not upside down.

Teach workers to work,—a wise saying; wise when applied to German boys and American girls; wiser when said of Negro boys, for they have less knowledge of working and none to teach them. Teach thinkers to think,—a needed knowledge in a day of loose and careless logic; and they whose lot is gravest must have the carefulest training to think aright. If these things are so, how foolish to ask what is the best education for one or seven or sixty million souls! shall we teach them trades, or train them in liberal arts? Neither and both: teach the workers to work and the thinkers to think; make carpenters of carpenters, and philosophers of philosophers, and fops of fools. Nor can we pause here. We are training not isolated men but a living group of men,—nay, a group within a group. And the final product of our training must be neither a psychologist nor a brickmason, but a man. And to make men, we must have ideals, broad, pure, and inspiring ends of living,—not sordid money-getting, not apples of gold. The worker must work for the glory of his handiwork, not simply for pay; the thinker must think for truth, not for fame. And all this is gained only by human strife and longing; by ceaseless training and education; by founding Right on righteousness and Truth on the unhampered search for Truth; by founding the common school on the university, and the industrial school on the common school; and weaving thus a system, not a distortion, and bringing a birth, not an abortion.

When night falls on the City of a Hundred Hills, a wind gathers itself from the seas and comes murmuring westward. And at its bidding, the smoke of the drowsy factories sweeps down upon the mighty city and covers it like a pall, while yonder at the University the stars twinkle above Stone Hall. And they say that yon gray mist is the tunic of Atalanta pausing over her golden apples. Fly, my maiden, fly, for yonder comes Hippomenes!

VI

Of the Training of Black Men[1]

Why, if the Soul can fling the Dust aside,
And naked on the Air of Heaven ride,
Were 't not a Shame—were 't not a Shame for him
In this clay carcase crippled to abide?
Omar Khayyam (Fitzgerald).[*]

FROM THE SHIMMERING SWIRL of waters where many, many thoughts ago the slave-ship first saw the square tower of Jamestown,[‡] have flowed down to our day three streams of thinking: one swollen from the larger world here and overseas, saying, the multiplying of human wants in culture-lands calls for the world-wide coöperation of men in satisfying them. Hence arises a new human unity, pulling the ends of earth nearer, and all men, black, yellow, and white. The larger humanity strives to feel in this contact of living Nations and sleeping hordes a thrill of new life in the world, crying, "If the contact of Life and Sleep be Death, shame on such Life." To be sure, behind this thought lurks the afterthought of force and dominion,—the making of brown men to delve when the temptation of beads and red calico cloys.

The second thought streaming from the death-ship and the curving river is the thought of the older South,—the sincere and

---

[*]From *The Rubaiyat of Omar Khayyam* (1859), translated by Edward Fitzgerald.
[†]From "March On."
[‡]In Virginia, where the first African captives arrived in 1619.

passionate belief that somewhere between men and cattle, God created a *tertium quid*,° and called it a Negro,—a clownish, simple creature, at times even lovable within its limitations, but straitly foreordained to walk within the Veil. To be sure, behind the thought lurks the afterthought,—some of them with favoring chance might become men, but in sheer self-defence we dare not let them, and we build about them walls so high, and hang between them and the light a veil so thick, that they shall not even think of breaking through.

And last of all there trickles down that third and darker thought,—the thought of the things themselves, the confused, half-conscious mutter of men who are black and whitened, crying "Liberty, Freedom, Opportunity—vouchsafe to us, O boastful World, the chance of living men!" To be sure, behind the thought lurks the afterthought,—suppose, after all, the World is right and we are less than men? Suppose this mad impulse within is all wrong, some mock mirage from the untrue?

So here we stand among thoughts of human unity, even through conquest and slavery; the inferiority of black men, even if forced by fraud; a shriek in the night for the freedom of men who themselves are not yet sure of their right to demand it. This is the tangle of thought and afterthought wherein we are called to solve the problem of training men for life.

Behind all its curiousness, so attractive alike to sage and *dilettante*, lie its dim dangers, throwing across us shadows at once grotesque and awful. Plain it is to us that what the world seeks through desert and wild we have within our threshold,—a stalwart laboring force, suited to the semi-tropics; if, deaf to the voice of the Zeitgeist, we refuse to use and develop these men, we risk poverty and loss. If, on the other hand, seized by the brutal afterthought, we debauch the race thus caught in our talons, selfishly sucking their blood and brains in the future as in the past, what shall save us from national decadence? Only that saner selfishness, which Education teaches men, can find the rights of all in the whirl of work.

°A third something (Latin).

Again, we may decry the color-prejudice of the South, yet it remains a heavy fact. Such curious kinks of the human mind exist
and must be reckoned with soberly. They cannot be laughed away,
nor always successfully stormed at, nor easily abolished by act of
legislature. And yet they must not be encouraged by being let
alone. They must be recognized as facts, but unpleasant facts;
things that stand in the way of civilization and religion and common decency. They can be met in but one way,—by the breadth
and broadening of human reason, by catholicity of taste and culture. And so, too, the native ambition and aspiration of men, even
though they be black, backward, and ungraceful, must not lightly
be dealt with. To stimulate wildly weak and untrained minds is to
play with mighty fires; to flout their striving idly is to welcome a
harvest of brutish crime and shameless lethargy in our very laps.
The guiding of thought and the deft coördination of deed is at
once the path of honor and humanity.

And so, in this great question of reconciling three vast and partially contradictory streams of thought, the one panacea of Education leaps to the lips of all:—such human training as will best
use the labor of all men without enslaving or brutalizing; such
training as will give us poise to encourage the prejudices that bul-
wark society, and to stamp out those that in sheer barbarity deafen
us to the wail of prisoned souls within the Veil, and the mounting
fury of shackled men.

But when we have vaguely said that Education will set this tangle straight, what have we uttered but a truism? Training for life
teaches living; but what training for the profitable living together
of black men and white? A hundred and fifty years ago our task
would have seemed easier. Then Dr. Johnson blandly assured us
that education was needful solely for the embellishments of life,
and was useless for ordinary vermin. To-day we have climbed to
heights where we would open at least the outer courts of knowledge to all, display its treasures to many, and select the few to
whom its mystery of Truth is revealed, not wholly by birth or the
accidents of the stock market, but at least in part according to
deftness and aim, talent and character. This programme, however,
we are sorely puzzled in carrying out through that part of the land
where the blight of slavery fell hardest, and where we are dealing
with two backward peoples. To make here in human education

that ever necessary combination of the permanent and the contingent—of the ideal and the practical in workable equilibrium—
has been there, as it ever must be in every age and place, a matter
of infinite experiment and frequent mistakes.

In rough approximation we may point out four varying decades
of work in Southern education since the Civil War. From the close
of the war until 1876, was the period of uncertain groping and
temporary relief. There were army schools, mission schools, and
schools of the Freedman's Bureau in chaotic disarrangement seeking system and coöperation. Then followed ten years of construc-
tive definite effort toward the building of complete school systems
in the South. Normal schools and colleges were founded for the
freedmen, and teachers trained there to man the public schools.
There was the inevitable tendency of war to underestimate the
prejudices of the master and the ignorance of the slave, and all
seemed clear sailing out of the wreckage of the storm. Meantime,
starting in this decade yet especially developing from 1885 to
1895, began the industrial revolution of the South. The land saw
glimpses of a new destiny and the stirring of new ideals. The educational system striving to complete itself saw new obstacles and a
field of work ever broader and deeper. The Negro colleges, hurriedly founded, were inadequately equipped, illogically distributed, and of varying efficiency and grade; the normal and high
schools were doing little more than common-school work, and the
common schools were training but a third of the children who
ought to be in them, and training these too often poorly. At the
same time the white South, by reason of its sudden conversion
from the slavery ideal, by so much the more became set and
strengthened in its racial prejudice, and crystallized it into harsh
law and harsher custom; while the marvellous pushing forward of
the poor white daily threatened to take even bread and butter
from the mouths of the heavily handicapped sons of the freedmen. In the midst, then, of the larger problem of Negro education
sprang up the more practical question of work, the inevitable economic quandary that faces a people in the transition from slavery
to freedom, and especially those who make that change amid hate
and prejudice, lawlessness and ruthless competition.

The industrial school springing to notice in this decade, but
coming to full recognition in the decade beginning with 1895, was

the proffered answer to this combined educational and economic crisis, and an answer of singular wisdom and timeliness. From the very first in nearly all the schools some attention had been given to training in handiwork, but now was this training first raised to a dignity that brought it in direct touch with the South's magnificent industrial development, and given an emphasis which reminded black folk that before the Temple of Knowledge swing the Gates of Toil.

Yet after all they are but gates, and when turning our eyes from the temporary and the contingent in the Negro problem to the broader question of the permanent uplifting and civilization of black men in America, we have a right to inquire, as this enthusiasm for material advancement mounts to its height, if after all the industrial school is the final and sufficient answer in the training of the Negro race; and to ask gently, but in all sincerity, the ever-recurring query of the ages, Is not life more than meat, and the body more than raiment?° And men ask this to-day all the more eagerly because of sinister signs in recent educational movements. The tendency is here, born of slavery and quickened to renewed life by the crazy imperialism of the day, to regard human beings as among the material resources of a land to be trained with an eye single to future dividends. Race-prejudices, which keep brown and black men in their "places," we are coming to regard as useful allies with such a theory, no matter how much they may dull the ambition and sicken the hearts of struggling human beings. And above all, we daily hear that an education that encourages aspiration, that sets the loftiest of ideals and seeks as an end culture and character rather than breadwinning, is the privilege of white men and the danger and delusion of black.

Especially has criticism been directed against the former educational efforts to aid the Negro. In the four periods I have mentioned, we find first, boundless, planless enthusiasm and sacrifice; then the preparation of teachers for a vast public-school system; then the launching and expansion of that school system amid increasing difficulties; and finally the training of workmen for the new and growing industries. This development has been sharply

---

°The reference is to the Bible, Matthew 6:25; "Is not the life more than meat, and the body than raiment?" (KJV).

ridiculed as a logical anomaly and flat reversal of nature. Soothly we have been told that first industrial and manual training should have taught the Negro to work, then simple schools should have taught him to read and write, and finally, after years, high and normal schools could have completed the system, as intelligence and wealth demanded.

That a system logically so complete was historically impossible, it needs but a little thought to prove. Progress in human affairs is more often a pull than a push, surging forward of the exceptional man, and the lifting of his duller brethren slowly and painfully to his vantage-ground. Thus it was no accident that gave birth to universities centuries before the common schools, that made fair Harvard the first flower of our wilderness. So in the South: the mass of the freedmen at the end of the war lacked the intelligence so necessary to modern workingmen. They must first have the common school to teach them to read, write, and cipher; and they must have higher schools to teach teachers for the common schools. The white teachers who flocked South went to establish such a common-school system. Few held the idea of founding colleges; most of them at first would have laughed at the idea. But they faced, as all men since them have faced, that central paradox of the South,—the social separation of the races. At that time it was the sudden volcanic rupture of nearly all relations between black and white, in work and government and family life. Since then a new adjustment of relations in economic and political affairs has grown up,—an adjustment subtle and difficult to grasp, yet singularly ingenious, which leaves still that frightful chasm at the color-line across which men pass at their peril. Thus, then and now, there stand in the South two separate worlds; and separate not simply in the higher realms of social intercourse, but also in church and school, on railway and street-car, in hotels and theatres, in streets and city sections, in books and newspapers, in asylums and jails, in hospitals and graveyards. There is still enough of contact for large economic and group coöperation, but the separation is so thorough and deep that it absolutely precludes for the present between the races anything like that sympathetic and effective group-training and leadership of the one by the other, such as the American Negro and all backward peoples must have for effectual progress.

This the missionaries of '68 soon saw; and if effective industrial and trade schools were impracticable before the establishment of a common-school system, just as certainly no adequate common schools could be founded until there were teachers to teach them. Southern whites would not teach them; Northern whites in sufficient numbers could not be had. If the Negro was to learn, he must teach himself, and the most effective help that could be given him was the establishment of schools to train Negro teachers. This conclusion was slowly but surely reached by every student of the situation until simultaneously, in widely separated regions, without consultation or systematic plan, there arose a series of institutions designed to furnish teachers for the untaught. Above the sneers of critics at the obvious defects of this procedure must ever stand its one crushing rejoinder: in a single generation they put thirty thousand black teachers in the South; they wiped out the illiteracy of the majority of the black people of the land, and they made Tuskegee possible.

Such higher training-schools tended naturally to deepen broader development: at first they were common and grammar schools, then some became high schools. And finally, by 1900, some thirty-four had one year or more of studies of college grade. This development was reached with different degrees of speed in different institutions: Hampton is still a high school, while Fisk University started her college in 1871, and Spelman Seminary about 1896.* In all cases the aim was identical,—to maintain the standards of the lower training by giving teachers and leaders the best practicable training; and above all, to furnish the black world with adequate standards of human culture and lofty ideals of life. It was not enough that the teachers of teachers should be trained in technical normal methods; they must also, so far as possible, be broad-minded, cultured men and women, to scatter civilization among a people whose ignorance was not simply of letters, but of life itself.

It can thus be seen that the work of education in the South began with higher institutions of training, which threw off as their foliage common schools, and later industrial schools, and at the

---

*The first college for black women; now Spelman College.

same time strove to shoot their roots ever deeper toward college
and university training. That this was an inevitable and necessary
development, sooner or later, goes without saying; but there has
been, and still is, a question in many minds if the natural growth
was not forced, and if the higher training was not either overdone
or done with cheap and unsound methods. Among white Southerners this feeling is widespread and positive. A prominent Southern journal voiced this in a recent editorial.

> *"The experiment that has been made to give the colored stu-
> dents classical training has not been satisfactory. Even
> though many were able to pursue the course, most of them
> did so in a parrot-like way, learning what was taught, but
> not seeming to appropriate the truth and import of their in-
> struction, and graduating without sensible aim or valuable
> occupation for their future. The whole scheme has proved a
> waste of time, efforts, and the money of the state."*

While most fair-minded men would recognize this as extreme
and overdrawn, still without doubt many are asking, Are there a
sufficient number of Negroes ready for college training to warrant
the undertaking? Are not too many students prematurely forced
into this work? Does it not have the effect of dissatisfying the
young Negro with his environment? And do these graduates succeed in real life? Such natural questions cannot be evaded, nor on
the other hand must a Nation naturally skeptical as to Negro ability assume an unfavorable answer without careful inquiry and
patient openness to conviction. We must not forget that most
Americans answer all queries regarding the Negro *a priori*, and
that the least that human courtesy can do is to listen to evidence.

The advocates of the higher education of the Negro would be
the last to deny the incompleteness and glaring defects of the
present system: too many institutions have attempted to do college work, the work in some cases has not been thoroughly done,
and quantity rather than quality has sometimes been sought. But
all this can be said of higher education throughout the land; it is
the almost inevitable incident of educational growth, and leaves
the deeper question of the legitimate demand for the higher training of Negroes untouched. And this latter question can be settled

in but one way,—by a first-hand study of the facts. If we leave out of view all institutions which have not actually graduated students from a course higher than that of a New England high school, even though they be called colleges; if then we take the thirty-four remaining institutions, we may clear up many misapprehensions by asking searchingly, What kind of institutions are they? what do they teach? and what sort of men do they graduate?

And first we may say that this type of college, including Atlanta, Fisk, and Howard, Wilberforce and Lincoln, Biddle, Shaw,[2] and the rest, is peculiar, almost unique. Through the shining trees that whisper before me as I write, I catch glimpses of a boulder of New England granite, covering a grave, which graduates of Atlanta University have placed there, with this inscription:

> *"IN GRATEFUL MEMORY OF THEIR*
> *FORMER TEACHER AND FRIEND*
> *AND OF THE UNSELFISH LIFE HE*
> *LIVED, AND THE NOBLE WORK HE*
> *WROUGHT; THAT THEY, THEIR*
> *CHILDREN, AND THEIR CHIL-*
> *DREN'S CHILDREN MIGHT BE*
> *BLESSED."*

This was the gift of New England to the freed Negro: not alms, but a friend; not cash, but character. It was not and is not money these seething millions want, but love and sympathy, the pulse of hearts beating with red blood;—a gift which to-day only their own kindred and race can bring to the masses, but which once saintly souls brought to their favored children in the crusade of the sixties, that finest thing in American history, and one of the few things untainted by sordid greed and cheap vainglory. The teachers in these institutions came not to keep the Negroes in their place, but to raise them out of the defilement of the places where slavery had wallowed them. The colleges they founded were social settlements; homes where the best of the sons of the freedmen came in close and sympathetic touch with the best traditions of New England. They lived and ate together, studied and worked, hoped and harkened in the dawning light. In actual formal content their curriculum was doubtless old-fashioned, but in educational power it was supreme, for it was the contact of living souls.

From such schools about two thousand Negroes have gone forth with the bachelor's degree. The number in itself is enough to put at rest the argument that too large a proportion of Negroes are receiving higher training. If the ratio to population of all Negro students throughout the land, in both college and secondary training, be counted, Commissioner Harris assures us "it must be increased to five times its present average" to equal the average of the land.

Fifty years ago the ability of Negro students in any appreciable numbers to master a modern college course would have been difficult to prove. To-day it is proved by the fact that four hundred Negroes, many of whom have been reported as brilliant students, have received the bachelor's degree from Harvard, Yale, Oberlin, and seventy other leading colleges. Here we have, then, nearly twenty-five hundred Negro graduates, of whom the crucial query must be made, How far did their training fit them for life? It is of course extremely difficult to collect satisfactory data on such a point,—difficult to reach the men, to get trustworthy testimony, and to gauge that testimony by any generally acceptable criterion of success. In 1900, the Conference at Atlanta University undertook to study these graduates, and published the results.[3] First they sought to know what these graduates were doing, and succeeded in getting answers from nearly two-thirds of the living. The direct testimony was in almost all cases corroborated by the reports of the colleges where they graduated, so that in the main the reports were worthy of credence. Fifty-three per cent of these graduates were teachers,—presidents of institutions, heads of normal schools, principals of city school-systems, and the like. Seventeen per cent were clergymen; another seventeen per cent were in the professions, chiefly as physicians. Over six per cent were merchants, farmers, and artisans, and four per cent were in the government civil service. Granting even that a considerable proportion of the third unheard from are unsuccessful, this is a record of usefulness. Personally I know many hundreds of these graduates, and have corresponded with more than a thousand; through others I have followed carefully the life-work of scores; I have taught some of them and some of the pupils whom they have taught, lived in homes which they have builded, and looked at life through their eyes. Comparing them as a class with my fellow students in New England and in Europe, I cannot hesitate in saying that nowhere have I met men and women with a broader spirit of helpfulness, with deeper devotion to their life-work, or with more consecrated determination to succeed in the face of bitter difficulties than among Negro college-bred men. They have, to be sure, their proportion of ne'er-do-wells, their pedants and lettered fools, but they have a surprisingly small proportion of them; they have not that culture of manner which we instinctively associate with university men, forgetting that in reality it is the heritage from cultured homes, and that no people a generation removed from slavery can escape a certain unpleasant rawness and *gaucherie*, despite the best of training.

With all their larger vision and deeper sensibility, these men have usually been conservative, careful leaders. They have seldom been agitators, have withstood the temptation to head the mob, and have worked steadily and faithfully in a thousand communities in the South. As teachers, they have given the South a commendable system of city schools and large numbers of private normal-schools and academies. Colored college-bred men have worked side by side with white college graduates at Hampton; almost from the beginning the backbone of Tuskegee's teaching force has been formed of graduates from Fisk and Atlanta. And today the institute is filled with college graduates, from the energetic wife of the principal[4] down to the teacher of agriculture, including nearly half of the executive council and a majority of the heads of departments. In the professions, college men are slowly but surely leavening the Negro church, are healing and preventing the devastations of disease, and beginning to furnish legal protection for the liberty and property of the toiling masses. All this is needful work. Who would do it if Negroes did not? How could Negroes do it if they were not trained carefully for it? If white people need colleges to furnish teachers, ministers, lawyers, and doctors, do black people need nothing of the sort?

If it is true that there are an appreciable number of Negro youth in the land capable by character and talent to receive that higher training, the end of which is culture, and if the two and a half thousand who have had something of this training in the past

have in the main proved themselves useful to their race and generation, the question then comes, What place in the future development of the South ought the Negro college and college-bred
man to occupy? That the present social separation and acute race-
sensitiveness must eventually yield to the influences of culture, as
the South grows civilized, is clear. But such transformation calls
for singular wisdom and patience. If, while the healing of this vast
sore is progressing, the races are to live for many years side by
side, united in economic effort, obeying a common government,
sensitive to mutual thought and feeling, yet subtly and silently
separate in many matters of deeper human intimacy,—if this unusual and dangerous development is to progress amid peace and
order, mutual respect and growing intelligence, it will call for social surgery at once the delicatest and nicest in modern history. It
will demand broad-minded, upright men, both white and black,
and in its final accomplishment American civilization will triumph. So far as white men are concerned, this fact is to-day being
recognized in the South, and a happy renaissance of university education seems imminent. But the very voices that cry hail to this
good work are, strange to relate, largely silent or antagonistic to
the higher education of the Negro.

Strange to relate! for this is certain, no secure civilization can
be built in the South with the Negro as an ignorant, turbulent proletariat. Suppose we seek to remedy this by making them laborers
and nothing more: they are not fools, they have tasted of the Tree
of Life, and they will not cease to think, will not cease attempting
to read the riddle of the world. By taking away their best equipped
teachers and leaders, by slamming the door of opportunity in the
faces of their bolder and brighter minds, will you make them sat-
isfied with their lot? or will you not rather transfer their leading
from the hands of men taught to think to the hands of untrained
demagogues? We ought not to forget that despite the pressure of
poverty, and despite the active discouragement and even ridicule
of friends, the demand for higher training steadily increases
among Negro youth: there were, in the years from 1875 to 1880,
22 Negro graduates from Northern colleges; from 1885 to 1890
there were 43, and from 1895 to 1900, nearly 100 graduates. From
Southern Negro colleges there were, in the same three periods,
143, 413, and over 500 graduates. Here, then, is the plain thirst for

training; by refusing to give this Talented Tenth[5] the key to knowledge, can any sane man imagine that they will lightly lay aside their yearning and contentedly become hewers of wood and drawers of water?

No. The dangerously clear logic of the Negro's position will more and more loudly assert itself in that day when increasing wealth and more intricate social organization preclude the South from being, as it so largely is, simply an armed camp for intimidating black folk. Such waste of energy cannot be spared if the South is to catch up with civilization. And as the black third of the land grows in thrift and skill, unless skilfully guided in its larger philosophy, it must more and more brood over the red past and the creeping, crooked present, until it grasps a gospel of revolt and revenge and throws its new-found energies athwart the current of advance. Even to-day the masses of the Negroes see all too clearly the anomalies of their position and the moral crookedness of yours. You may marshal strong indictments against them, but their counter-cries, lacking though they be in formal logic, have burning truths within them which you may not wholly ignore, O Southern Gentlemen! If you deplore their presence here, they ask, Who brought us? When you cry, Deliver us from the vision of intermarriage, they answer that legal marriage is infinitely better than systematic concubinage and prostitution. And if in just fury you accuse their vagabonds of violating women, they also in fury quite as just may reply: The wrong which your gentlemen have done against helpless black women in defiance of your own laws is written on the foreheads of two millions of mulattoes, and written in ineffaceable blood. And finally, when you fasten crime upon this race as its peculiar trait, they answer that slavery was the arch-crime, and lynching and lawlessness its twin abortion; that color and race are not crimes, and yet they it is which in this land receives most unceasing condemnation, North, East, South, and West.

I will not say such arguments are wholly justified,—I will not insist that there is no other side to the shield; but I do say that of the nine millions of Negroes in this nation, there is scarcely one out of the cradle to whom these arguments do not daily present themselves in the guise of terrible truth. I insist that the question of the future is how best to keep these millions from brooding over the wrongs of the past and the difficulties of the present, so that all their energies may be bent toward a cheerful striving and coöperation with their white neighbors toward a larger, juster, and fuller future. That one wise method of doing this lies in the closer knitting of the Negro to the great industrial possibilities of the South is a great truth. And this the common schools and the manual training and trade schools are working to accomplish. But these alone are not enough. The foundations of knowledge in this race, as in others, must be sunk deep in the college and university if we would build a solid, permanent structure. Internal problems of social advance must inevitably come,—problems of work and wages, of families and homes, of morals and the true valuing of the things of life; and all these and other inevitable problems of civilization the Negro must meet and solve largely for himself, by reason of his isolation; and can there be any possible solution other than by study and thought and an appeal to the rich experience of the past? Is there not, with such a group and in such a crisis, infinitely more danger to be apprehended from half-trained minds and shallow thinking than from over-education and over-refinement? Surely we have wit enough to found a Negro college so manned and equipped as to steer successfully between the *dilettante* and the fool. We shall hardly induce black men to believe that if their stomachs be full, it matters little about their brains. They already dimly perceive that the paths of peace winding between honest toil and dignified manhood call for the guidance of skilled thinkers, the loving, reverent comradeship between the black lowly and the black men emancipated by training and culture.

The function of the Negro college, then, is clear: it must maintain the standards of popular education, it must seek the social regeneration of the Negro, and it must help in the solution of problems of race contact and coöperation. And finally, beyond all this, it must develop men. Above our modern socialism, and out of the worship of the mass, must persist and evolve that higher individualism which the centres of culture protect; there must come a loftier respect for the sovereign human soul that seeks to know itself and the world about it; that seeks a freedom for expansion and self-development; that will love and hate and labor in its own way, untrammeled alike by old and new. Such souls aforetime

have inspired and guided worlds, and if we be not wholly be-
witched by our Rhine-gold, they shall again. Herein the longing of
black men must have respect: the rich and bitter depth of their experience, the unknown treasures of their inner life, the strange
rendings of nature they have seen, may give the world new points
of view and make their loving, living, and doing precious to all
human hearts. And to themselves in these the days that try their
souls, the chance to soar in the dim blue air above the smoke is to
their finer spirits boon and guerdon for what they lose on earth by
being black.

I sit with Shakespeare and he winces not. Across the color-line I
move arm in arm with Balzac and Dumas, where smiling men and
welcoming women glide in gilded halls. From out the caves of
evening that swing between the strong-limbed earth and the trac-
ery of the stars, I summon Aristotle and Aurelius and what soul I
will, and they come all graciously with no scorn nor condescen-
sion. So, wed with Truth, I dwell above the Veil. Is this the life you
grudge us, O knightly America? Is this the life you long to change
into the dull red hideousness of Georgia? Are you so afraid lest
peering from this high Pisgah, between Philistine and Amalekite,
we sight the Promised Land? [6]

VII

Of the Black Belt[1]

I am black but comely, O ye daughters of Jerusalem,
As the tents of Kedar, as the curtains of Solomon.
Look not upon me, because I am black,
Because the sun hath looked upon me:
My mother's children were angry with me;
They made me the keeper of the vineyards;
But mine own vineyard have I not kept.

The Song of Solomon.*

OUT OF THE NORTH the train thundered, and we woke to see the crimson soil of Georgia stretching away bare and monotonous right and left. Here and there lay straggling, unlovely villages, and lean men loafed leisurely at the depots; then again came the stretch of pines and clay. Yet we did not nod, nor weary of the scene; for this is historic ground. Right across our track, three hundred and sixty years ago, wandered the cavalcade of Hernando de Soto, looking for gold and the Great Sea; and he and his foot-sore captives disappeared yonder in the grim forests to the west. Here sits Atlanta, the city of

---

*From the Song of Solomon; see the Bible, Solomon 1:5–6 (KJV).
†From "Bright Sparkles in the Churchyard."

a hundred hills, with something Western, something Southern, and something quite its own, in its busy life. And a little past Atlanta, to the southwest, is the land of the Cherokees, and there, not far from where Sam Hose was crucified, you may stand on a spot which is to-day the centre of the Negro problem,—the centre of those nine million men who are America's dark heritage from slavery and the slave-trade.

Not only is Georgia thus the geographical focus of our Negro population, but in many other respects, both now and yesterday, the Negro problems have seemed to be centered in this State. No other State in the Union can count a million Negroes among its citi-zens,—a population as large as the slave population of the whole Union in 1800; no other State fought so long and strenuously to gather this host of Africans. Oglethorpe thought slavery against law and gospel; but the circumstances which gave Georgia its first in-habitants were not calculated to furnish citizens over-nice in their ideas about rum and slaves. Despite the prohibitions of the trustees, these Georgians, like some of their descendants, proceeded to take the law into their own hands; and so pliant were the judges, and so flagrant the smuggling, and so earnest were the prayers of White-field, that by the middle of the eighteenth century all restrictions were swept away, and the slave-trade went merrily on for fifty years and more.

Down in Darien, where the Delegal riots[2] took place some sum-mers ago, there used to come a strong protest against slavery from the Scotch Highlanders; and the Moravians of Ebenezea[3] did not like the system. But not till the Haytian Terror of Toussaint was the trade in men even checked; while the national statute of 1808[4] did not suffice to stop it. How the Africans poured in!—fifty thousand between 1790 and 1810, and then, from Virginia and from smug-glers, two thousand a year for many years more. So the thirty thou-sand Negroes of Georgia in 1790 were doubled in a decade,—were over a hundred thousand in 1810, had reached two hundred thou-sand in 1820, and half a million at the time of the war. Thus like a snake the black population writhed upward.

But we must hasten on our journey. This that we pass as we leave Atlanta is the ancient land of the Cherokees,—that brave Indian na-tion which strove so long for its fatherland, until Fate and the United States Government drove them beyond the Mississippi. If you wish to ride with me you must come into the "Jim Crow Car." There will be no objection,—already four other white men, and a little white girl with her nurse, are in there. Usually the races are mixed in there; but the white coach is all white. Of course this car is not so good as the other, but it is fairly clean and comfortable. The discomfort lies chiefly in the hearts of those four black men yonder—and in mine.

We rumble south in quite a business-like way. The bare red clay and pines of Northern Georgia begin to disappear, and in their place appears a rich rolling land, luxuriant, and here and there well tilled. This is the land of the Creek Indians; and a hard time the Georgians had to seize it. The towns grow more frequent and more interesting, and brand-new cotton mills rise on every side. Below Macon the world grows darker; for now we approach the Black Belt,—that strange land of shadows, at which even slaves paled in the past, and whence come now only faint and half-intelligible murmurs to the world beyond. The "Jim Crow Car" grows larger and a shade better; three rough field-hands and two or three white loafers accompany us, and the newsboy still spreads his wares at one end. The sun is setting, but we can see the great cotton country as we enter it,—the soil now dark and fertile, now thin and gray, with fruit-trees and dilapidated buildings,—all the way to Albany.

At Albany, in the heart of the Black Belt, we stop. Two hundred miles south of Atlanta, two hundred miles west of the Atlantic, and one hundred miles north of the Great Gulf lies Dougherty County, with ten thousand Negroes and two thousand whites. The Flint River winds down from Andersonville, and, turning suddenly at Albany, the county-seat, hurries on to join the Chattahoochee and the sea. Andrew Jackson knew the Flint well, and marched across it once to avenge the Indian Massacre at Fort Mims.° That was in 1814, not long before the battle of New Orleans; and by the Creek treaty that followed this campaign, all Dougherty County, and much other rich land, was ceded to Georgia. Still, settlers fought shy of this land, for the Indians were all about, and they were unpleasant neighbors in those days. The panic of 1837,† which Jackson bequeathed to Van Buren, turned the planters from the impoverished lands of Virginia, the Carolinas, and east Georgia, toward the West. The Indians were

---

°Creek Indian uprising on August 30, 1813, at Fort Mims, Alabama.
†Economic crisis resulting in bank failures.

removed to Indian Territory, and settlers poured into these coveted lands to retrieve their broken fortunes. For a radius of a hundred miles about Albany, stretched a great fertile land, luxuriant with forests of pine, oak, ash, hickory, and poplar; hot with the sun and damp with the rich black swamp-land; and here the corner-stone of the Cotton Kingdom was laid.

Albany is to-day a wide-streeted, placid, Southern town, with a broad sweep of stores and saloons, and flanking rows of homes,— whites usually to the north, and blacks to the south. Six days in the week the town looks decidedly too small for itself, and takes frequent and prolonged naps. But on Saturday suddenly the whole county disgorges itself upon the place, and a perfect flood of black peasantry pours through the streets, fills the stores, blocks the sidewalks, chokes the thoroughfares, and takes full possession of the town. They are black, sturdy, uncouth country folk, good-natured and simple, talkative to a degree, and yet far more silent and brooding than the crowds of the Rhine-pfalz, or Naples, or Cracow. They drink considerable quantities of whiskey, but do not get very drunk; they talk and laugh loudly at times, but seldom quarrel or fight. They walk up and down the streets, meet and gossip with friends, stare at the shop windows, buy coffee, cheap candy, and clothes, and at dusk drive home—happy? well no, not exactly happy, but much happier than as though they had not come.

Thus Albany is a real capital,—a typical Southern county town, the centre of the life of ten thousand souls; their point of contact with the outer world, their centre of news and gossip, their market for buying and selling, borrowing and lending, their fountain of justice and law. Once upon a time we knew country life so well and city life so little, that we illustrated city life as that of a closely crowded country district. Now the world has well-nigh forgotten what the country is, and we must imagine a little city of black people scattered far and wide over three hundred lonesome square miles of land, without train or trolley, in the midst of cotton and corn, and wide patches of sand and gloomy soil.

It gets pretty hot in Southern Georgia in July,—a sort of dull, determined heat that seems quite independent of the sun; so it took us some days to muster courage enough to leave the porch and venture out on the long country roads, that we might see this unknown world. Finally we started. It was about ten in the morning, bright with a faint breeze, and we jogged leisurely southward in the valley of the Flint. We passed the scattered box-like cabins of the brick-yard hands, and the long tenement-row facetiously called "The Ark," and were soon in the open country, and on the confines of the great plantations of other days. There is the "Joe Fields place"; a rough old fellow was he, and had killed many a "nigger" in his day. Twelve miles his plantation used to run,—a regular barony. It is nearly all gone now; only straggling bits belong to the family, and the rest has passed to Jews and Negroes. Even the bits which are left are heavily mortgaged, and, like the rest of the land, tilled by tenants. Here is one of them now,—a tall brown man, a hard worker and a hard drinker, illiterate, but versed in farm-lore, as his nodding crops de-clare. This distressingly new board house is his, and he has just moved out of yonder moss-grown cabin with its one square room.

From the curtains in Benton's house, down the road, a dark comely face is staring at the strangers; for passing carriages are not every-day occurrences here. Benton is an intelligent yellow man with a good-sized family, and manages a plantation blasted by the war and now the broken staff of the widow. He might be well-to-do, they say; but he carouses too much in Albany. And the half-desolate spirit of neglect born of the very soil seems to have settled on these acres. In times past there were cotton-gins and machinery here; but they have rotted away.

The whole land seems forlorn and forsaken. Here are the rem-nants of the vast plantations of the Sheldons, the Pellots, and the Rensons; but the souls of them are passed. The houses lie in half ruin, or have wholly disappeared; the fences have flown, and the families are wandering in the world. Strange vicissitudes have met these whilom masters. Yonder stretch the wide acres of Bildad Rea-sor; he died in war-time, but the upstart overseer hastened to wed the widow. Then he went, and his neighbors too, and now only the black tenant remains; but the shadow-hand of the master's grand-nephew or cousin or creditor stretches out of the gray distance to collect the rack-rent remorselessly, and so the land is uncared-for and poor. Only black tenants can stand such a system, and they only because they must. Ten miles we have ridden to-day and have seen no white face.

A resistless feeling of depression falls slowly upon us, despite the gaudy sunshine and the green cotton-fields. This, then, is the Cotton

Kingdom,—the shadow of a marvellous dream. And where is the
King? Perhaps this is he,—the sweating ploughman, tilling his eighty
acres with two lean mules, and fighting a hard battle with debt. So
we sit musing, until, as we turn a corner on the sandy road, there
comes a fairer scene suddenly in view,—a neat cottage snugly en-
sconced by the road, and near it a little store. A tall bronzed man
rises from the porch as we hail him, and comes out to our carriage.
He is six feet in height, with a sober face that smiles gravely. He
walks too straight to be a tenant,—yes, he owns two hundred and
forty acres. "The land is run down since the boom-days of eighteen
hundred and fifty," he explains, and cotton is low. Three black tenants live on his place, and in his little store he keeps a small stock of
tobacco, snuff, soap, and soda, for the neighborhood. Here is his gin-
house with new machinery just installed. Three hundred bales of
cotton went through it last year. Two children he has sent away to
school. Yes, he says sadly, he is getting on, but cotton is down to four
cents; I know how Debt sits staring at him.

Wherever the King may be, the parks and palaces of the Cotton
Kingdom have not wholly disappeared. We plunge even now into
great groves of oak and towering pine, with an undergrowth of myr-
tle and shrubbery. This was the "home-house" of the Thompsons,—
slave-barons who drove their coach and four in the merry past. All is
silence now, and ashes, and tangled weeds. The owner put his whole
fortune into the rising cotton industry of the fifties, and with the
falling prices of the eighties he packed up and stole away. Yonder is
another grove, with unkempt lawn, great magnolias, and grass-
grown paths. The Big House stands in half-ruin, its great front door
staring blankly at the street, and the back part grotesquely restored
for its black tenant. A shabby, well-built Negro he is, unlucky and ir-
resolute. He digs hard to pay rent to the white girl who owns the
remnant of the place. She married a policeman, and lives in Savannah.

Now and again we come to churches. Here is one now,—Shepherd's, they call it,—a great whitewashed barn of a thing, perched on
stilts of stone, and looking for all the world as though it were just
resting here a moment and might be expected to waddle off down
the road at almost any time. And yet it is the centre of a hundred
cabin homes; and sometimes, of a Sunday, five hundred persons
from far and near gather here and talk and eat and sing. There is

a school-house near,—a very airy, empty shed; but even this is an improvement, for usually the school is held in the church. The churches vary from log-huts to those like Shepherd's, and the schools from nothing to this little house that sits demurely on the county line. It is a tiny plank-house, perhaps ten by twenty, and has within a double row of rough unplaned benches, resting mostly on legs, sometimes on boxes. Opposite the door is a square home-made desk. In one corner are the ruins of a stove, and in the other a dim blackboard. It is the cheerfulest schoolhouse I have seen in Dougherty, save in town. Back of the schoolhouse is a lodge-house two stories high and not quite finished. Societies meet there,—societies "to care for the sick and bury the dead"; and these societies grow and flourish.

We had come to the boundaries of Dougherty, and were about to turn west along the county-line, when all these sights were pointed out to us by a kindly old man, black, white-haired, and seventy. Forty-five years he had lived here, and now supports himself and his old wife by the help of the steer tethered yonder and the charity of his black neighbors. He shows us the farm of the Hills just across the county line in Baker,—a widow and two strapping sons, who raised ten bales (one need not add "cotton" down here) last year. There are fences and pigs and cows, and the soft-voiced, velvet-skinned young Memnon,* who sauntered half-bashfully over to greet the strangers, is proud of his home. We turn now to the west along the county-line. Great dismantled trunks of pines tower above the green cotton fields, cracking their naked gnarled fingers toward the border of living forest beyond. There is little beauty in this region, only a sort of crude abandon that suggests power,—a naked grandeur, as it were. The houses are bare and straight; there are no hammocks or easy-chairs, and few flowers. So when, as here at Rawdon's, one sees a vine clinging to a little porch, and home-like windows peeping over the fences, one takes a long breath. I think I never before quite realized the place of the Fence in civilization. This is the Land of the Unfenced, where crouch on either hand scores of ugly one-room cabins, cheerless and dirty. Here lies the Negro problem in its naked dirt and penury. And here are no fences. But now and then the criss-cross rails or straight palings break into view, and then we know a

---

*Ethiopian king of Greek mythology.

touch of culture is near. Of course Harrison Gohagen,—a quiet yellow man, young, smooth-faced, and diligent,—of course he is lord of some hundred acres, and we expect to see a vision of well-kept rooms and fat beds and laughing children. For has he not fine fences? And those over yonder, why should they build fences on the rack-rented land? It will only increase their rent.

On we wind, through sand and pines and glimpses of old plantations, till there creeps into sight a cluster of buildings,—wood and brick, mills and houses, and scattered cabins. It seemed quite a village. As it came nearer and nearer, however, the aspect changed: the buildings were rotten, the bricks were falling out, the mills were silent, and the store was closed. Only in the cabins appeared now and then a bit of lazy life. I could imagine the place under some weird spell, and was half-minded to search out the princess. An old ragged black man, honest, simple, and improvident, told us the tale. The Wizard of the North—the Capitalist—had rushed down in the seventies to woo this coy dark soil. He bought a square mile or more, and for a time the field-hands sang, the gins groaned, and the mills buzzed. Then came a change. The agent's son embezzled the funds and ran off with them. Then the agent himself disappeared. Finally the new agent stole even the books, and the company in wrath closed its business and its houses, refused to sell, and let houses and furniture and machinery rust and rot. So the Waters-Loring plantation was stilled by the spell of dishonesty, and stands like some gaunt rebuke to a scarred land.

Somehow that plantation ended our day's journey; for I could not shake off the influence of that silent scene. Back toward town we glided, past the straight and thread-like pines, past a dark tree-dotted pond where the air was heavy with a dead sweet perfume. White slender-legged curlews flitted by us, and the garnet blooms of the cotton looked gay against the green and purple stalks. A peasant girl was hoeing in the field, white-turbaned and black-limbed. All this we saw, but the spell still lay upon us.

How curious a land is this,—how full of untold story, of tragedy and laughter, and the rich legacy of human life; shadowed with a tragic past, and big with future promise! This is the Black Belt of Georgia. Dougherty County is the west end of the Black Belt, and men once called it the Egypt of the Confederacy. It is full of historic interest. First there is the Swamp, to the west, where the Chicka-

sawhatchee flows sullenly southward. The shadow of an old plantation lies at its edge, forlorn and dark. Then comes the pool; pendent
gray moss and brackish waters appear, and forests filled with wild-
fowl. In one place the wood is on fire, smouldering in dull red anger;
but nobody minds. Then the swamp grows beautiful; a raised road,
built by chained Negro convicts, dips down into it, and forms a way
walled and almost covered in living green. Spreading trees spring
from a prodigal luxuriance of undergrowth; great dark green shadows fade into the black background, until all is one mass of tangled
semi-tropical foliage, marvellous in its weird savage splendor. Once
we crossed a black silent stream, where the sad trees and writhing
creepers, all glinting fiery yellow and green, seemed like some vast
cathedral,—some green Milan builded of wildwood. And as I
crossed, I seemed to see again that fierce tragedy of seventy years
ago. Osceola, the Indian-Negro chieftain, had risen in the swamps of
Florida, vowing vengeance. His war-cry reached the red Creeks of
Dougherty, and their war-cry rang from the Chattahoochee to the
sea. Men and women and children fled and fell before them as they
swept into Dougherty. In yonder shadows a dark and hideously
painted warrior glided stealthily on,—another and another, until
three hundred had crept into the treacherous swamp. Then the false
slime closing about them called the white men from the east. Waist-
deep, they fought beneath the tall trees, until the war-cry was
hushed and the Indians glided back into the west. Small wonder the
wood is red.

Then came the black slaves. Day after day the clank of chained
feet marching from Virginia and Carolina to Georgia was heard in
these rich swamp lands. Day after day the songs of the callous, the
wail of the motherless, and the muttered curses of the wretched
echoed from the Flint to the Chickasawhatchee, until by 1860 there
had risen in West Dougherty perhaps the richest slave kingdom the
modern world ever knew. A hundred and fifty barons commanded
the labor of nearly six thousand Negroes, held sway over farms with
ninety thousand acres of tilled land, valued even in times of cheap
soil at three millions of dollars. Twenty thousand bales of ginned cotton went yearly to England, New and Old; and men that came there
bankrupt made money and grew rich. In a single decade the cotton
output increased four-fold and the value of lands was tripled. It was
the heyday of the *nouveau riche*, and a life of careless extravagance

reigned among the masters. Four and six bob-tailed thoroughbreds rolled their coaches to town; open hospitality and gay entertainment were the rule. Parks and groves were laid out, rich with flower and vine, and in the midst stood the low wide-halled "big house," with its porch and columns and great fire-places.

And yet with all this there was something sordid, something forced,—a certain feverish unrest and recklessness; for was not all this show and tinsel built upon a groan? "This land was a little Hell," said a ragged, brown, and grave-faced man to me. We were seated near a roadside blacksmith shop, and behind was the bare ruin of some master's home. "I've seen niggers drop dead in the furrow, but they were kicked aside, and the plough never stopped. And down in the guardhouse, there's where the blood ran."

With such foundations a kingdom must in time sway and fall. The masters moved to Macon and Augusta, and left only the irresponsible overseers on the land. And the result is such ruin as this, the Lloyd "home-place":—great waving oaks, a spread of lawn, myrtles and chestnuts, all ragged and wild; a solitary gate-post standing where once was a castle entrance; an old rusty anvil lying amid rotting bellows and wood in the ruins of a blacksmith shop; a wide rambling old mansion, brown and dingy, filled now with the grand-children of the slaves who once waited on its tables; while the family of the master has dwindled to two lone women, who live in Macon and feed hungrily off the remnants of an earldom. So we ride on, past phantom gates and falling homes,—past the once flourishing farms of the Smiths, the Gandys, and the Lagores,—and find all dilapidated and half ruined, even there where a solitary white woman, a relic of other days, sits alone in state among miles of Negroes and rides to town in her ancient coach each day.

This was indeed the Egypt of the Confederacy,—the rich granary whence potatoes and corn and cotton poured out to the famished and ragged Confederate troops as they battled for a cause lost long before 1861. Sheltered and secure, it became the place of refuge for families, wealth, and slaves. Yet even then the hard ruthless rape of the land began to tell. The red-clay sub-soil already had begun to peer above the loam. The harder the slaves were driven the more careless and fatal was their farming. Then came the revolution of war and Emancipation, the bewilderment of Reconstruction,—and now, what is the Egypt of the Confederacy, and what meaning has it for the nation's weal or woe?

It is a land of rapid contrasts and of curiously mingled hope and pain. Here sits a pretty blue-eyed quadroon hiding her bare feet; she was married only last week, and yonder in the field is her dark young husband, hoeing to support her, at thirty cents a day without board. Across the way is Gatesby, brown and tall, lord of two thousand acres shrewdly won and held. There is a store conducted by his black son, a blacksmith shop, and a ginnery. Five miles below here is a town owned and controlled by one white New Englander. He owns almost a Rhode Island county, with thousands of acres and hundreds of black laborers. Their cabins look better than most, and the farm, with machinery and fertilizers, is much more business-like than any in the county, although the manager drives hard bargains in wages. When now we turn and look five miles above, there on the edge of town are five houses of prostitutes,—two of blacks and three of whites; and in one of the houses of the whites a worthless black boy was harbored too openly two years ago; so he was hanged for rape. And here, too, is the high whitewashed fence of the "stockade," as the county prison is called; the white folks say it is ever full of black criminals,—the black folks say that only colored boys are sent to jail, and they not because they are guilty, but because the State needs criminals to eke out its income by their forced labor.

The Jew is the heir of the slave-baron in Dougherty; and as we ride westward, by wide stretching cornfields and stubby orchards of peach and pear, we see on all sides within the circle of dark forest a Land of Canaan. Here and there are tales of projects for money-getting, born in the swift days of Reconstruction,—"improvement" companies, wine companies, mills and factories; nearly all failed, and the Jew° fell heir. It is a beautiful land, this Dougherty, west of the Flint. The forests are wonderful, the solemn pines have disappeared, and this is the "Oakey Woods," with its wealth of hickories, beeches, oaks, and palmettos. But a pall of debt hangs over the beautiful land; the merchants are in debt to the wholesalers, the planters are in debt to the merchants, the tenants owe the planters, and laborers bow and bend beneath the burden of it all. Here and there a man has

---

°In later editions of *The Souls of Black Folk*, Du Bois changes all references to "Jews" to "immigrants."

raised his head above these murky waters. We passed one fenced stock-farm, with grass and grazing cattle, that looked very homelike after endless corn and cotton. Here and there are black freeholders: there is the gaunt dull-black Jackson, with his hundred acres. "I says, 'Look up! If you don't look up you can't get up,'" remarks Jackson, philosophically. And he's gotten up. Dark Carter's neat barns would do credit to New England. His master helped him to get a start, but when the black man died last fall the master's sons immediately laid claim to the estate. "And them white folks will get it, too," said my yellow gossip.

I turn from these well-tended acres with a comfortable feeling that the Negro is rising. Even then, however, the fields, as we proceed, begin to redden and the trees disappear. Rows of old cabins appear filled with renters and laborers,—cheerless, bare, and dirty, for the most part, although here and there the very age and decay makes the scene picturesque. A young black fellow greets us. He is twenty-two, and just married. Until last year he had good luck renting; then cotton fell, and the sheriff seized and sold all he had. So he moved here, where the rent is higher, the land poorer, and the owner inflexible; he rents a forty-dollar mule for twenty dollars a year. Poor lad!—a slave at twenty-two. This plantation, owned now by a Russian Jew, was a part of the famous Bolton estate. After the war it was for many years worked by gangs of Negro convicts,—and black convicts then were even more plentiful than now; it was a way of making Negroes work, and the question of guilt was a minor one. Hard tales of cruelty and mistreatment of the chained freemen are told, but the county authorities were deaf until the free-labor market was nearly ruined by wholesale migration. Then they took the convicts from the plantations, but not until one of the fairest regions of the "Oakey Woods" had been ruined and ravished into a red waste, out of which only a Yankee or a Jew could squeeze more blood from debt-cursed tenants.

No wonder that Luke Black, slow, dull, and discouraged, shuffles to our carriage and talks hopelessly. Why should he strive? Every year finds him deeper in debt. How strange that Georgia, the world-heralded refuge of poor debtors, should bind her own to sloth and misfortune as ruthlessly as ever England did! The poor land groans with its birth-pains, and brings forth scarcely a hundred pounds of cotton to the acre, where fifty years ago it yielded eight times as much. Of this meagre yield the tenant pays from a quarter to a third in rent, and most of the rest in interest on food and supplies bought on credit. Twenty years yonder sunken-cheeked, old black man has labored under that system, and now, turned day-laborer, is supporting his wife and boarding himself on his wages of a dollar and a half a week, received only part of the year.

The Bolton convict farm formerly included the neighboring plantation. Here it was that the convicts were lodged in the great log prison still standing. A dismal place it still remains, with rows of ugly huts filled with surly ignorant tenants. "What rent do you pay here?" I inquired. "I don't know,—what is it, Sam?" "All we make," answered Sam. It is a depressing place,—bare, unshaded, with no charm of past association, only a memory of forced human toil,— now, then, and before the war. They are not happy, these black men whom we meet throughout this region. There is little of the joyous abandon and playfulness which we are wont to associate with the plantation Negro. At best, the natural good-nature is edged with complaint or has changed into sullenness and gloom. And now and then it blazes forth in veiled but hot anger. I remember one big red-eyed black whom we met by the roadside. Forty-five years he had labored on this farm, beginning with nothing, and still having nothing. To be sure, he had given four children a common-school training, and perhaps if the new fence-law had not allowed unfenced crops in West Dougherty he might have raised a little stock and kept ahead. As it is, he is hopelessly in debt, disappointed, and embittered. He stopped us to inquire after the black boy in Albany, whom it was said a policeman had shot and killed for loud talking on the sidewalk. And then he said slowly: "Let a white man touch me, and he dies; I don't boast this,—I don't say it around loud, or before the children,—but I mean it. I've seen them whip my father and my old mother in them cotton-rows till the blood ran; by—" and we passed on.

Now Sears, whom we met next lolling under the chubby oak-trees, was of quite different fibre. Happy?—Well, yes; he laughed and flipped pebbles, and thought the world was as it was. He had worked here twelve years and has nothing but a mortgaged mule. Children? Yes, seven; but they hadn't been to school this year,— could n't afford books and clothes, and could n't spare their work. There go part of them to the fields now,—three big boys astride mules, and a strapping girl with bare brown legs. Careless ignorance and laziness here, fierce hate and vindictiveness there;—these are the extremes of the Negro problem which we met that day, and we scarce knew which we preferred.

Here and there we meet distinct characters quite out of the ordinary. One came out of a piece of newly cleared ground, making a wide detour to avoid the snakes. He was an old, hollow-cheeked man, with a drawn and characterful brown face. He had a sort of self-contained quaintness and rough humor impossible to describe; a certain cynical earnestness that puzzled one. "The niggers were jealous of me over on the other place," he said, "and so me and the old woman begged this piece of woods, and I cleared it up myself. Made nothing for two years, but I reckon I've got a crop now." The cotton looked tall and rich, and we praised it. He curtsied low, and then bowed almost to the ground, with an imperturbable gravity that seemed almost suspicious. Then he continued, "My mule died last week,"—a calamity in this land equal to a devastating fire in town,— "but a white man loaned me another." Then he added, eyeing us, "Oh, I gets along with white folks." We turned the conversation. "Bears? deer?" he answered, "well, I should say there were," and he let fly a string of brave oaths, as he told hunting-tales of the swamp. We left him standing still in the middle of the road looking after us, and yet apparently not noticing us.

The Whistle place, which includes his bit of land, was bought soon after the war by an English syndicate, the "Dixie Cotton and Corn Company." A marvellous deal of style their factor put on, with his servants and coach-and-six; so much so that the concern soon landed in inextricable bankruptcy. Nobody lives in the old house now, but a man comes each winter out of the North and collects his high rents. I know not which are the more touching,—such old empty houses, or the homes of the masters' sons. Sad and bitter tales lie hidden back of those white doors,—tales of poverty, of struggle, of disappointment. A revolution such as that of '63 is a terrible thing; they that rose rich in the morning often slept in paupers' beds. Beggars and vulgar speculators rose to rule over them, and their children went astray. See yonder sad-colored house, with its cabins and fences and glad crops? It is not glad within; last month the prodigal son of the struggling father wrote home from the city for money. Money! Where was it to come from? And so the son rose in the night and killed his baby, and killed his wife, and shot himself dead. And the world passed on.

I remember wheeling around a bend in the road beside a graceful bit of forest and a singing brook. A long low house faced us, with porch and flying pillars, great oaken door, and a broad lawn shining in the evening sun. But the windowpanes were gone, the pillars were worm-eaten, and the moss-grown roof was falling in. Half curiously I peered through the unhinged door, and saw where, on the wall across the hall, was written in once gay letters a faded "Welcome."

Quite a contrast to the southwestern part of Dougherty County is the northwest. Soberly timbered in oak and pine, it has none of that half-tropical luxuriance of the southwest. Then, too, there are fewer signs of a romantic past, and more of systematic modern land-grabbing and money-getting. White people are more in evidence here, and farmer and hired labor replace to some extent the absentee landlord and rack-rented tenant. The crops have neither the luxuriance of the richer land nor the signs of neglect so often seen, and there were fences and meadows here and there. Most of this land was poor, and beneath the notice of the slave-baron, before the war. Since then his nephews and the poor whites and the Jews have seized it. The returns of the farmer are too small to allow much for wages, and yet he will not sell off small farms. There is the Negro Sanford; he has worked fourteen years as overseer on the Ladson place, and "paid out enough for fertilizers to have bought a farm," but the owner will not sell off a few acres.

Two children—a boy and a girl—are hoeing sturdily in the fields on the farm where Corliss works. He is smooth-faced and brown, and is fencing up his pigs. He used to run a successful cotton-gin, but the Cotton Seed Oil Trust has forced the price of ginning so low that he says it hardly pays him. He points out a stately old house over the way as the home of "Pa Willis." We eagerly ride over, for "Pa Willis" was the tall and powerful black Moses who led the Negroes for a generation, and led them well. He was a Baptist preacher, and when he died two thousand black people followed him to the grave; and now they preach his funeral sermon each year. His widow lives here,—a weazened, sharp-featured little woman, who curtsied quaintly as we greeted her. Further on lives Jack Delson, the most prosperous Negro farmer in the county. It is a joy to meet him,—a great broad-shouldered, handsome black man, intelligent and jovial.

Six hundred and fifty acres he owns, and has eleven black tenants. A neat and tidy home nestled in a flower-garden, and a little store stands beside it.

We pass the Munson place, where a plucky white widow is renting and struggling; and the eleven hundred acres of the Sennet plantation, with its Negro overseer. Then the character of the farms begins to change. Nearly all the lands belong to Russian Jews; the overseers are white, and the cabins are bare board-houses scattered here and there. The rents are high, and day-laborers and "contract" hands abound. It is a keen, hard struggle for living here, and few have time to talk. Tired with the long ride, we gladly drive into Gillonsville. It is a silent cluster of farm-houses standing on the cross-roads, with one of its stores closed and the other kept by a Negro preacher. They tell great tales of busy times at Gillonsville before all the railroads came to Albany; now it is chiefly a memory. Riding down the street, we stop at the preacher's and seat ourselves before the door. It was one of those scenes one cannot soon forget:— a wide, low, little house, whose motherly roof reached over and sheltered a snug little porch. There we sat, after the long hot drive, drinking cool water,—the talkative little storekeeper who is my daily companion; the silent old black woman patching pantaloons and saying never a word; the ragged picture of helpless misfortune who called in just to see the preacher; and finally the neat matronly preacher's wife, plump, yellow, and intelligent. "Own land?" said the wife; "well, only this house." Then she added quietly, "We did buy seven hundred acres up yonder, and paid for it; but they cheated us out of it. Sells was the owner." "Sells!" echoed the ragged misfortune, who was leaning against the balustrade and listening, "he's a regular cheat. I worked for him thirty-seven days this spring, and he paid me in cardboard checks which were to be cashed at the end of the month. But he never cashed them,—kept putting me off. Then the sheriff came and took my mule and corn and furniture—" "Furniture?" I asked; "but furniture is exempt from seizure by law." "Well, he took it just the same," said the hard-faced man.

VIII

Of the Quest of the Golden Fleece[1]

But the Brute said in his breast, "Till the mills I grind have ceased,
The riches shall be dust of dust, dry ashes be the feast!

   "On the strong and cunning few
     Cynic favors I will strew;
I will stuff their maw with overplus until their spirit dies;
     From the patient and the low
     I will take the joys they know;
     They shall hunger after vanities and still an-hungered go.
Madness shall be on the people, ghastly jealousies arise;
Brother's blood shall cry on brother up the dead and empty skies."
                     William Vaughn Moody.*

HAVE YOU EVER SEEN A COTTON-FIELD white with the harvest,—its golden fleece hovering above the black earth like a silvery cloud edged with dark green, its bold white signals waving like the foam of billows from Carolina to Texas across that Black and human Sea? I have sometimes half suspected that here the winged ram Chrysomallus left that Fleece after which Jason and his Argonauts[2] went vaguely wandering into the shadowy East three thousand years ago; and certainly one might frame a pretty and

---

*From "The Brute" (1901), by William Vaughn Moody.
†From "Children, You'll Be Called On."

not far-fetched analogy of witchery and dragon's teeth, and blood and armed men, between the ancient and the modern Quest of the Golden Fleece in the Black Sea.

And now the golden fleece is found; not only found, but, in its birthplace, woven. For the hum of the cotton-mills is the newest and most significant thing in the New South to-day. All through the Carolinas and Georgia, away down to Mexico, rise these gaunt red buildings, bare and homely, and yet so busy and noisy withal that they scarce seem to belong to the slow and sleepy land. Perhaps they sprang from dragons' teeth. So the Cotton Kingdom still lives; the world still bows beneath her sceptre. Even the markets that once defied the *parvenu*° have crept one by one across the seas, and then slowly and reluctantly, but surely, have started toward the Black Belt.

To be sure, there are those who wag their heads knowingly and tell us that the capital of the Cotton Kingdom has moved from the Black to the White Belt,—that the Negro of to-day raises not more than half of the cotton crop. Such men forget that the cotton crop has doubled, and more than doubled, since the era of slavery, and that, even granting their contention, the Negro is still supreme in a Cotton Kingdom larger than that on which the Confederacy builded its hopes. So the Negro forms to-day one of the chief figures in a great world-industry; and this, for its own sake, and in the light of historic interest, makes the field-hands of the cotton country worth studying.

We seldom study the condition of the Negro to-day honestly and carefully. It is so much easier to assume that we know it all. Or perhaps, having already reached conclusions in our own minds, we are loth to have them disturbed by facts. And yet how little we really know of these millions,—of their daily lives and longings, of their homely joys and sorrows, of their real shortcomings and the meaning of their crimes! All this we can only learn by intimate contact with the masses, and not by wholesale arguments covering millions separate in time and space, and differing widely in training and culture. To-day, then, my reader, let us turn our faces to

---

°One who rises above his birth but lacks the social skills of his new position.

the Black Belt of Georgia and seek simply to know the condition of the black farm-laborers of one county there.

Here in 1890 lived ten thousand Negroes and two thousand whites. The country is rich, yet the people are poor. The keynote of the Black Belt is debt; not commercial credit, but debt in the sense of continued inability on the part of the mass of the population to make income cover expense. This is the direct heritage of the South from the wasteful economies of the slave *régime*; but it was emphasized and brought to a crisis by the Emancipation of the slaves. In 1860, Dougherty County had six thousand slaves, worth at least two and a half millions of dollars; its farms were estimated at three millions,—making five and a half millions of property, the value of which depended largely on the slave system, and on the speculative demand for land once marvellously rich but already partially devitalized by careless and exhaustive culture. The war then meant a financial crash; in place of the five and a half millions of 1860, there remained in 1870 only farms valued at less than two millions. With this came increased competition in cotton culture from the rich lands of Texas; a steady fall in the normal price of cotton followed, from about fourteen cents a pound in 1860 until it reached four cents in 1898. Such a financial revolution was it that involved the owners of the cotton-belt in debt. And if things went ill with the master, how fared it with the man?

The plantations of Dougherty County in slavery days were not as imposing and aristocratic as those of Virginia. The Big House was smaller and usually one-storied, and sat very near the slave cabins. Sometimes these cabins stretched off on either side like wings; sometimes only on one side, forming a double row, or edging the road that turned into the plantation from the main thoroughfare. The form and disposition of the laborers' cabins throughout the Black Belt is to-day the same as in slavery days. Some live in the self-same cabins, others in cabins rebuilt on the sites of the old. All are sprinkled in little groups over the face of the land, centering about some dilapidated Big House where the head-tenant or agent lives. The general character and arrangement of these dwellings remains on the whole unaltered. There were in the county, outside the corporate town of Albany, about fifteen hundred Negro families in 1898. Out of all these, only a single family occupied a house with seven rooms; only fourteen have five rooms or more. The mass live in one- and two-room homes.

The size and arrangements of a people's homes are no unfair index of their condition. If, then, we inquire more carefully into these Negro homes, we find much that is unsatisfactory. All over the face of the land is the one-room cabin,—now standing in the shadow of the Big House, now staring at the dusty road, now rising dark and sombre amid the green of the cotton-fields. It is nearly always old and bare, built of rough boards, and neither plastered nor ceiled. Light and ventilation are supplied by the single door and by the square hole in the wall with its wooden shutter. There is no glass, porch, or ornamentation without. Within is a fireplace, black and smoky, and usually unsteady with age. A bed or two, a table, a wooden chest, and a few chairs compose the furniture; while a stray show-bill or a newspaper makes up the decorations for the walls. Now and then one may find such a cabin kept scrupulously neat, with merry steaming fire-place and hospitable door; but the majority are dirty and dilapidated, smelling of eating and sleeping, poorly ventilated, and anything but homes.

Above all, the cabins are crowded. We have come to associate crowding with homes in cities almost exclusively. This is primarily because we have so little accurate knowledge of country life. Here in Dougherty County one may find families of eight and ten occupying one or two rooms, and for every ten rooms of house accommodation for the Negroes there are twenty-five persons. The worst tenement abominations of New York do not have above twenty-two persons for every ten rooms. Of course, one small, close room in a city, without a yard, is in many respects worse than the larger single country room. In other respects it is better; it has glass windows, a decent chimney, and a trustworthy floor. The single great advantage of the Negro peasant is that he may spend most of his life outside his hovel, in the open fields.

There are four chief causes of these wretched homes: First, long custom born of slavery has assigned such homes to Negroes; white laborers would be offered better accommodations, and might, for that and similar reasons, give better work. Secondly, the Negroes, used to such accommodations, do not as a rule demand better; they do not know what better houses mean. Thirdly, the landlords as a class have not yet come to realize that it is a good

business investment to raise the standard of living among labor by
slow and judicious methods; that a Negro laborer who demands
three rooms and fifty cents a day would give more efficient work
and leave a larger profit than a discouraged toiler herding his family in one room and working for thirty cents. Lastly, among such
conditions of life there are few incentives to make the laborer become a better farmer. If he is ambitious, he moves to town or tries
other labor; as a tenant-farmer his outlook is almost hopeless, and
following it as a makeshift, he takes the house that is given him
without protest.

In such homes, then, these Negro peasants live. The families
are both small and large; there are many single tenants,—widows
and bachelors, and remnants of broken groups. The system of
labor and the size of the houses both tend to the breaking up of
family groups: the grown children go away as contract hands or
migrate to town, the sister goes into service; and so one finds
many families with hosts of babies, and many newly married cou-
ples, but comparatively few families with half-grown and grown
sons and daughters. The average size of Negro families has undoubtedly decreased since the war, primarily from economic
stress. In Russia over a third of the bridegrooms and over half the
brides are under twenty; the same was true of the ante-bellum
Negroes. To-day, however, very few of the boys and less than a
fifth of the Negro girls under twenty are married. The young men
marry between the ages of twenty-five and thirty-five; the young
women between twenty and thirty. Such postponement is due to
the difficulty of earning sufficient to rear and support a family;
and it undoubtedly leads, in the country districts, to sexual immorality. The form of this immorality, however, is very seldom that
of prostitution, and less frequently that of illegitimacy than one
would imagine. Rather, it takes the form of separation and desertion after a family group has been formed. The number of separated persons is thirty-five to the thousand,—a very large number.
It would of course be unfair to compare this number with divorce
statistics, for many of these separated women are in reality widowed, were the truth known, and in other cases the separation is
not permanent. Nevertheless, here lies the seat of greatest moral
danger. There is little or no prostitution among these Negroes,
and over three-fourths of the families, as found by house-to-house

investigation, deserve to be classed as decent people with considerable regard for female chastity. To be sure, the ideas of the mass would not suit New England, and there are many loose habits and notions. Yet the rate of illegitimacy is undoubtedly lower than in Austria or Italy, and the women as a class are modest. The plague-spot in sexual relations is easy marriage and easy separation. This is no sudden development, nor the fruit of Emancipation. It is the plain heritage from slavery. In those days Sam, with his master's consent, "took up" with Mary. No ceremony was necessary, and in the busy life of the great plantations of the Black Belt it was usually dispensed with. If now the master needed Sam's work in another plantation or in another part of the same plantation, or if he took a notion to sell the slave, Sam's married life with Mary was usually unceremoniously broken, and then it was clearly to the master's interest to have both of them take new mates. This widespread custom of two centuries has not been eradicated in thirty years. To-day Sam's grandson "takes up" with a woman without license or ceremony; they live together decently and honestly, and are, to all intents and purposes, man and wife. Sometimes these unions are never broken until death; but in too many cases family quarrels, a roving spirit, a rival suitor, or perhaps more frequently the hopeless battle to support a family, lead to separation, and a broken household is the result. The Negro church has done much to stop this practice, and now most marriage ceremonies are performed by the pastors. Nevertheless, the evil is still deep seated, and only a general raising of the standard of living will finally cure it.

Looking now at the county black population as a whole, it is fair to characterize it as poor and ignorant. Perhaps ten per cent compose the well-to-do and the best of the laborers, while at least nine per cent are thoroughly lewd and vicious. The rest, over eighty per cent, are poor and ignorant, fairly honest and well meaning, plodding, and to a degree shiftless, with some but not great sexual looseness. Such class lines are by no means fixed; they vary, one might almost say, with the price of cotton. The degree of ignorance cannot easily be expressed. We may say, for instance, that nearly two-thirds of them cannot read or write. This but partially expresses the fact. They are ignorant of the world about them, of modern economic organization, of the function of government, of individual worth and possibilities,—of nearly all those things which slavery in self-defence had to keep them from learning. Much that the white boy imbibes from his earliest social atmosphere forms the puzzling problems of the black boy's mature years. America is not another word for Opportunity to *all* her sons.

It is easy for us to lose ourselves in details in endeavoring to grasp and comprehend the real condition of a mass of human beings. We often forget that each unit in the mass is a throbbing human soul. Ignorant it may be, and poverty stricken, black and curious in limb and ways and thought; and yet it loves and hates, it toils and tires, it laughs and weeps its bitter tears, and looks in vague and awful longing at the grim horizon of its life,—all this, even as you and I. These black thousands are not in reality lazy; they are improvident and careless; they insist on breaking the monotony of toil with a glimpse at the great town-world on Saturday; they have their loafers and their rascals; but the great mass of them work continuously and faithfully for a return, and under circumstances that would call forth equal voluntary effort from few if any other modern laboring class. Over eighty-eight per cent of them—men, women, and children—are farmers. Indeed, this is almost the only industry. Most of the children get their schooling after the "crops are laid by," and very few there are that stay in school after the spring work has begun. Child-labor is to be found here in some of its worst phases, as fostering ignorance and stunting physical development. With the grown men of the county there is little variety in work: thirteen hundred are farmers, and two hundred are laborers, teamsters, etc., including twenty-four artisans, ten merchants, twenty-one preachers, and four teachers. This narrowness of life reaches its maximum among the women: thirteen hundred and fifty of these are farm laborers, one hundred are servants and washerwomen, leaving sixty-five housewives, eight teachers, and six seamstresses.

Among this people there is no leisure class. We often forget that in the United States over half the youth and adults are not in the world earning incomes, but are making homes, learning of the world, or resting after the heat of the strife. But here ninety-six per cent are toiling; no one with leisure to turn the bare and cheerless cabin into a home, no old folks to sit beside the fire and hand down traditions of the past; little of careless, happy childhood and dreaming youth. The dull monotony of daily toil is broken only by the gayety of the thoughtless and the Saturday trip to town. The toil, like all farm toil, is monotonous, and here there are little machinery and few tools to relieve its burdensome drudgery. But with all this, it is work in the pure open air, and this is something in a day when fresh air is scarce.

The land on the whole is still fertile, despite long abuse. For nine or ten months in succession the crops will come if asked: garden vegetables in April, grain in May, melons in June and July, hay in August, sweet potatoes in September, and cotton from then to Christmas. And yet on two-thirds of the land there is but one crop, and that leaves the toilers in debt. Why is this?

Away down the Baysan road, where the broad flat fields are flanked by great oak forests, is a plantation; many thousands of acres it used to run, here and there, and beyond the great wood. Thirteen hundred human beings here obeyed the call of one,— were his in body, and largely in soul. One of them lives there yet,—a short, stocky man, his dull-brown face seamed and drawn, and his tightly curled hair gray-white. The crops? Just tolerable, he said; just tolerable. Getting on? No—he was n't getting on at all. Smith of Albany "furnishes" him, and his rent is eight hundred pounds of cotton. Can't make anything at that. Why did n't he buy land? *Humph!* Takes money to buy land. And he turns away. Free! The most piteous thing amid all the black ruin of war-time, amid the broken fortunes of the masters, the blighted hopes of mothers and maidens, and the fall of an empire,—the most piteous thing amid all this was the black freedman who threw down his hoe because the world called him free. What did such a mockery of freedom mean? Not a cent of money, not an inch of land, not a mouthful of victuals,—not even ownership of the rags on his back. Free! On Saturday, once or twice a month, the old master, before the war, used to dole out bacon and meal to his Negroes. And after the first flush of freedom wore off, and his true helplessness dawned on the freedman, he came back and picked up his hoe, and old master still doled out his bacon and meal. The legal form of service was theoretically far different; in practice, task-work or "cropping" was substituted for daily toil in gangs; and the slave gradually became a metayer, or tenant on shares, in name, but a laborer with indeterminate wages in fact.

Still the price of cotton fell, and gradually the landlords deserted their plantations, and the reign of the merchant began. The
merchant of the Black Belt is a curious institution,—part banker,
part landlord, part contractor, and part despot. His store, which
used most frequently to stand at the cross-roads and become the
centre of a weekly village, has now moved to town; and thither
the Negro tenant follows him. The merchant keeps everything,—
clothes and shoes, coffee and sugar, pork and meal, canned and
dried goods, wagons and ploughs, seed and fertilizer,—and what
he has not in stock he can give you an order for at the store across
the way. Here, then, comes the tenant, Sam Scott, after he has
contracted with some absent landlord's agent for hiring forty acres
of land; he fingers his hat nervously until the merchant finishes his
morning chat with Colonel Sanders, and calls out, "Well, Sam,
what do you want?" Sam wants him to "furnish" him,—*i.e.*, to advance him food and clothing for the year, and perhaps seed and
tools, until his crop is raised and sold. If Sam seems a favorable
subject, he and the merchant go to a lawyer, and Sam executes a
chattel mortgage on his mule and wagon in return for seed and a
week's rations. As soon as the green cotton-leaves appear above
the ground, another mortgage is given on the "crop." Every Saturday, or at longer intervals, Sam calls upon the merchant for his
"rations"; a family of five usually gets about thirty pounds of fat
side-pork and a couple of bushels of corn-meal a month. Besides
this, clothing and shoes must be furnished; if Sam or his family is
sick, there are orders on the druggist and doctor; if the mule wants
shoeing, an order on the blacksmith, etc. If Sam is a hard worker
and crops promise well, he is often encouraged to buy more,—
sugar, extra clothes, perhaps a buggy. But he is seldom encouraged
to save. When cotton rose to ten cents last fall, the shrewd merchants of Dougherty County sold a thousand buggies in one season, mostly to black men.

The security offered for such transactions—a crop and chattel
mortgage—may at first seem slight. And, indeed, the merchants
tell many a true tale of shiftlessness and cheating; of cotton picked
at night, mules disappearing, and tenants absconding. But on the
whole the merchant of the Black Belt is the most prosperous man
in the section. So skilfully and so closely has he drawn the bonds
of the law about the tenant, that the black man has often simply to

choose between pauperism and crime; he "waives" all homestead exemptions in his contract; he cannot touch his own mortgaged crop, which the laws put almost in the full control of the land-owner and of the merchant. When the crop is growing the merchant watches it like a hawk; as soon as it is ready for market he takes possession of it, sells it, pays the land-owner his rent, subtracts his bill for supplies, and if, as sometimes happens, there is anything left, he hands it over to the black serf for his Christmas celebration.

The direct result of this system is an all-cotton scheme of agriculture and the continued bankruptcy of the tenant. The currency of the Black Belt is cotton. It is a crop always salable for ready money, not usually subject to great yearly fluctuations in price, and one which the Negroes know how to raise. The landlord therefore demands his rent in cotton, and the merchant will accept mortgages on no other crop. There is no use asking the black tenant, then, to diversify his crops,—he cannot under this system. Moreover, the system is bound to bankrupt the tenant. I remember once meeting a little one-mule wagon on the River road. A young black fellow sat in it driving listlessly, his elbows on his knees. His dark-faced wife sat beside him, stolid, silent.

"Hello!" cried my driver,—he has a most impudent way of addressing these people, though they seem used to it,—"what have you got there?"

"Meat and meal," answered the man, stopping. The meat lay uncovered in the bottom of the wagon,—a great thin side of fat pork covered with salt; the meal was in a white bushel bag.

"What did you pay for that meat?"

"Ten cents a pound." It could have been bought for six or seven cents cash.

"And the meal?"

"Two dollars." One dollar and ten cents is the cash price in town. Here was a man paying five dollars for goods which he could have bought for three dollars cash, and raised for one dollar or one dollar and a half.

Yet it is not wholly his fault. The Negro farmer started behind,—started in debt. This was not his choosing, but the crime of this happy-go-lucky nation which goes blundering along with its Reconstruction tragedies, its Spanish war interludes and Philippine matinees, just as though God really were dead. Once in debt, it is no easy matter for a whole race to emerge.

In the year of low-priced cotton, 1898, out of three hundred tenant families one hundred and seventy-five ended their year's work in debt to the extent of fourteen thousand dollars; fifty cleared nothing, and the remaining seventy-five made a total profit of sixteen hundred dollars. The net indebtedness of the black tenant families of the whole county must have been at least sixty thousand dollars. In a more prosperous year the situation is far better; but on the average the majority of tenants end the year even, or in debt, which means that they work for board and clothes. Such an economic organization is radically wrong. Whose is the blame?

The underlying causes of this situation are complicated but discernible. And one of the chief, outside the carelessness of the nation in letting the slave start with nothing, is the widespread opinion among the merchants and employers of the Black Belt that only by the slavery of debt can the Negro be kept at work. Without doubt, some pressure was necessary at the beginning of the free-labor system to keep the listless and lazy at work; and even to-day the mass of the Negro laborers need stricter guardianship than most Northern laborers. Behind this honest and widespread opinion dishonesty and cheating of the ignorant laborers have a good chance to take refuge. And to all this must be added the obvious fact that a slave ancestry and a system of unrequited toil has not improved the efficiency or temper of the mass of black laborers. Nor is this peculiar to Sambo;* it has in history been just as true of John and Hans, of Jacques and Pat, of all grounddown peasantries. Such is the situation of the mass of the Negroes in the Black Belt to-day; and they are thinking about it. Crime, and a cheap and dangerous socialism, are the inevitable results of this pondering. I see now that ragged black man sitting on a log, aimlessly whittling a stick. He muttered to me with the murmur of many ages, when he said: "White man sit down whole year; Nigger work day and night and make crop; Nigger hardly gits bread and meat; white man sittin' down gits all. *It's wrong.*" And what do

---

*Derogatory name for an African-American man.

the better classes of Negroes do to improve their situation? One of two things: if any way possible, they buy land; if not, they migrate to town. Just as centuries ago it was no easy thing for the serf to escape into the freedom of town-life, even so to-day there are hindrances laid in the way of county laborers. In considerable parts of all the Gulf States, and especially in Mississippi, Louisiana, and Arkansas, the Negroes on the plantations in the back-country districts are still held at forced labor practically without wages. Especially is this true in districts where the farmers are composed of the more ignorant class of poor whites, and the Negroes are beyond the reach of schools and intercourse with their advancing fellows. If such a peon should run away, the sheriff, elected by white suffrage, can usually be depended on to catch the fugitive, return him, and ask no questions. If he escape to another county, a charge of petty thieving, easily true, can be depended upon to secure his return. Even if some unduly officious person insist upon a trial, neighborly comity will probably make his conviction sure, and then the labor due the county can easily be bought by the master. Such a system is impossible in the more civilized parts of the South, or near the large towns and cities; but in those vast stretches of land beyond the telegraph and the newspaper the spirit of the Thirteenth Amendment is sadly broken. This represents the lowest economic depths of the black American peasant; and in a study of the rise and condition of the Negro freeholder we must trace his economic progress from this modern serfdom.

Even in the better-ordered country districts of the South the free movement of agricultural laborers is hindered by the migration-agent laws. The "Associated Press" recently informed the world of the arrest of a young white man in Southern Georgia who represented the "Atlantic Naval Supplies Company," and who "was caught in the act of enticing hands from the turpentine farm of Mr. John Greer." The crime for which this young man was arrested is taxed five hundred dollars for each county in which the employment agent proposes to gather laborers for work outside the State. Thus the Negroes' ignorance of the labor-market outside his own vicinity is increased rather than diminished by the laws of nearly every Southern State.

Similar to such measures is the unwritten law of the back districts and small towns of the South, that the character of all Negroes unknown to the mass of the community must be vouched for by some white man. This is really a revival of the old Roman idea of the patron under whose protection the new-made freedman was put. In many instances this system has been of great good to the Negro, and very often under the protection and guidance of the former master's family, or other white friends, the freedman progressed in wealth and morality. But the same system has in other cases resulted in the refusal of whole communities to recognize the right of a Negro to change his habitation and to be master of his own fortunes. A black stranger in Baker County, Georgia, for instance, is liable to be stopped anywhere on the public highway and made to state his business to the satisfaction of any white interrogator. If he fails to give a suitable answer, or seems too independent or "sassy," he may be arrested or summarily driven away.

Thus it is that in the country districts of the South, by written or unwritten law, peonage,° hindrances to the migration of labor, and a system of white patronage exists over large areas. Besides this, the chance for lawless oppression and illegal exactions is vastly greater in the country than in the city, and nearly all the more serious race disturbances of the last decade have arisen from disputes in the county between master and man,—as, for instance, the Sam Hose affair. As a result of such a situation, there arose, first, the Black Belt; and, second, the Migration to Town. The Black Belt was not, as many assumed, a movement toward fields of labor under more genial climatic conditions; it was primarily a huddling for self-protection,—a massing of the black population for mutual defence in order to secure the peace and tranquillity necessary to economic advance. This movement took place between Emancipation and 1880, and only partially accomplished the desired results. The rush to town since 1880 is the countermovement of men disappointed in the economic opportunities of the Black Belt.

°System in which a person is forced to work without compensation until a debt is paid; served as a new form of slavery following Reconstruction.

In Dougherty County, Georgia, one can see easily the results of this experiment in huddling for protection. Only ten per cent of the adult population was born in the county, and yet the blacks outnumber the whites four or five to one. There is undoubtedly a security to the blacks in their very numbers,—a personal freedom from arbitrary treatment, which makes hundreds of laborers cling to Dougherty in spite of low wages and economic distress. But a change is coming, and slowly but surely even here the agricultural laborers are drifting to town and leaving the broad acres behind. Why is this? Why do not the Negroes become land-owners, and build up the black landed peasantry, which has for a generation and more been the dream of philanthropist and statesman?

To the car-window sociologist, to the man who seeks to understand and know the South by devoting the few leisure hours of a holiday trip to unravelling the snarl of centuries,—to such men very often the whole trouble with the black field-hand may be summed up by Aunt Ophelia's word, "Shiftless!"* They have noted repeatedly scenes like one I saw last summer. We were riding along the highroad to town at the close of a long hot day. A couple of young black fellows passed us in a mule-team, with several bushels of loose corn in the ear. One was driving, listlessly bent forward, his elbows on his knees,—a happy-go-lucky, careless picture of irresponsibility. The other was fast asleep in the bottom of the wagon. As we passed we noticed an ear of corn fall from the wagon. They never saw it,—not they. A rod farther on we noted another ear on the ground; and between that creeping mule and town we counted twenty-six ears of corn. Shiftless? Yes, the personification of shiftlessness. And yet follow those boys: they are not lazy; to-morrow morning they'll be up with the sun; they work hard when they do work, and they work willingly. They have no sordid, selfish, money-getting ways, but rather a fine disdain for mere cash. They 'll loaf before your face and work behind your back with good-natured honesty. They 'll steal a watermelon, and hand you back your lost purse intact. Their great defect as laborers lies in their lack of incentive to work beyond the mere pleasure of physical exertion. They are careless because they have not

---

*Ophelia St. Clair; a northern character in *Uncle Tom's Cabin* (1852), by Harriet Beecher Stowe.

found that it pays to be careful; they are improvident because the improvident ones of their acquaintance get on about as well as the provident. Above all, they cannot see why they should take unusual pains to make the white man's land better, or to fatten his mule, or save his corn. On the other hand, the white land-owner argues that any attempt to improve these laborers by increased responsibility, or higher wages, or better homes, or land of their own, would be sure to result in failure. He shows his Northern visitor the scarred and wretched land; the ruined mansions, the worn-out soil and mortgaged acres, and says, This is Negro freedom!

Now it happens that both master and man have just enough argument on their respective sides to make it difficult for them to understand each other. The Negro dimly personifies in the white man all his ills and misfortunes; if he is poor, it is because the white man seizes the fruit of his toil; if he is ignorant, it is because the white man gives him neither time nor facilities to learn; and, indeed, if any misfortune happens to him, it is because of some hidden machinations of "white folks." On the other hand, the masters and the masters' sons have never been able to see why the Negro, instead of settling down to be day-laborers for bread and clothes, are infected with a silly desire to rise in the world, and why they are sulky, dissatisfied, and careless, where their fathers were happy and dumb and faithful. "Why, you niggers have an easier time than I do," said a puzzled Albany merchant to his black customer. "Yes," he replied, "and so does yo' hogs."

Taking, then, the dissatisfied and shiftless field-hand as a starting-point, let us inquire how the black thousands of Dougherty have struggled from him up toward their ideal, and what that ideal is. All social struggle is evidenced by the rise, first of economic, then of social classes, among a homogeneous population. To-day the following economic classes are plainly differentiated among these Negroes.

A "submerged tenth" of croppers, with a few paupers; forty per cent who are metayers and thirty-nine per cent of semi-metayers and wage-laborers. There are left five per cent of money-renters and six per cent of freeholders—the "Upper Ten" of the land. The croppers are entirely without capital, even in the limited sense of food or money to keep them from seed-time to harvest. All they furnish is their labor; the land-owner furnishes land, stock, tools, seed, and house; and at the end of the year the laborer gets from a third to a half of the crop. Out of his share, however, comes pay and interest for food and clothing advanced him during the year. Thus we have a laborer without capital and without wages, and an employer whose capital is largely his employees' wages. It is an unsatisfactory arrangement, both for hirer and hired, and is usually in vogue on poor land with hard-pressed owners.

Above the croppers come the great mass of the black population who work the land on their own responsibility, paying rent in cotton and supported by the crop-mortgage system. After the war this system was attractive to the freedmen on account of its larger freedom and its possibilities for making a surplus. But with the carrying out of the crop-lien system, the deterioration of the land, and the slavery of debt, the position of the metayers has sunk to a dead level of practically unrewarded toil. Formerly all tenants had some capital, and often considerable; but absentee landlordism, rising rack-rent, and falling cotton have stripped them well-nigh of all, and probably not over half of them to-day own their mules. The change from cropper to tenant was accomplished by fixing the rent. If, now, the rent fixed was reasonable, this was an incentive to the tenant to strive. On the other hand, if the rent was too high, or if the land deteriorated, the result was to discourage and check the efforts of the black peasantry. There is no doubt that the latter case is true; that in Dougherty County every economic advantage of the price of cotton in market and of the strivings of the tenant has been taken advantage of by the landlords and merchants, and swallowed up in rent and interest. If cotton rose in price, the rent rose even higher; if cotton fell, the rent remained or followed reluctantly. If a tenant worked hard and raised a large crop, his rent was raised the next year; if that year the crop failed, his corn was confiscated and his mule sold for debt. There were, of course, exceptions to this,—cases of personal kindness and forbearance; but in the vast majority of cases the rule was to extract the uttermost farthing from the mass of the black farm laborers.

The average metayer pays from twenty to thirty per cent of his crop in rent. The result of such rack-rent can only be evil,—abuse and neglect of the soil, deterioration in the character of the laborers, and a wide-spread sense of injustice. "Wherever the country is poor," cried Arthur Young, "it is in the hands of metayers" and "their condition is more wretched than that of day-laborers." He was talking of Italy a century ago; but he might have been talking of Dougherty County to-day. And especially is that true to-day which he declares was true in France before the Revolution: "The metayers are considered as little better than menial servants, removable at pleasure, and obliged to conform in all things to the will of the landlords." On this low plane half the black population of Dougherty County—perhaps more than half the black millions of this land—are to-day struggling.

A degree above these we may place those laborers who receive money wages for their work. Some receive a house with perhaps a garden-spot; then supplies of food and clothing are advanced, and certain fixed wages are given at the end of the year, varying from thirty to sixty dollars, out of which the supplies must be paid for, with interest. About eighteen per cent of the population belong to this class of semi-metayers, while twenty-two per cent are laborers paid by the month or year, and are either "furnished" by their own savings or perhaps more usually by some merchant who takes his chances of payment. Such laborers receive from thirty-five to fifty cents a day during the working season. They are usually young unmarried persons, some being women; and when they marry they sink to the class of metayers, or, more seldom, become renters.

The renters for fixed money rentals are the first of the emerging classes, and form five per cent of the families. The sole advantage of this small class is their freedom to choose their crops, and the increased responsibility which comes through having money transactions. While some of the renters differ little in condition from the metayers, yet on the whole they are more intelligent and responsible persons, and are the ones who eventually become land-owners. Their better character and greater shrewdness enable them to gain, perhaps to demand, better terms in rents; rented farms, varying from forty to a hundred acres, bear an average rental of about fifty-four dollars a year. The men who conduct such farms do not long remain renters; either they sink to metayers, or with a successful series of harvests rise to be land-owners.

In 1870 the tax-books of Dougherty report no Negroes as land-holders. If there were any such at that time,—and there may have been a few,—their land was probably held in the name of some white patron,—a method not uncommon during slavery. In 1875 ownership of land had begun with seven hundred and fifty acres; ten years later this had increased to over sixty-five hundred acres, to nine thousand acres in 1890 and ten thousand in 1900. The total assessed property has in this same period risen from eighty thousand dollars in 1875 to two hundred and forty thousand dollars in 1900.

Two circumstances complicate this development and make it in some respects difficult to be sure of the real tendencies; they are the panic of 1893,* and the low price of cotton in 1898. Besides this, the system of assessing property in the country districts of Georgia is somewhat antiquated and of uncertain statistical value; there are no assessors, and each man makes a sworn return to a tax-receiver. Thus public opinion plays a large part, and the re-turns vary strangely from year to year. Certainly these figures show the small amount of accumulated capital among the Ne-groes, and the consequent large dependence of their property on temporary prosperity. They have little to tide over a few years of economic depression, and are at the mercy of the cotton-market far more than the whites. And thus the land-owners, despite their marvellous efforts, are really a transient class, continually being depleted by those who fall back into the class of renters or metay-ers, and augmented by newcomers from the masses. Of the one hundred land-owners in 1898, half had bought their land since 1893, a fourth between 1890 and 1893, a fifth between 1884 and 1890, and the rest between 1870 and 1884. In all, one hundred and eighty-five Negroes have owned land in this county since 1875.

If all the black land-owners who had ever held land here had kept it or left it in the hands of black men, the Negroes would have owned nearer thirty thousand acres than the fifteen thou-sand they now hold. And yet these fifteen thousand acres are a creditable showing,—a proof of no little weight of the worth and

---

*Economic depression following the collapse of the stock market.

ability of the Negro people. If they had been given an economic
start at Emancipation, if they had been in an enlightened and rich
community which really desired their best good, then we might
perhaps call such a result small or even insignificant. But for a few
thousand poor ignorant field-hands, in the face of poverty, a falling
market, and social stress, to save and capitalize two hundred thousand dollars in a generation has meant a tremendous effort. The
rise of a nation, the pressing forward of a social class, means a bitter struggle, a hard and soul-sickening battle with the world such
as few of the more favored classes know or appreciate.

Out of the hard economic conditions of this portion of the
Black Belt, only six per cent of the population have succeeded in
emerging into peasant proprietorship; and these are not all firmly
fixed, but grow and shrink in number with the wavering of the cotton-market. Fully ninety-four per cent have struggled for land and
failed, and half of them sit in hopeless serfdom. For these there is
one other avenue of escape toward which they have turned in increasing numbers, namely, migration to town. A glance at the dis-
tribution of land among the black owners curiously reveals this
fact. In 1898 the holdings were as follows: Under forty acres,
forty-nine families; forty to two hundred and fifty acres, seventeen
families; two hundred and fifty to one thousand acres, thirteen
families; one thousand or more acres, two families. Now in 1890
there were forty-four holdings, but only nine of these were under
forty acres. The great increase of holdings, then, has come in the
buying of small homesteads near town, where their owners really
share in the town life; this is a part of the rush to town. And for
every land-owner who has thus hurried away from the narrow and
hard conditions of country life, how many field-hands, how many
tenants, how many ruined renters, have joined that long proces-
sion? Is it not strange compensation? The sin of the country districts is visited on the town, and the social sores of city life to-day
may, here in Dougherty County, and perhaps in many places near
and far, look for their final healing without the city walls.

IX

Of the Sons of Master and Man[1]

Life treads on life, and heart on heart;
We press too close in church and mart
To keep a dream or grave apart.
                                    Mrs. Browning.[*]

THE WORLD-OLD PHENOMENON of the contact of diverse races of men is to have new exemplification during the new century. Indeed, the characteristic of our age is the contact of European civilization with the world's undeveloped peoples. Whatever we may say of the results of such contact in the past, it certainly forms a chapter in human action not pleasant to look back upon. War, murder, slavery, extermination, and debauchery,—this has again and again been the result of carrying civilization and the blessed gospel to the isles of the sea and the heathen without the law. Nor does it altogether satisfy the conscience of the modern world to be told complacently that all this has been right and proper, the fated triumph of strength over weakness, of righteousness over evil, of superiors over inferiors. It would certainly be soothing if one could readily believe all this; and yet there are too many ugly facts for everything to be thus easily explained away. We feel and know that there are many delicate differences

---

[*]From *A Vision of Poets* (1844), by Elizabeth Barrett Browning.
[†]From "I'm a Rolling."

117

in race psychology, numberless changes that our crude social measurements are not yet able to follow minutely, which explain much of history and social development. At the same time, too, we know that these considerations have never adequately explained or excused the triumph of brute force and cunning over weakness and innocence.

It is, then, the strife of all honorable men of the twentieth century to see that in the future competition of races the survival of the fittest shall mean the triumph of the good, the beautiful, and the true; that we may be able to preserve for future civilization all that is really fine and noble and strong, and not continue to put a premium on greed and impudence and cruelty. To bring this hope to fruition, we are compelled daily to turn more and more to a conscientious study of the phenomena of race-contact,—to a study frank and fair, and not falsified and colored by our wishes or our fears. And we have in the South as fine a field for such a study as the world affords,—a field, to be sure, which the average American scientist deems somewhat beneath his dignity, and which the average man who is not a scientist knows all about, but nevertheless a line of study which by reason of the enormous race complications with which God seems about to punish this nation must increasingly claim our sober attention, study, and thought, we must ask, what are the actual relations of whites and blacks in the South? and we must be answered, not by apology or fault-finding, but by a plain, unvarnished tale.

In the civilized life of to-day the contact of men and their relations to each other fall in a few main lines of action and communication: there is, first, the physical proximity of homes and dwelling-places, the way in which neighborhoods group themselves, and the contiguity of neighborhoods. Secondly, and in our age chiefest, there are the economic relations,—the methods by which individuals coöperate for earning a living, for the mutual satisfaction of wants, for the production of wealth. Next, there are the political relations, the coöperation in social control, in group government, in laying and paying the burden of taxation. In the fourth place there are the less tangible but highly important forms of intellectual contact and commerce, the interchange of ideas through conversation and conference, through periodicals and libraries; and, above all, the gradual formation for each community of that curious *tertium quid* which we call public opinion. Closely allied with this come the various forms of social contact in everyday life, in travel, in theatres, in house gatherings, in marrying and giving in marriage. Finally, there are the varying forms of religious enterprise, of moral teaching and benevolent endeavor. These are the principal ways in which men living in the same communities are brought into contact with each other. It is my present task, therefore, to indicate, from my point of view, how the black race in the South meet and mingle with the whites in these matters of everyday life.

First, as to physical dwelling. It is usually possible to draw in nearly every Southern community a physical color-line on the map, on the one side of which whites dwell and on the other Negroes. The winding and intricacy of the geographical color-line varies, of course, in different communities. I know some towns where a straight line drawn through the middle of the main street separates nine-tenths of the whites from nine-tenths of the blacks. In other towns the older settlement of whites has been encircled by a broad band of blacks; in still other cases little settlements or nuclei of blacks have sprung up amid surrounding whites. Usually in cities each street has its distinctive color, and only now and then do the colors meet in close proximity. Even in the country something of this segregation is manifest in the smaller areas, and of course in the larger phenomena of the Black Belt.

All this segregation by color is largely independent of that natural clustering by social grades common to all communities. A Negro slum may be in dangerous proximity to a white residence quarter, while it is quite common to find a white slum planted in the heart of a respectable Negro district. One thing, however, seldom occurs: the best of the whites and the best of the Negroes almost never live in anything like close proximity. It thus happens that in nearly every Southern town and city, both whites and blacks see commonly the worst of each other. This is a vast change from the situation in the past, when, through the close contact of master and house-servant in the patriarchal big house, one found the best of both races in close contact and sympathy, while at the same time the squalor and dull round of toil among the field-hands was removed from the sight and hearing of the family. One can easily see how a person who saw slavery thus from his father's parlors, and sees freedom on the streets of a great city, fails to grasp or comprehend the whole of the new picture. On the other hand, the settled belief of the mass of the Negroes that the Southern white people do not have the black man's best interests at heart has been intensified in later years by this continual daily contact of the better class of blacks with the worst representatives of the white race.

Coming now to the economic relations of the races, we are on ground made familiar by study, much discussion, and no little philanthropic effort. And yet with all this there are many essential elements in the coöperation of Negroes and whites for work and wealth that are too readily overlooked or not thoroughly understood. The average American can easily conceive of a rich land awaiting development and filled with black laborers. To him the Southern problem is simply that of making efficient workingmen out of this material, by giving them the requisite technical skill and the help of invested capital. The problem, however, is by no means as simple as this, from the obvious fact that these workingmen have been trained for centuries as slaves. They exhibit, therefore, all the advantages and defects of such training; they are willing and good-natured, but not self-reliant, provident, or careful. If now the economic development of the South is to be pushed to the verge of exploitation, as seems probable, then we have a mass of workingmen thrown into relentless competition with the workingmen of the world, but handicapped by a training the very opposite to that of the modern self-reliant democratic laborer. What the black laborer needs is careful personal guidance, group leadership of men with hearts in their bosoms, to train them to foresight, carefulness, and honesty. Nor does it require any fine-spun theories of racial differences to prove the necessity of such group training after the brains of the race have been knocked out by two hundred and fifty years of assiduous education in submission, carelessness, and stealing. After Emancipation, it was the plain duty of some one to assume this group leadership and training of the Negro laborer. I will not stop here to inquire whose duty it was,— whether that of the white ex-master who had profited by unpaid toil, or the Northern philanthropist whose persistence brought on the crisis, or the National Government whose edict freed the bondmen; I will not stop to ask whose duty it was, but I insist it was the duty of some one to see that these workingmen were not left alone and unguided, without capital, without land, without skill, without economic organization, without even the bald protection of law, order, and decency,—left in a great land, not to settle down to slow and careful internal development, but destined to be thrown almost immediately into relentless and sharp competition with the best of modern workingmen under an economic system where every participant is fighting for himself, and too often utterly regardless of the rights or welfare of his neighbor.

For we must never forget that the economic system of the South to-day which has succeeded the old *régime* is not the same system as that of the old industrial North, of England, or of France, with their trades-unions, their restrictive laws, their written and unwritten commercial customs, and their long experience. It is, rather, a copy of that England of the early nineteenth century, before the factory acts,—the England that wrung pity from thinkers and fired the wrath of Carlyle. The rod of empire that passed from the hands of Southern gentlemen in 1865, partly by force, partly by their own petulance, has never returned to them. Rather it has passed to those men who have come to take charge of the industrial exploitation of the New South,—the sons of poor whites fired with a new thirst for wealth and power, thrifty and avaricious Yankees, shrewd and unscrupulous Jews. Into the hands of these men the Southern laborers, white and black, have fallen; and this to their sorrow. For the laborers as such there is in these new captains of industry neither love nor hate, neither sympathy nor romance; it is a cold question of dollars and dividends. Under such a system all labor is bound to suffer. Even the white laborers are not yet intelligent, thrifty, and well trained enough to maintain themselves against the powerful inroads of organized capital. The results among them, even, are long hours of toil, low wages, child labor, and lack of protection against usury and cheating. But among the black laborers all this is aggravated, first, by a race prejudice which varies from a doubt and distrust among the best element of whites to a frenzied hatred among the worst; and, secondly, it is aggravated, as I have said before, by the wretched economic heritage of the freedmen from slavery. With this training it is difficult for the freedman to learn to grasp the opportunities already opened to him, and the new opportunities are seldom given him, but go by favor to the whites.

Left by the best elements of the South with little protection or oversight, he has been made in law and custom the victim of the worst and most unscrupulous men in each community. The crop-lien system* which is depopulating the fields of the South is not simply the result of shiftlessness on the part of Negroes, but is also the result of cunningly devised laws as to mortgages, liens, and misdemeanors, which can be made by conscienceless men to entrap and snare the unwary until escape is impossible, further toil a farce, and protest a crime. I have seen, in the Black Belt of Georgia, an ignorant, honest Negro buy and pay for a farm in installments three separate times, and then in the face of law and decency the enterprising Russian Jew who sold it to him pocketed money and deed and left the black man landless, to labor on his own land at thirty cents a day. I have seen a black farmer fall in debt to a white storekeeper, and that storekeeper go to his farm and strip it of every single marketable article,—mules, ploughs, stored crops, tools, furniture, bedding, clocks, looking-glass,—and all this without a warrant, without process of law, without a sheriff or officer, in the face of the law for homestead exemptions, and without rendering to a single responsible person any account or reckoning. And such proceedings can happen, and will happen, in any community where a class of ignorant toilers are placed by custom and race-prejudice beyond the pale of sympathy and race-brotherhood. So long as the best elements of a community do not feel in duty bound to protect and train and care for the weaker members of their group, they leave them to be preyed upon by these swindlers and rascals.

This unfortunate economic situation does not mean the hindrance of all advance in the black South, or the absence of a class of black landlords and mechanics who, in spite of disadvantages, are accumulating property and making good citizens. But it does mean that this class is not nearly so large as a fairer economic system might easily make it, that those who survive in the competition are handicapped so as to accomplish much less than they deserve to, and that, above all, the *personnel* of the successful class is left to chance and accident, and not to any intelligent culling or reasonable methods of selection. As a remedy for this, there is but one possible procedure. We must accept some of the race prejudice in the South as a fact,— deplorable in its intensity, unfortunate in results, and dangerous for the future, but nevertheless a hard fact which only time can efface.

---

*System in which farmers receive food, supplies, seeds, and credit; they repay the debt after their crop is harvested; usually results in long terms of indebtedness.

We cannot hope, then, in this generation, or for several generations, that the mass of the whites can be brought to assume that close sympathetic and self-sacrificing leadership of the blacks which their present situation so eloquently demands. Such leadership, such social teaching and example, must come from the blacks themselves. For some time men doubted as to whether the Negro could develop such leaders; but to-day no one seriously disputes the capability of individual Negroes to assimilate the culture and common sense of modern civilization, and to pass it on, to some extent at least, to their fellows. If this is true, then here is the path out of the economic situation, and here is the imperative demand for trained Negro leaders of character and intelligence,—men of skill, men of light and leading, college-bred men, black captains of industry, and missionaries of culture; men who thoroughly comprehend and know modern civilization, and can take hold of Negro communities and raise and train them by force of precept and example, deep sympathy, and the inspiration of common blood and ideals. But if such men are to be effective they must have some power,—they must be backed by the best public opinion of these communities, and able to wield for their objects and aims such weapons as the experience of the world has taught are indispensable to human progress.

Of such weapons the greatest, perhaps, in the modern world is the power of the ballot; and this brings me to a consideration of the third form of contact between whites and blacks in the South,—political activity.

In the attitude of the American mind toward Negro suffrage can be traced with unusual accuracy the prevalent conceptions of government. In the fifties we were near enough the echoes of the French Revolution to believe pretty thoroughly in universal suffrage. We argued, as we thought then rather logically, that no social class was so good, so true, and so disinterested as to be trusted wholly with the political destiny of its neighbors; that in every state the best arbiters of their own welfare are the persons directly affected; consequently that it is only by arming every hand with a ballot,—with the right to have a voice in the policy of the state,—that the greatest good to the greatest number could be attained. To be sure, there were objections to these arguments, but we thought we had answered them tersely and convincingly; if some one complained of the ignorance of voters, we answered, "Educate them." If another complained of their venality, we replied, "Disfranchise them or put them in jail." And, finally, to the men who feared demagogues and the natural perversity of some human beings we insisted that time and bitter experience would teach the most hardheaded. It was at this time that the question of Negro suffrage in the South was raised. Here was a defenceless people suddenly made free. How were they to be protected from those who did not believe in their freedom and were determined to thwart it? Not by force, said the North; not by government guardianship, said the South; then by the ballot, the sole and legitimate defence of a free people, said the Common Sense of the Nation. No one thought, at the time, that the ex-slaves could use the ballot intelligently or very effectively; but they did think that the possession of so great power by a great class in the nation would compel their fellows to educate this class to its intelligent use.

Meantime, new thoughts came to the nation: the inevitable period of moral retrogression and political trickery that ever follows in the wake of war overtook us. So flagrant became the political scandals that reputable men began to leave politics alone, and politics consequently became disreputable. Men began to pride themselves on having nothing to do with their own government, and to agree tacitly with those who regarded public office as a private perquisite. In this state of mind it became easy to wink at the suppression of the Negro vote in the South, and to advise self-respecting Negroes to leave politics entirely alone. The decent and reputable citizens of the North who neglected their own civic duties grew hilarious over the exaggerated importance with which the Negro regarded the franchise. Thus it easily happened that more and more the better class of Negroes followed the advice from abroad and the pressure from home, and took no further interest in politics, leaving to the careless and the venal of their race the exercise of their rights as voters. The black vote that still remained was not trained and educated, but further debauched by open and unblushing bribery, or force and fraud; until the Negro voter was thoroughly inoculated with the idea that politics was a method of private gain by disreputable means.

And finally, now, to-day, when we are awakening to the fact that the perpetuity of republican institutions on this continent depends on the purification of the ballot, the civic training of voters, and the raising of voting to the plane of a solemn duty which a patriotic citizen neglects to his peril and to the peril of his children's children,—

in this day, when we are striving for a renaissance of civic virtue, what are we going to say to the black voter of the South? Are we going to tell him still that politics is a disreputable and useless form of human activity? Are we going to induce the best class of Negroes to take less and less interest in government, and to give up their right to take such an interest, without a protest? I am not saying a word against all legitimate efforts to purge the ballot of ignorance, pauperism, and crime. But few have pretended that the present movement for disfranchisement in the South is for such a purpose; it has been plainly and frankly declared in nearly every case that the object of the disfranchising laws is the elimination of the black man from politics.

Now, is this a minor matter which has no influence on the main question of the industrial and intellectual development of the Negro? Can we establish a mass of black laborers and artisans and landholders in the South who, by law and public opinion, have absolutely no voice in shaping the laws under which they live and work? Can the modern organization of industry, assuming as it does free democratic government and the power and ability of the laboring classes to compel respect for their welfare,—can this system be carried out in the South when half its laboring force is voiceless in the public councils and powerless in its own defence? To-day the black man of the South has almost nothing to say as to how much he shall be taxed, or how those taxes shall be expended; as to who shall execute the laws, and how they shall do it; as to who shall make the laws, and how they shall be made. It is pitiable that frantic efforts must be made at critical times to get law-makers in some States even to listen to the respectful presentation of the black man's side of a current controversy. Daily the Negro is coming more and more to look upon law and justice, not as protecting safeguards, but as sources of humiliation and oppression. The laws are made by men who have little interest in him; they are executed by men who have absolutely no motive for treating the black people with courtesy or consideration; and, finally, the accused law-breaker is tried, not by his peers, but too often by men who would rather punish ten innocent Negroes than let one guilty one escape.

I should be the last one to deny the patent weaknesses and shortcomings of the Negro people; I should be the last to withhold sympathy from the white South in its efforts to solve its intricate social problems. I freely acknowledge that it is possible, and sometimes best, that a partially undeveloped people should be ruled by the best of their stronger and better neighbors for their own good, until such time as they can start and fight the world's battles alone. I have already pointed out how sorely in need of such economic and spiritual guidance the emancipated Negro was, and I am quite willing to admit that if the representatives of the best white Southern public opinion were the ruling and guiding powers in the South to-day the conditions indicated would be fairly well fulfilled. But the point I have insisted upon, and now emphasize again, is that the best opinion of the South to-day is not the ruling opinion. That to leave the Negro helpless and without a ballot to-day is to leave him, not to the guidance of the best, but rather to the exploitation and debauchment of the worst; that this is no truer of the South than of the North,— of the North than of Europe: in any land, in any country under modern free competition, to lay any class of weak and despised people, be they white, black, or blue, at the political mercy of their stronger, richer, and more resourceful fellows, is a temptation which human nature seldom has withstood and seldom will withstand.

Moreover, the political status of the Negro in the South is closely connected with the question of Negro crime. There can be no doubt that crime among Negroes has sensibly increased in the last thirty years, and that there has appeared in the slums of great cities a distinct criminal class among the blacks. In explaining this unfortunate development, we must note two things: (1) that the inevitable result of Emancipation was to increase crime and criminals, and (2) that the police system of the South was primarily designed to control slaves. As to the first point, we must not forget that under a strict slave system there can scarcely be such a thing as crime. But when these variously constituted human particles are suddenly thrown broadcast on the sea of life, some swim, some sink, and some hang suspended, to be forced up or down by the chance currents of a busy hurrying world. So great an economic and social revolution as swept the South in '63 meant a weeding out among the Negroes of the incompetents and vicious, the beginning of a differentiation of social grades. Now a rising group of people are not lifted bodily from the ground like an inert solid mass, but rather stretch upward like a living plant with its roots still clinging in the mould. The appearance, therefore, of the Negro criminal was a phenomenon to be awaited; and while it causes anxiety, it should not occasion surprise.

Here again the hope for the future depended peculiarly on careful and delicate dealing with these criminals. Their offences at first were those of laziness, carelessness, and impulse, rather than of malignity or ungoverned viciousness. Such misdemeanors needed discriminating treatment, firm but reformatory, with no hint of injustice, and full proof of guilt. For such dealing with criminals, white or black, the South had no machinery, no adequate jails or reformatories; its police system was arranged to deal with blacks alone, and tacitly assumed that every white man was *ipso facto** a member of that police. Thus grew up a double system of justice, which erred on the white side by undue leniency and the practical immunity of red-handed criminals, and erred on the black side by undue severity, injustice, and lack of discrimination. For, as I have said, the police system of the South was originally designed to keep track of all Negroes, not simply of criminals; and when the Negroes were freed and the whole South was convinced of the impossibility of free Negro labor, the first and almost universal device was to use the courts as a means of reënslaving the blacks. It was not then a question of crime, but rather one of color, that settled a man's conviction on almost any charge. Thus Negroes came to look upon courts as instruments of injustice and oppression, and upon those convicted in them as martyrs and victims.

When, now, the real Negro criminal appeared, and instead of petty stealing and vagrancy we began to have highway robbery, burglary, murder, and rape, there was a curious effect on both sides the color-line: the Negroes refused to believe the evidence of white witnesses or the fairness of white juries, so that the greatest deterrent to crime, the public opinion of one's own social caste, was lost, and the criminal was looked upon as crucified rather than hanged. On the other hand, the whites, used to being careless as to the guilt or innocence of accused Negroes, were swept in moments of passion beyond law, reason, and decency. Such a situation is bound to increase crime, and has increased it. To natural viciousness and vagrancy are being daily added motives of revolt and revenge which stir up all the latent savagery of both races and make peaceful attention to economic development often impossible.

---

*By that very fact (Latin).

But the chief problem in any community cursed with crime is not the punishment of the criminals, but the preventing of the young from being trained to crime. And here again the peculiar conditions of the South have prevented proper precautions. I have seen twelve-year-old boys working in chains on the public streets of Atlanta, directly in front of the schools, in company with old and hardened criminals; and this indiscriminate mingling of men and women and children makes the chain-gangs perfect schools of crime and debauchery. The struggle for reformatories, which has gone on in Virginia, Georgia, and other States, is the one encouraging sign of the awakening of some communities to the suicidal results of this policy.

It is the public schools, however, which can be made, outside the homes, the greatest means of training decent self-respecting citizens. We have been so hotly engaged recently in discussing trade-schools and the higher education that the pitiable plight of the public-school system in the South has almost dropped from view. Of every five dollars spent for public education in the State of Georgia, the white schools get four dollars and the Negro one dollar; and even then the white public-school system, save in the cities, is bad and cries for reform. If this is true of the whites, what of the blacks? I am becoming more and more convinced, as I look upon the system of common-school training in the South, that the national government must soon step in and aid popular education in some way. To-day it has been only by the most strenuous efforts on the part of the thinking men of the South that the Negro's share of the school fund has not been cut down to a pittance in some half-dozen States; and that movement not only is not dead, but in many communities is gaining strength. What in the name of reason does this nation expect of a people, poorly trained and hard pressed in severe economic competition, without political rights, and with ludicrously inadequate common-school facilities? What can it expect but crime and listlessness, offset here and there by the dogged struggles of the fortunate and more determined who are themselves buoyed by the hope that in due time the country will come to its senses?

I have thus far sought to make clear the physical, economic, and political relations of the Negroes and whites in the South, as I have conceived them, including, for the reasons set forth, crime and education. But after all that has been said on these more tangible matters of human contact, there still remains a part essential to a proper description of the South which it is difficult to describe or fix in terms easily understood by strangers. It is, in fine, the atmosphere of the land, the thought and feeling, the thousand and one little actions which go to make up life. In any community or nation it is these little things which are most elusive to the grasp and yet most essential to any clear conception of the group life taken as a whole. What is thus true of all communities is peculiarly true of the South, where, outside of written history and outside of printed law, there has been going on for a generation as deep a storm and stress of human souls, as intense a ferment of feeling, as intricate a writhing of spirit, as ever a people experienced. Within and without the sombre veil of color vast social forces have been at work,—efforts for human betterment, movements toward disintegration and despair, tragedies and comedies in social and economic life, and a swaying and lifting and sinking of human hearts which have made this land a land of mingled sorrow and joy, of change and excitement and unrest.

The centre of this spiritual turmoil has ever been the millions of black freedmen and their sons, whose destiny is so fatefully bound up with that of the nation. And yet the casual observer visiting the South sees at first little of this. He notes the growing frequency of dark faces as he rides along,—but otherwise the days slip lazily on, the sun shines, and this little world seems as happy and contented as other worlds he has visited. Indeed, on the question of questions—the Negro problem—he hears so little that there almost seems to be a conspiracy of silence; the morning papers seldom mention it, and then usually in a far-fetched academic way, and indeed almost every one seems to forget and ignore the darker half of the land, until the astonished visitor is inclined to ask if after all there *is* any problem here. But if he lingers long enough there comes the awakening: perhaps in a sudden whirl of passion which leaves him gasping at its bitter intensity; more likely in a gradually dawning sense of things he had not at first noticed. Slowly but surely his eyes begin to catch the shadows of the color-line: here he meets crowds of Negroes and whites; then he is suddenly aware that he cannot discover a single dark face; or again at the close of a day's wandering he may find himself in some strange assembly, where all faces are tinged brown or black, and where he has the vague, uncomfortable feeling of the stranger. He realizes at last that silently, resistlessly, the world about flows by him in two great streams: they ripple on in the same sun-

shine, they approach and mingle their waters in seeming carelessness,—then they divide and flow wide apart. It is done quietly; no
mistakes are made, or if one occurs, the swift arm of the law and of
public opinion swings down for a moment, as when the other day a
black man and a white woman were arrested for talking together on
Whitehall Street in Atlanta.

Now if one notices carefully one will see that between these two
worlds, despite much physical contact and daily intermingling, there
is almost no community of intellectual life or point of transference
where the thoughts and feelings of one race can come into direct
contact and sympathy with the thoughts and feelings of the other.
Before and directly after the war, when all the best of the Negroes
were domestic servants in the best of the white families, there were
bonds of intimacy, affection, and sometimes blood relationship, between the races. They lived in the same home, shared in the family
life, often attended the same church, and talked and conversed with
each other. But the increasing civilization of the Negro since then
has naturally meant the development of higher classes: there are increasing numbers of ministers, teachers, physicians, merchants, mechanics, and independent farmers, who by nature and training are
the aristocracy and leaders of the blacks. Between them, however,
and the best element of the whites, there is little or no intellectual
commerce. They go to separate churches, they live in separate sections, they are strictly separated in all public gatherings, they travel
separately, and they are beginning to read different papers and
books. To most libraries, lectures, concerts, and museums, Negroes
are either not admitted at all, or on terms peculiarly galling to the
pride of the very classes who might otherwise be attracted. The daily
paper chronicles the doings of the black world from afar with no
great regard for accuracy; and so on, throughout the category of
means for intellectual communication,—schools, conferences, efforts for social betterment, and the like,—it is usually true that the
very representatives of the two races, who for mutual benefit and the
welfare of the land ought to be in complete understanding and sympathy, are so far strangers that one side thinks all whites are narrow
and prejudiced, and the other thinks educated Negroes dangerous
and insolent. Moreover, in a land where the tyranny of public opinion and the intolerance of criticism is for obvious historical reasons
so strong as in the South, such a situation is extremely difficult to cor-

rect. The white man, as well as the Negro, is bound and barred by the color-line, and many a scheme of friendliness and philanthropy, of broad-minded sympathy and generous fellowship between the two has dropped still-born because some busybody has forced the color-question to the front and brought the tremendous force of un-written law against the innovators.

It is hardly necessary for me to add very much in regard to the so-cial contact between the races. Nothing has come to replace that finer sympathy and love between some masters and house servants which the radical and more uncompromising drawing of the color-line in recent years has caused almost completely to disappear. In a world where it means so much to take a man by the hand and sit be-side him, to look frankly into his eyes and feel his heart beating with red blood; in a world where a social cigar or a cup of tea together means more than legislative halls and magazine articles and speeches,—one can imagine the consequences of the almost utter absence of such social amenities between estranged races, whose separation extends even to parks and street-cars.

Here there can be none of that social going down to the people,—the opening of heart and hand of the best to the worst, in generous acknowledgment of a common humanity and a common destiny. On the other hand, in matters of simple almsgiving, where there can be no question of social contact, and in the succor of the aged and sick, the South, as if stirred by a feeling of its unfortunate limitations, is generous to a fault. The black beggar is never turned away without a good deal more than a crust, and a call for help for the unfortunate meets quick response. I remember, one cold winter, in Atlanta, when I refrained from contributing to a public relief fund lest Negroes should be discriminated against, I afterward inquired of a friend: "Were any black people receiving aid?" "Why," said he, "they were *all* black."

And yet this does not touch the kernel of the problem. Human advancement is not a mere question of almsgiving, but rather of sympathy and cooperation among classes who would scorn charity. And here is a land where, in the higher walks of life, in all the higher striving for the good and noble and true, the color-line comes to sep-arate natural friends and co-workers; while at the bottom of the so-cial group, in the saloon, the gambling-hell, and the brothel, that same line wavers and disappears.

❖   ❖   ❖

I have sought to paint an average picture of real relations between the sons of master and man in the South. I have not glossed over matters for policy's sake, for I fear we have already gone too far in that sort of thing. On the other hand, I have sincerely sought to let no unfair exaggerations creep in. I do not doubt that in some Southern communities conditions are better than those I have indicated; while I am no less certain that in other communities they are far worse.

Nor does the paradox and danger of this situation fail to interest and perplex the best conscience of the South. Deeply religious and intensely democratic as are the mass of the whites, they feel acutely the false position in which the Negro problems place them. Such an essentially honest-hearted and generous people cannot cite the caste-levelling precepts of Christianity, or believe in equality of opportunity for all men, without coming to feel more and more with each generation that the present drawing of the color-line is a flat contradiction to their beliefs and professions. But just as often as they come to this point, the present social condition of the Negro stands as a menace and a portent before even the most open-minded: if there were nothing to charge against the Negro but his blackness or other physical peculiarities, they argue, the problem would be comparatively simple; but what can we say to his ignorance, shiftlessness, poverty, and crime? can a self-respecting group hold anything but the least possible fellowship with such persons and survive? and shall we let a mawkish sentiment sweep away the culture of our fathers or the hope of our children? The argument so put is of great strength, but it is not a whit stronger than the argument of thinking Negroes: granted, they reply, that the condition of our masses is bad; there is certainly on the one hand adequate historical cause for this, and unmistakable evidence that no small number have, in spite of tremendous disadvantages, risen to the level of American civilization. And when, by proscription and prejudice, these same Negroes are classed with and treated like the lowest of their people, simply *because* they are Negroes, such a policy not only discourages thrift and intelligence among black men, but puts a direct premium on the very things you complain of,—inefficiency and crime. Draw lines of crime, of incompetency, of vice, as tightly and uncompromisingly as you will, for these things must be proscribed;

but a color-line not only does not accomplish this purpose, but thwarts it.

In the face of two such arguments, the future of the South depends on the ability of the representatives of these opposing views to see and appreciate and sympathize with each other's position,—for the Negro to realize more deeply than he does at present the need of uplifting the masses of his people, for the white people to realize more vividly than they have yet done the deadening and disastrous effect of a color-prejudice that classes Phillis Wheatley and Sam Hose in the same despised class.

It is not enough for the Negroes to declare that color-prejudice is the sole cause of their social condition, nor for the white South to reply that their social condition is the main cause of prejudice. They both act as reciprocal cause and effect, and a change in neither alone will bring the desired effect. Both must change, or neither can improve to any great extent. The Negro cannot stand the present reactionary tendencies and unreasoning drawing of the color-line indefinitely without discouragement and retrogression. And the condition of the Negro is ever the excuse for further discrimination. Only by a union of intelligence and sympathy across the color-line in this critical period of the Republic shall justice and right triumph,—

"That mind and soul according well,
May make one music as before,
But vaster." *

In Memoriam (1850), by Alfred, Lord Tennyson.

X

Of the Faith of the Fathers[1]

Dim face of Beauty haunting all the world,
* Fair face of Beauty all too fair to see,*
Where the lost stars adown the heavens are hurled,—
* There, there alone for thee*
* May white peace be.*

Beauty, sad face of Beauty, Mystery, Wonder,
* What are these dreams to foolish babbling men*
Who cry with little noises 'neath the thunder
* Of Ages ground to sand,*
* To a little sand.*

        Fiona Macleod.*

IT WAS OUT IN THE COUNTRY, far from home, far from my foster home, on a dark Sunday night. The road wandered from our rambling log-house up the stony bed of a creek, past wheat and corn, until we could hear dimly across the fields a rhythmic cadence of song,—soft, thrilling, powerful, that swelled and died sorrowfully in our ears. I was a country school-teacher then, fresh from the East, and had never seen a Southern Negro revival. To be sure, we in Berkshire† were not perhaps as stiff and formal as they in Suffolk§ of olden time; yet we were very quiet and subdued, and I

---

*From "Dim Face of Beauty," by Fiona Macleod (pen name of William Sharp).
†From "Steal Away."
‡Berkshire County is where Great Barrington, Massachusetts, Du Bois's birthplace, is located.
§Suffolk County in England.

134

know not what would have happened those clear Sabbath mornings had some one punctuated the sermon with a wild scream, or interrupted the long prayer with a loud Amen! And so most striking to me, as I approached the village and the little plain church perched aloft, was the air of intense excitement that possessed that mass of black folk. A sort of suppressed terror hung in the air and seemed to seize us,—a pythian madness, a demoniac possession, that lent terrible reality to song and word. The black and massive form of the preacher swayed and quivered as the words crowded to his lips and flew at us in singular eloquence. The people moaned and fluttered, and then the gaunt-cheeked brown woman beside me suddenly leaped straight into the air and shrieked like a lost soul, while round about came wail and groan and outcry, and a scene of human passion such as I had never conceived before.

Those who have not thus witnessed the frenzy of a Negro revival in the untouched backwoods of the South can but dimly realize the religious feeling of the slave; as described, such scenes appear grotesque and funny, but as seen they are awful. Three things characterized this religion of the slave,—the Preacher, the Music, and the Frenzy. The Preacher is the most unique personality developed by the Negro on American soil. A leader, a politician, an orator, a "boss," an intriguer, an idealist,—all these he is, and ever, too, the centre of a group of men, now twenty, now a thousand in number. The combination of a certain adroitness with deep-seated earnestness, of tact with consummate ability, gave him his preëminence, and helps him maintain it. The type, of course, varies according to time and place, from the West Indies in the sixteenth century to New England in the nineteenth, and from the Mississippi bottoms to cities like New Orleans or New York.

The Music of Negro religion is that plaintive rhythmic melody, with its touching minor cadences, which, despite caricature and defilement,* still remains the most original and beautiful expression of human life and longing yet born on American soil. Sprung

---

*Du Bois refers to the caricature of black religious music in minstrel shows, in which white actors in blackface presented stereotypes of black speech and song.

from the African forests, where its counterpart can still be heard, it was adapted, changed, and intensified by the tragic soul-life of the slave, until, under the stress of law and whip, it became the one true expression of a people's sorrow, despair, and hope.

Finally the Frenzy or "Shouting," when the Spirit of the Lord passed by, and, seizing the devotee, made him mad with supernatural joy, was the last essential of Negro religion and the one more devoutly believed in than all the rest. It varied in expression from the silent rapt countenance or the low murmur and moan to the mad abandon of physical fervor,—the stamping, shrieking, and shouting, the rushing to and fro and wild waving of arms, the weeping and laughing, the vision and the trance. All this is nothing new in the world, but old as religion, as Delphi and Endor. And so firm a hold did it have on the Negro, that many generations firmly believed that without this visible manifestation of the God there could be no true communion with the Invisible.

These were the characteristics of Negro religious life as developed up to the time of Emancipation. Since under the peculiar circumstances of the black man's environment they were the one expression of his higher life, they are of deep interest to the student of his development, both socially and psychologically. Numerous are the attractive lines of inquiry that here group themselves. What did slavery mean to the African savage? What was his attitude toward the World and Life? What seemed to him good and evil,—God and Devil? Whither went his longings and strivings, and wherefore were his heart-burnings and disappointments? Answers to such questions can come only from a study of Negro religion as a development, through its gradual changes from the heathenism of the Gold Coast to the institutional Negro church of Chicago.

Moreover, the religious growth of millions of men, even though they be slaves, cannot be without potent influence upon their contemporaries. The Methodists and Baptists of America owe much of their condition to the silent but potent influence of their millions of Negro converts. Especially is this noticeable in the South, where theology and religious philosophy are on this account a long way behind the North, and where the religion of the poor whites is a plain copy of Negro thought and methods. The mass of "gospel" hymns which has swept through American churches and well-nigh ruined our sense of song consists largely of debased imitations of Negro melodies made by ears that caught the jingle but not the music, the body but not the soul, of the Jubilee songs. It is thus clear that the study of Negro religion is not only a vital part of the history of the Negro in America, but no uninteresting part of American history.

The Negro church of to-day is the social centre of Negro life in the United States, and the most characteristic expression of African character. Take a typical church in a small Virginian town: it is the "First Baptist"—a roomy brick edifice seating five hundred or more persons, tastefully finished in Georgia pine, with a carpet, a small organ, and stained-glass windows. Underneath is a large assembly room with benches. This building is the central club-house of a community of a thousand or more Negroes. Various organizations meet here,—the church proper, the Sunday-school, two or three insurance societies, women's societies, secret societies, and mass meetings of various kinds. Entertainments, suppers, and lectures are held beside the five or six regular weekly religious services. Considerable sums of money are collected and expended here, employment is found for the idle, strangers are introduced, news is disseminated and charity distributed. At the same time this social, intellectual, and economic centre is a religious centre of great power. Depravity, Sin, Redemption, Heaven, Hell, and Damnation are preached twice a Sunday with much fervor, and revivals take place every year after the crops are laid by; and few indeed of the community have the hardihood to withstand conversion. Back of this more formal religion, the Church often stands as a real conserver of morals, a strengthener of family life, and the final authority on what is Good and Right.

Thus one can see in the Negro church to-day, reproduced in microcosm, all that great world from which the Negro is cut off by color-prejudice and social condition. In the great city churches the same tendency is noticeable and in many respects emphasized. A great church like the Bethel of Philadelphia* has over eleven hundred members, an edifice seating fifteen hundred persons and val-

---

*Founded by Richard Allen in 1794, Mother Bethel A.M.E. (African Methodist Episcopal) was the first urban black church in the United States.

ued at one hundred thousand dollars, an annual budget of five thousand dollars, and a government consisting of a pastor with several assisting local preachers, an executive and legislative board, financial boards and tax collectors; general church meetings for making laws; subdivided groups led by class leaders, a company of militia, and twenty-four auxiliary societies. The activity of a church like this is immense and far-reaching, and the bishops who preside over these organizations throughout the land are among the most powerful Negro rulers in the world.

Such churches are really governments of men, and consequently a little investigation reveals the curious fact that, in the South, at least, practically every American Negro is a church member. Some, to be sure, are not regularly enrolled, and a few do not habitually attend services; but, practically, a proscribed people must have a social centre, and that centre for this people is the Negro church. The census of 1890 showed nearly twenty-four thousand Negro churches in the country, with a total enrolled membership of over two and a half millions, or ten actual church members to every twenty-eight persons, and in some Southern States one in every two persons. Besides these there is the large number who, while not enrolled as members, attend and take part in many of the activities of the church. There is an organized Negro church for every sixty black families in the nation, and in some States for every forty families, owning, on an average, a thousand dollars' worth of property each, or nearly twenty-six million dollars in all.

Such, then, is the large development of the Negro church since Emancipation. The question now is, What have been the successive steps of this social history and what are the present tendencies? First, we must realize that no such institution as the Negro church could rear itself without definite historical foundations. These foundations we can find if we remember that the social history of the Negro did not start in America. He was brought from a definite social environment,—the polygamous clan life under the headship of the chief and the potent influence of the priest. His religion was nature-worship, with profound belief in invisible surrounding influences, good and bad, and his worship was through incantation and sacrifice. The first rude change in this life was the slave ship and the West Indian sugar-fields. The planta-

tion organization replaced the clan and tribe, and the white master replaced the chief with far greater and more despotic powers.
Forced and long-continued toil became the rule of life, the old
ties of blood relationship and kinship disappeared, and instead of
the family appeared a new polygamy and polyandry, which, in
some cases, almost reached promiscuity. It was a terrific social
revolution, and yet some traces were retained of the former group
life, and the chief remaining institution was the Priest or Medi-
cine-man. He early appeared on the plantation and found his
function as the healer of the sick, the interpreter of the Unknown,
the comforter of the sorrowing, the supernatural avenger of
wrong, and the one who rudely but picturesquely expressed the
longing, disappointment, and resentment of a stolen and oppressed people. Thus, as bard, physician, judge, and priest, within
the narrow limits allowed by the slave system, rose the Negro
preacher, and under him the first Afro-American institution, the
Negro church. This church was not at first by any means Christian nor definitely organized; rather it was an adaptation and mingling of heathen rites among the members of each plantation, and
roughly designated as Voodooism. Association with the masters,
missionary effort and motives of expediency gave these rites an
early veneer of Christianity, and after the lapse of many generations the Negro church became Christian.

Two characteristic things must be noticed in regard to this
church. First, it became almost entirely Baptist and Methodist in
faith; secondly, as a social institution it antedated by many decades
the monogamic Negro home. From the very circumstances of its
beginning, the church was confined to the plantation, and consisted primarily of a series of disconnected units; although, later
on, some freedom of movement was allowed, still this geographical limitation was always important and was one cause of the
spread of the decentralized and democratic Baptist faith among
the slaves. At the same time, the visible rite of baptism appealed
strongly to their mystic temperament. To-day the Baptist Church
is still largest in membership among Negroes, and has a million
and a half communicants. Next in popularity came the churches
organized in connection with the white neighboring churches,
chiefly Baptist and Methodist, with a few Episcopalian and others.
The Methodists still form the second greatest denomination, with

nearly a million members. The faith of these two leading denominations was more suited to the slave church from the prominence
they gave to religious feeling and fervor. The Negro membership
in other denominations has always been small and relatively unimportant, although the Episcopalians and Presbyterians are gaining
among the more intelligent classes to-day, and the Catholic
Church is making headway in certain sections. After Emancipation, and still earlier in the North, the Negro churches largely severed such affiliations as they had had with the white churches,
either by choice or by compulsion. The Baptist churches became
independent, but the Methodists were compelled early to unite
for purposes of episcopal government. This gave rise to the great
African Methodist Church, the greatest Negro organization in the
world, to the Zion Church and the Colored Methodist, and to the
black conferences and churches in this and other denominations.

The second fact noted, namely, that the Negro church antedates the Negro home, leads to an explanation of much that is
paradoxical in this communistic institution and in the morals of its
members. But especially it leads us to regard this institution as peculiarly the expression of the inner ethical life of a people in a
sense seldom true elsewhere. Let us turn, then, from the outer
physical development of the church to the more important inner
ethical life of the people who compose it. The Negro has already
been pointed out many times as a religious animal,—a being of
that deep emotional nature which turns instinctively toward the
supernatural. Endowed with a rich tropical imagination and a
keen, delicate appreciation of Nature, the transplanted African
lived in a world animate with gods and devils, elves and witches;
full of strange influences,—of Good to be implored, of Evil to be
propitiated. Slavery, then, was to him the dark triumph of Evil
over him. All the hateful powers of the Under-world were striving
against him, and a spirit of revolt and revenge filled his heart. He
called up all the resources of heathenism to aid,—exorcism and
witchcraft, the mysterious Obi* worship with its barbarous rites,
spells, and blood-sacrifice even, now and then, of human victims.
Weird midnight orgies and mystic conjurations were invoked, the

---

*Africa-based religion; also known as "obeah" in Jamaica.

witch-woman and the voodoo-priest became the centre of Negro group life, and that vein of vague superstition which characterizes the unlettered Negro even to-day was deepened and strengthened.

In spite, however, of such success as that of the fierce Maroons, the Danish blacks, and others, the spirit of revolt gradually died away under the untiring energy and superior strength of the slave masters. By the middle of the eighteenth century the black slave had sunk, with hushed murmurs, to his place at the bottom of a new economic system, and was unconsciously ripe for a new philosophy of life. Nothing suited his condition then better than the doctrines of passive submission embodied in the newly learned Christianity. Slave masters early realized this, and cheerfully aided religious propaganda within certain bounds. The long system of repression and degradation of the Negro tended to emphasize the elements in his character which made him a valuable chattel: courtesy became humility, moral strength degenerated into submission, and the exquisite native appreciation of the beautiful became an infinite capacity for dumb suffering. The Negro, losing the joy of this world, eagerly seized upon the offered conceptions of the next; the avenging Spirit of the Lord enjoining patience in this world, under sorrow and tribulation until the Great Day when He should lead His dark children home,—this became his comforting dream. His preacher repeated the prophecy, and his bards sang,—

> *"Children, we all shall be free*
> *When the Lord shall appear!"* *

This deep religious fatalism, painted so beautifully in "Uncle Tom,"† came soon to breed, as all fatalistic faiths will, the sensualist side by side with the martyr. Under the lax moral life of the plantation, where marriage was a farce, laziness a virtue, and property a theft, a religion of resignation and submission degenerated easily, in less strenuous minds, into a philosophy of indulgence and crime. Many of the worst characteristics of the Negro

---

*From "Children, We All Shall Be Free."
† Religious protagonist of *Uncle Tom's Cabin* (1852), by Harriet Beecher Stowe.

masses of to-day had their seed in this period of the slave's ethical growth. Here it was that the Home was ruined under the very shadow of the Church, white and black; here habits of shiftlessness took root, and sullen hopelessness replaced hopeful strife.

With the beginning of the abolition movement and the gradual growth of a class of free Negroes came a change. We often neglect the influence of the freedman before the war, because of the paucity of his numbers and the small weight he had in the history of the nation. But we must not forget that his chief influence was internal,—was exerted on the black world; and that there he was the ethical and social leader. Huddled as he was in a few centres like Philadelphia, New York, and New Orleans, the masses of the freedmen sank into poverty and listlessness; but not all of them. The free Negro leader early arose and his chief characteristic was intense earnestness and deep feeling on the slavery question. Freedom became to him a real thing and not a dream. His religion became darker and more intense, and into his ethics crept a note of revenge, into his songs a day of reckoning close at hand. The "Coming of the Lord" swept this side of Death, and came to be a thing to be hoped for in this day. Through fugitive slaves and irrepressible discussion this desire for freedom seized the black millions still in bondage, and became their one ideal of life. The black bards caught new notes, and sometimes even dared to sing,—

> *"O Freedom, O Freedom, O Freedom over me!*
> *Before I'll be a slave*
> *I'll be buried in my grave,*
> *And go home to my Lord*
> *And be free."* °

For fifty years Negro religion thus transformed itself and identified itself with the dream of Abolition, until that which was a radical fad in the white North and an anarchistic plot in the white South had become a religion to the black world. Thus, when Emancipation finally came, it seemed to the freedman a literal

---

°From "O Freedom"; this spiritual became a staple of the civil rights movement of the 1950s and 1960s.

Coming of the Lord. His fervid imagination was stirred as never before, by the tramp of armies, the blood and dust of battle, and the wail and whirl of social upheaval. He stood dumb and motionless before the whirlwind: what had he to do with it? Was it not the Lord's doing, and marvellous in his eyes? Joyed and bewildered with what came, he stood awaiting new wonders till the inevitable Age of Reaction swept over the nation and brought the crisis of to-day.

It is difficult to explain clearly the present critical stage of Negro religion. First, we must remember that living as the blacks do in close contact with a great modern nation, and sharing, although imperfectly, the soul-life of that nation, they must necessarily be affected more or less directly by all the religious and ethical forces that are to-day moving the United States. These questions and movements are, however, over-shadowed and dwarfed by the (to them) all-important question of their civil, political, and economic status. They must perpetually discuss the "Negro Problem,"—must live, move, and have their being in it, and interpret all else in its light or darkness. With this come, too, peculiar problems of their inner life,—of the status of women, the maintenance of Home, the training of children, the accumulation of wealth, and the prevention of crime. All this must mean a time of intense ethical ferment, of religious heart-searching and intellectual unrest. From the double life every American Negro must live, as a Negro and as an American, as swept on by the current of the nineteenth while yet struggling in the eddies of the fifteenth century,—from this must arise a painful self-consciousness, an almost morbid sense of personality and a moral hesitancy which is fatal to self-confidence. The worlds within and without the Veil of Color are changing, and changing rapidly, but not at the same rate, not in the same way; and this must produce a peculiar wrenching of the soul, a peculiar sense of doubt and bewilderment. Such a double life, with double thoughts, double duties, and double social classes, must give rise to double words and double ideals, and tempt the mind to pretence or to revolt, to hypocrisy or to radicalism.

In some such doubtful words and phrases can one perhaps most clearly picture the peculiar ethical paradox that faces the Negro of to-day and is tingeing and changing his religious life.

Feeling that his rights and his dearest ideals are being trampled upon, that the public conscience is ever more deaf to his righteous appeal, and that all the reactionary forces of prejudice, greed, and revenge are daily gaining new strength and fresh allies, the Negro faces no enviable dilemma. Conscious of his impotence, and pessimistic, he often becomes bitter and vindictive; and his religion, instead of a worship, is a complaint and a curse, a wail rather than a hope, a sneer rather than a faith. On the other hand, another type of mind, shrewder and keener and more tortuous too, sees in the very strength of the anti-Negro movement its patent weaknesses, and with Jesuitic casuistry is deterred by no ethical considerations in the endeavor to turn this weakness to the black man's strength. Thus we have two great and hardly reconcilable streams of thought and ethical strivings; the danger of the one lies in anarchy, that of the other in hypocrisy. The one type of Negro stands almost ready to curse God and die, and the other is too often found a traitor to right and a coward before force; the one is wedded to ideals remote, whimsical, perhaps impossible of realization; the other forgets that life is more than meat and the body more than raiment. But, after all, is not this simply the writhing of the age translated into black,—the triumph of the Lie which to-day, with its false culture, faces the hideousness of the anarchist assassin?

To-day the two groups of Negroes, the one in the North, the other in the South, represent these divergent ethical tendencies, the first tending toward radicalism, the other toward hypocritical compromise. It is no idle regret with which the white South mourns the loss of the old-time Negro,—the frank, honest, simple old servant who stood for the earlier religious age of submission and humility. With all his laziness and lack of many elements of true manhood, he was at least open-hearted, faithful, and sincere. To-day he is gone, but who is to blame for his going? Is it not those very persons who mourn for him? Is it not the tendency, born of Reconstruction and Reaction, to found a society on lawlessness and deception, to tamper with the moral fibre of a naturally honest and straightforward people until the whites threaten to become ungovernable tyrants and the blacks criminals and hypocrites? Deception is the natural defence of the weak against the strong, and the South used it for many years against its conquerors; to-day it must be prepared to see its black proletariat turn that same two-edged weapon against itself. And how natural this is! The death of Denmark Vesey and Nat Turner proved long since to the Negro the present hopelessness of physical defence. Political defence is becoming less and less available, and economic defence is still only partially effective. But there is a patent defence at hand,—the defence of deception and flattery, of cajoling and lying. It is the same defence which the Jews of the Middle Age used and which left its stamp on their character for centuries. To-day the young Negro of the South who would succeed cannot be frank and outspoken, honest and self-assertive, but rather he is daily tempted to be silent and wary, politic and sly; he must flatter and be pleasant, endure petty insults with a smile, shut his eyes to wrong; in too many cases he sees positive personal advantage in deception and lying. His real thoughts, his real aspirations, must be guarded in whispers; he must not criticise, he must not complain. Patience, humility, and adroitness must, in these growing black youth, replace impulse, manliness, and courage. With this sacrifice there is an economic opening, and perhaps peace and some prosperity. Without this there is riot, migration, or crime. Nor is this situation peculiar to the Southern United States,—is it not rather the only method by which undeveloped races have gained the right to share modern culture? The price of culture is a Lie.

On the other hand, in the North the tendency is to emphasize the radicalism of the Negro. Driven from his birthright in the South by a situation at which every fibre of his more outspoken and assertive nature revolts, he finds himself in a land where he can scarcely earn a decent living amid the harsh competition and the color discrimination. At the same time, through schools and periodicals, discussions and lectures, he is intellectually quickened and awakened. The soul, long pent up and dwarfed, suddenly expands in new-found freedom. What wonder that every tendency is to excess,—radical complaint, radical remedies, bitter denunciation or angry silence. Some sink, some rise. The criminal and the sensualist leave the church for the gambling-hell and the brothel, and fill the slums of Chicago and Baltimore; the better classes segregate themselves from the group-life of both white and black, and form an aristocracy, cultured but pessimistic, whose bitter criticism stings while it points out no way of escape. They despise the submission and subserviency of the Southern Negroes, but offer no other means by which a poor and oppressed minority can exist side by side with its masters. Feeling deeply and keenly the tendencies and opportunities of the age in which they live, their souls are bitter at the fate which drops the Veil between; and the very fact that this bitterness is natural and justifiable only serves to intensify it and make it more maddening.

Between the two extreme types of ethical attitude which I have thus sought to make clear wavers the mass of the millions of Negroes, North and South; and their religious life and activity partake of this social conflict within their ranks. Their churches are differentiating,—now into groups of cold, fashionable devotees, in no way distinguishable from similar white groups save in color of skin; now into large social and business institutions catering to the desire for information and amusement of their members, warily avoiding unpleasant questions both within and without the black world, and preaching in effect if not in word: *Dum vivimus, vivamus.*°

But back of this still broods silently the deep religious feeling of the real Negro heart, the stirring, unguided might of powerful human souls who have lost the guiding star of the past and are seeking in the great night a new religious ideal. Some day the Awakening will come, when the pent-up vigor of ten million souls shall sweep irresistibly toward the Goal, out of the Valley of the Shadow of Death, where all that makes life worth living—Liberty, Justice, and Right—is marked "For White People Only."

°While we live, let us live (Latin).

XI

Of the Passing of the First-Born

O sister, sister, thy first-begotten,
The hands that cling and the feet that follow,
The voice of the child's blood crying yet,
Who hath remembered me? who hath forgotten?
Thou hast forgotten, O summer swallow,
But the world shall end when I forget.

Swinburne.°

UNTO YOU A CHILD IS BORN,"[†] sang the bit of yellow paper that fluttered into my room one brown October morning. Then the fear of fatherhood mingled wildly with the joy of creation; I wondered how it looked and how it felt,—what were its eyes, and how its hair curled and crumpled itself. And I thought in awe of her,—she who had slept with Death to tear a man-child from underneath her heart, while I was unconsciously wandering. I fled to my wife and child, repeating the while to myself half wonderingly, "Wife and child? Wife and child?"—fled fast and faster than boat and steam-car, and yet must ever impatiently await them; away from the hard-voiced city, away from the flickering sea into my own Berkshire Hills that sit all sadly guarding the gates of Massachusetts.

°From "Itylus" (1866), by Algernon Charles Swinburne.
[†]From "I Hope My Mother Will Be There."
[‡]See the Bible, Isaiah 9:6: "For unto us a child is born, unto us a son is given: and the government shall be upon his shoulder" (KJV).

Up the stairs I ran to the wan mother and whimpering babe, to the sanctuary on whose altar a life at my bidding had offered itself to win a life, and won. What is this tiny formless thing, this new-born wail from an unknown world,—all head and voice? I handle it curiously, and watch perplexed its winking, breathing, and sneezing. I did not love it then; it seemed a ludicrous thing to love; but her I loved, my girl-mother, she whom now I saw unfolding like the glory of the morning—the transfigured woman.

Through her I came to love the wee thing, as it grew and waxed strong; as its little soul unfolded itself in twitter and cry and half-formed word, and as its eyes caught the gleam and flash of life. How beautiful he was, with his olive-tinted flesh and dark gold ringlets, his eyes of mingled blue and brown, his perfect little limbs, and the soft voluptuous roll which the blood of Africa had moulded into his features! I held him in my arms, after we had sped far away to our Southern home,—held him, and glanced at the hot red soil of Georgia and the breathless city of a hundred hills, and felt a vague unrest. Why was his hair tinted with gold? An evil omen was golden hair in my life. Why had not the brown of his eyes crushed out and killed the blue?—for brown were his father's eyes, and his father's father's. And thus in the Land of the Color-line I saw, as it fell across my baby, the shadow of the Veil.

Within the Veil was he born, said I; and there within shall he live,—a Negro and a Negro's son. Holding in that little head—ah, bitterly!—the unbowed pride of a hunted race, clinging with that tiny dimpled hand—ah, wearily!—to a hope not hopeless but un-hopeful, and seeing with those bright wondering eyes that peer into my soul a land whose freedom is to us a mockery and whose liberty a lie. I saw the shadow of the Veil as it passed over my baby, I saw the cold city towering above the blood-red land. I held my face beside his little cheek, showed him the star-children and the twinkling lights as they began to flash, and stilled with an even-song the unvoiced terror of my life.

So sturdy and masterful he grew, so filled with bubbling life so tremulous with the unspoken wisdom of a life but eighteen months distant from the All-life,—we were not far from worship-ping this revelation of the divine, my wife and I. Her own life builded and moulded itself upon the child; he tinged her every dream and idealized her every effort. No hands but hers must touch and garnish those little limbs; no dress or frill must touch them that had not wearied her fingers; no voice but hers could coax him off to Dreamland, and she and he together spoke some soft and unknown tongue and in it held communion. I too mused above his little white bed; saw the strength of my own arm stretched onward through the ages through the newer strength of his; saw the dream of my black fathers stagger a step onward in the wild phantasm of the world; heard in his baby voice the voice of the Prophet that was to rise within the Veil.

And so we dreamed and loved and planned by fall and winter, and the full flush of the long Southern spring, till the hot winds rolled from the fetid Gulf, till the roses shivered and the still stern sun quivered its awful light over the hills of Atlanta. And then one night the little feet pattered wearily to the wee white bed, and the tiny hands trembled; and a warm flushed face tossed on the pillow, and we knew baby was sick. Ten days he lay there,—a swift week and three endless days, wasting, wasting away. Cheerily the mother nursed him the first days, and laughed into the little eyes that smiled again. Tenderly then she hovered round him, till the smile fled away and Fear crouched beside the little bed.

Then the day ended not, and night was a dreamless terror, and joy and sleep slipped away. I hear now that Voice at midnight calling me from dull and dreamless trance,—crying, "The Shadow of Death! The Shadow of Death!" Out into the starlight I crept, to rouse the gray physician,—the Shadow of Death, the Shadow of Death. The hours trembled on; the night listened; the ghastly dawn glided like a tired thing across the lamplight. Then we two alone looked upon the child as he turned toward us with great eyes, and stretched his string-like hands,—the Shadow of Death![1] And we spoke no word, and turned away.

He died at eventide, when the sun lay like a brooding sorrow above the western hills, veiling its face; when the winds spoke not, and the trees, the great green trees he loved, stood motionless. I saw his breath beat quicker and quicker, pause, and then his little soul leapt like a star that travels in the night and left a world of darkness in its train. The day changed not; the same tall trees peeped in at the windows, the same green grass glinted in the setting sun. Only in the chamber of death writhed the world's most piteous thing—a childless mother.

I shirk not. I long for work. I pant for a life full of striving. I am no coward, to shrink before the rugged rush of the storm, nor even quail before the awful shadow of the Veil. But hearken, O Death! Is not this my life hard enough,—is not that dull land that stretches its sneering web about me cold enough,—is not all the world beyond these four little walls pitiless enough, but that thou must needs enter here,—thou, O Death? About my head the thundering storm beat like a heartless voice, and the crazy forest pulsed with the curses of the weak; but what cared I, within my home beside my wife and baby boy? Wast thou so jealous of one little coign of happiness that thou must needs enter there,—thou, O Death?

A perfect life was his, all joy and love, with tears to make it brighter,—sweet as a summer's day beside the Housatonic. The world loved him; the women kissed his curls, the men looked gravely into his wonderful eyes, and the children hovered and fluttered about him. I can see him now, changing like the sky from sparkling laughter to darkening frowns, and then to wondering thoughtfulness as he watched the world. He knew no color-line, poor dear,—and the Veil, though it shadowed him, had not yet darkened half his sun. He loved the white matron, he loved his black nurse; and in his little world walked souls alone, uncolored and unclothed. I—yea, all men—are larger and purer by the infinite breadth of that one little life. She who in simple clearness of vision sees beyond the stars said when he had flown, "He will be happy There; he ever loved beautiful things." And I, far more ignorant, and blind by the web of mine own weaving, sit alone winding words and muttering, "If still he be, and he be There, and there be a There, let him be happy, O Fate!"

Blithe was the morning of his burial, with bird and song and sweet-smelling flowers. The trees whispered to the grass, but the children sat with hushed faces. And yet it seemed a ghostly unreal day,—the wraith of Life. We seemed to rumble down an unknown street behind a little white bundle of posies, with the shadow of a song in our ears. The busy city dinned about us; they did not say much, those pale-faced hurrying men and women; they did not say much,—they only glanced and said, "Niggers!"

We could not lay him in the ground there in Georgia, for the earth there is strangely red; so we bore him away to the northward, with his flowers and his little folded hands. In vain, in vain!—for where, O God! beneath thy broad blue sky shall my dark baby rest in peace,—where Reverence dwells, and Goodness, and a Freedom that is free?

All that day and all that night there sat an awful gladness in my heart,—nay, blame me not if I see the world thus darkly through the Veil,—and my soul whispers ever to me, saying, "Not dead, not dead, but escaped; not bond, but free." No bitter meanness now shall sicken his baby heart till it die a living death, no taunt shall madden his happy boyhood. Fool that I was to think or wish that this little soul should grow choked and deformed within the Veil! I might have known that yonder deep unworldly look that ever and anon floated past his eyes was peering far beyond this narrow Now. In the poise of his little curl-crowned head did there not sit all that wild pride of being which his father had hardly crushed in his own heart? For what, forsooth, shall a Negro want with pride amid the studied humiliations of fifty million fellows? Well sped, my boy, before the world had dubbed your ambition insolence, had held your ideals unattainable, and taught you to cringe and bow. Better far this nameless void that stops my life than a sea of sorrow for you.

Idle words; he might have borne his burden more bravely than we,—aye, and found it lighter too, some day; for surely, surely this is not the end. Surely there shall yet dawn some mighty morning to lift the Veil and set the prisoned free. Not for me,—I shall die in my bonds,—but for fresh young souls who have not known the night and waken to the morning; a morning when men ask of the workman, not "Is he white?" but "Can he work?" When men ask artists, not "Are they black?" but "Do they know?" Some morning this may be, long, long years to come. But now there wails, on that dark shore within the Veil, the same deep voice, *Thou shalt forego!* And all have I foregone at that command, and with small complaint,—all save that fair young form that lies so coldly wed with death in the nest I had builded.

If one must have gone, why not I? Why may I not rest me from this restlessness and sleep from this wide waking? Was not the world's alembic, Time, in his young hands, and is not my time waning? Are there so many workers in the vineyard that the fair promise of this little body could lightly be tossed away? The wretched of my race that line the alleys of the nation sit fatherless and unmothered; but Love sat beside his cradle, and in his ear Wisdom waited to speak. Perhaps now he knows the All-love, and needs not to be wise. Sleep, then, child,—sleep till I sleep and waken to a baby voice and the ceaseless patter of little feet— above the Veil.

XII

Of Alexander Crummell

*Then from the Dawn it seemed there came, but faint
As from beyond the limit of the world,
Like the last echo born of a great cry,
Sounds, as if some fair city were one voice
Around a king returning from his wars.*

Tennyson.*

THIS IS THE HISTORY of a human heart,—the tale of a black boy who many long years ago began to struggle with life that he might know the world and know himself. Three temptations he met on those dark dunes that lay gray and dismal before the wonder-eyes of the child: the temptation of Hate, that stood out against the red dawn; the temptation of Despair, that darkened noonday; and the temptation of Doubt, that ever steals along with twilight. Above all, you must hear of the vales he crossed,—the Valley of Humiliation and the Valley of the Shadow of Death.

I saw Alexander Crummell first at a Wilberforce commencement season, amid its bustle and crush. Tall, frail, and black he stood, with simple dignity and an unmistakable air of good breeding. I talked with him apart, where the storming of the lusty young orators could not harm us. I spoke to him politely, then curiously,

---

*From "The Passing of Arthur," in *Idylls of the King* (1869), by Alfred, Lord Tennyson.
†From "Swing Low, Sweet Chariot."

then eagerly, as I began to feel the fineness of his character,—his calm courtesy, the sweetness of his strength, and his fair blending of the hope and truth of life. Instinctively I bowed before this man, as one bows before the prophets of the world. Some seer he seemed, that came not from the crimson Past or the gray To-come, but from the pulsing Now,—that mocking world which seemed to me at once so light and dark, so splendid and sordid. Fourscore years had he wandered in this same world of mine, within the Veil.

He was born with the Missouri Compromise* and lay a-dying amid the echoes of Manila and El Caney:† stirring times for living, times dark to look back upon, darker to look forward to. The black-faced lad that paused over his mud and marbles seventy years ago saw puzzling vistas as he looked down the world. The slave-ship still groaned across the Atlantic, faint cries burdened the Southern breeze, and the great black father whispered mad tales of cruelty into those young ears. From the low doorway the mother silently watched her boy at play, and at nightfall sought him eagerly lest the shadows bear him away to the land of slaves.

So his young mind worked and winced and shaped curiously a vision of Life; and in the midst of that vision ever stood one dark figure alone,—ever with the hard, thick countenance of that bitter father, and a form that fell in vast and shapeless folds. Thus the temptation of Hate grew and shadowed the growing child,—gliding stealthily into his laughter, fading into his play, and seizing his dreams by day and night with rough, rude turbulence. So the black boy asked of sky and sun and flower the never-answered Why? and loved, as he grew, neither the world nor the world's rough ways.

Strange temptation for a child, you may think; and yet in this wide land to-day a thousand thousand dark children brood before this same temptation, and feel its cold and shuddering arms. For them, perhaps, some one will some day lift the Veil,—will come tenderly and cheerily into those sad little lives and brush the brooding hate away, just as Beriah Green strode in upon the life of Alexander Crummell. And before the bluff, kind-hearted man

---

*Congressional act of 1820 that admitted Missouri to the Union as a slave state and Maine as a free state.
†Sites of U.S. victories in the Philippines and Cuba during the Spanish-American War (1898).

the shadow seemed less dark. Beriah Green had a school in Oneida County, New York, with a score of mischievous boys. "I'm going to bring a black boy here to educate," said Beriah Green, as only a crank and an abolitionist would have dared to say. "Oho!" laughed the boys. "Ye-es," said his wife; and Alexander came. Once before, the black boy had sought a school, had travelled, cold and hungry, four hundred miles up into free New Hampshire, to Canaan. But the godly farmers hitched ninety yoke of oxen to the abolition schoolhouse and dragged it into the middle of the swamp.[1] The black boy trudged away.

The nineteenth was the first century of human sympathy,—the age when half wonderingly we began to descry in others that transfigured spark of divinity which we call Myself; when clodhoppers and peasants, and tramps and thieves, and millionaires and—sometimes—Negroes, became throbbing souls whose warm pulsing life touched us so nearly that we half gasped with surprise, crying, "Thou too! Hast Thou seen Sorrow and the dull waters of Hopelessness? Hast Thou known Life?" And then all helplessly we peered into those Other-worlds, and wailed, "O World of Worlds, how shall man make you one?"

So in that little Oneida school there came to those schoolboys a revelation of thought and longing beneath one black skin, of which they had not dreamed before. And to the lonely boy came a new dawn of sympathy and inspiration. The shadowy, formless thing—the temptation of Hate, that hovered between him and the world—grew fainter and less sinister. It did not wholly fade away, but diffused itself and lingered thick at the edges. Through it the child now first saw the blue and gold of life,—the sun-swept road that ran 'twixt heaven and earth until in one far-off wan wavering line they met and kissed. A vision of life came to the growing boy,—mystic, wonderful. He raised his head, stretched himself, breathed deep of the fresh new air. Yonder, behind the forests, he heard strange sounds; then glinting through the trees he saw, far, far away, the bronzed hosts of a nation calling,—calling faintly, calling loudly. He heard the hateful clank of their chains, he felt them cringe and grovel, and there rose within him a protest and a prophecy. And he girded himself to walk down the world.

A voice and vision called him to be a priest,—a seer to lead the uncalled out of the house of bondage. He saw the headless host turn toward him like the whirling of mad waters,—he stretched forth his hands eagerly, and then, even as he stretched them, suddenly there swept across the vision the temptation of Despair.

They were not wicked men,—the problem of life is not the problem of the wicked,—they were calm, good men, Bishops of the Apostolic Church of God, and strove toward righteousness. They said slowly, "It is all very natural—it is even commendable; but the General Theological Seminary of the Episcopal Church cannot admit a Negro."[2] And when that thin, half-grotesque figure still haunted their doors, they put their hands kindly, half sorrowfully, on his shoulders, and said, "Now,—of course, we—we know how *you* feel about it; but you see it is impossible,—that is—well—it is premature. Sometime, we trust—sincerely trust—all such distinctions will fade away; but now the world is as it is."

This was the temptation of Despair; and the young man fought it doggedly. Like some grave shadow he flitted by those halls, pleading, arguing, half angrily demanding admittance, until there came the final *No*; until men hustled the disturber away, marked him as foolish, unreasonable, and injudicious, a vain rebel against God's law. And then from that Vision Splendid all the glory faded slowly away, and left an earth gray and stern rolling on beneath a dark despair. Even the kind hands that stretched themselves toward him from out the depths of that dull morning seemed but parts of the purple shadows. He saw them coldly, and asked, "Why should I strive by special grace when the way of the world is closed to me?" All gently yet, the hands urged him on,—the hands of young John Jay, that daring father's daring son; the hands of the good folk of Boston, that free city. And yet, with a way to the priesthood of the Church open at last before him, the cloud lingered there; and even when in old St. Paul's the venerable Bishop raised his white arms above the Negro deacon*—even then the burden had not lifted from that heart, for there had passed a glory from the earth.

And yet the fire through which Alexander Crummell went did not burn in vain. Slowly and more soberly he took up again his plan of life. More critically he studied the situation. Deep down

---

*Crummell was ordained in St. Paul's Church in Philadelphia in 1844.

below the slavery and servitude of the Negro people he saw their fatal weaknesses, which long years of mistreatment had emphasized. The dearth of strong moral character, of unbending righteousness, he felt, was their great shortcoming, and here he would begin. He would gather the best of his people into some little Episcopal chapel and there lead, teach, and inspire them, till the leaven spread, till the children grew, till the world hearkened, till—till—and then across his dream gleamed some faint afterglow of that first fair vision of youth—only an after-glow, for there had passed a glory from the earth.

One day—it was in 1842, and the springtide was struggling merrily with the May winds of New England—he stood at last in his own chapel in Providence, a priest of the Church.* The days sped by, and the dark young clergyman labored; he wrote his sermons carefully; he intoned his prayers with a soft, earnest voice; he haunted the streets and accosted the wayfarers; he visited the sick, and knelt beside the dying. He worked and toiled, week by week, day by day, month by month. And yet month by month the congregation dwindled, week by week the hollow walls echoed more sharply, day by day the calls came fewer and fewer, and day by day the third temptation sat clearer and still more clearly within the Veil; a temptation, as it were, bland and smiling, with just a shade of mockery in its smooth tones. First it came casually, in the cadence of a voice: "Oh, colored folks? Yes." Or perhaps more definitely: "What do you *expect?*" In voice and gesture lay the doubt—the temptation of Doubt. How he hated it, and stormed at it furiously! "Of course they are capable," he cried; "of course they can learn and strive and achieve—" and "Of course," added the temptation softly, "they do nothing of the sort." Of all the three temptations, this one struck the deepest. Hate? He had outgrown so childish a thing. Despair? He had steeled his right arm against it, and fought it with the vigor of determination. But to doubt the worth of his life-work,—to doubt the destiny and capability of the race his soul loved because it was his; to find listless squalor instead of eager endeavor; to hear his own lips whispering, "They do not care; they cannot know; they are dumb driven cattle,—why cast

---

*Christ Church, in Providence, Rhode Island.

your pearls before swine?"*—this, this seemed more than man could bear; and he closed the door, and sank upon the steps of the chancel, and cast his robe upon the floor and writhed.

The evening sunbeams had set the dust to dancing in the gloomy chapel when he arose. He folded his vestments, put away the hymn-books, and closed the great Bible. He stepped out into the twilight, looked back upon the narrow little pulpit with a weary smile, and locked the door. Then he walked briskly to the Bishop, and told the Bishop what the Bishop already knew. "I have failed," he said simply. And gaining courage by the confession, he added: "What I need is a larger constituency. There are comparatively few Negroes here, and perhaps they are not of the best. I must go where the field is wider, and try again." So the Bishop sent him to Philadelphia, with a letter to Bishop Onderdonk.

Bishop Onderdonk lived at the head of six white steps,—corpulent, red-faced, and the author of several thrilling tracts on Apostolic Succession. It was after dinner, and the Bishop had settled himself for a pleasant season of contemplation, when the bell must needs ring, and there must burst in upon the Bishop a letter and a thin, ungainly Negro. Bishop Onderdonk read the letter hastily and frowned. Fortunately, his mind was already clear on this point; and he cleared his brow and looked at Crummell. Then he said, slowly and impressively: "I will receive you into this diocese on one condition: no Negro priest can sit in my church convention, and no Negro church must ask for representation there."

I sometimes fancy I can see that tableau: the frail black figure, nervously twitching his hat before the massive abdomen of Bishop Onderdonk; his threadbare coat thrown against the dark woodwork of the book-cases, where Fox's "Lives of the Martyrs"† nestled happily beside "The Whole Duty of Man." I seem to see the wide eyes of the Negro wander past the Bishop's broadcloth to where the swinging glass doors of the cabinet glow in the sunlight. A little blue fly is trying to cross the yawning keyhole. He marches briskly up to it, peers into the chasm in a surprised sort of way, and rubs his feelers reflectively; then he essays its depths, and, finding

---

*See the Bible, Matthew 7:6: "Give not that which is holy unto the dogs, neither cast ye your pearls before swine" (KJV).
†*Book of Martyrs* (1563), by John Fox.

it bottomless, draws back again. The dark-faced priest finds himself wondering if the fly too has faced its Valley of Humiliation, and if it will plunge into it,—when lo! it spreads its tiny wings and buzzes merrily across, leaving the watcher wingless and alone.

Then the full weight of his burden fell upon him. The rich walls wheeled away, and before him lay the cold rough moor winding on through life, cut in twain by one thick granite ridge,—here, the Valley of Humiliation; yonder, the Valley of the Shadow of Death. And I know not which be darker,—no, not I. But this I know: in yonder Vale of the Humble stand to-day a million swarthy men, who willingly would

> "... *bear the whips and scorns of time,*
> *The oppressor's wrong, the proud man's contumely,*
> *The pangs of despised love, the law's delay,*
> *The insolence of office, and the spurns*
> *That patient merit of the unworthy takes,"* °

all this and more would they bear did they but know that this were sacrifice and not a meaner thing. So surged the thought within that lone black breast. The Bishop cleared his throat suggestively; then, recollecting that there was really nothing to say, considerately said nothing, only sat tapping his foot impatiently. But Alexander Crummell said, slowly and heavily: "I will never enter your diocese on such terms." And saying this, he turned and passed into the Valley of the Shadow of Death. You might have noted only the physical dying, the shattered frame and hacking cough; but in that soul lay deeper death than that. He found a chapel in New York,—the church of his father;[†] he labored for it in poverty and starvation, scorned by his fellow priests. Half in despair, he wandered across the sea, a beggar with outstretched hands. Englishmen clasped them,—Wilberforce and Stanley, Thirwell and Ingles, and even Froude and Macaulay; Sir Benjamin Brodie bade him rest awhile at Queen's College in Cambridge, and there he lingered, struggling for health of body and

---

°From act 3, scene 1 of *Hamlet,* by William Shakespeare.
[†]Church of the Messiah.

mind, until he took his degree in '53. Restless still and unsatisfied, he turned toward Africa, and for long years, amid the spawn of the slave-smugglers, sought a new heaven and a new earth.[3]

So the man groped for light; all this was not Life,—it was the world-wandering of a soul in search of itself, the striving of one who vainly sought his place in the world, ever haunted by the shadow of a death that is more than death,—the passing of a soul that has missed its duty. Twenty years he wandered,—twenty years and more; and yet the hard rasping question kept gnawing within him, "What, in God's name, am I on earth for?" In the narrow New York parish his soul seemed cramped and smothered. In the fine old air of the English University he heard the millions wailing over the sea. In the wild fever-cursed swamps of West Africa he stood helpless and alone.

You will not wonder at his weird pilgrimage,—you who in the swift whirl of living, amid its cold paradox and marvellous vision, have fronted life and asked its riddle face to face. And if you find that riddle hard to read, remember that yonder black boy finds it just a little harder; if it is difficult for you to find and face your duty, it is a shade more difficult for him; if your heart sickens in the blood and dust of battle, remember that to him the dust is thicker and the battle fiercer. No wonder the wanderers fall! No wonder we point to thief and murderer, and haunting prostitute, and the never-ending throng of unhearsed dead! The Valley of the Shadow of Death gives few of its pilgrims back to the world.

But Alexander Crummell it gave back. Out of the temptation of Hate, and burned by the fire of Despair, triumphant over Doubt, and steeled by Sacrifice against Humiliation, he turned at last home across the waters, humble and strong, gentle and determined. He bent to all the gibes and prejudices, to all hatred and discrimination, with that rare courtesy which is the armor of pure souls. He fought among his own, the low, the grasping, and the wicked, with that unbending righteousness which is the sword of the just. He never faltered, he seldom complained; he simply worked, inspiring the young, rebuking the old, helping the weak, guiding the strong.

So he grew, and brought within his wide influence all that was best of those who walk within the Veil. They who live without knew not nor dreamed of that full power within, that mighty inspiration which the dull gauze of caste decreed that most men

should not know. And now that he is gone, I sweep the Veil away
and cry, Lo! the soul to whose dear memory I bring this little tribute. I can see his face still, dark and heavy-lined beneath his snowy
hair; lighting and shading, now with inspiration for the future, now
in innocent pain at some human wickedness, now with sorrow at
some hard memory from the past. The more I met Alexander
Crummell, the more I felt how much that world was losing which
knew so little of him. In another age he might have sat among the
elders of the land in purple-bordered toga; in another country
mothers might have sung him to the cradles.

He did his work,—he did it nobly and well; and yet I sorrow
that here he worked alone, with so little human sympathy. His
name to-day, in this broad land, means little, and comes to fifty
million ears laden with no incense of memory or emulation. And
herein lies the tragedy of the age: not that men are poor,—all men
know something of poverty; not that men are wicked,—who is
good? not that men are ignorant,—what is Truth? Nay, but that
men know so little of men.

He sat one morning gazing toward the sea. He smiled and said,
"The gate is rusty on the hinges." That night at star-rise a wind came
moaning out of the west to blow the gate ajar, and then the soul I
loved fled like a flame across the Seas, and in its seat sat Death.

I wonder where he is to-day? I wonder if in that dim world
beyond, as he came gliding in, there rose on some wan throne a
King,—a dark and pierced Jew, who knows the writhings of the
earthly damned, saying, as he laid those heart-wrung talents down,
"Well done!" while round about the morning stars sat singing.*

---

*See the Bible, Matthew 25:21, the parable of the talents: "His lord said unto him,
Well done, thou good and faithful servant: thou hast been faithful over a few
things, I will make thee ruler over many things: enter thou into the joy of thy lord"
(KJV).

XIII

Of the Coming of John

What bring they 'neath the midnight,
Beside the River-sea?
They bring the human heart wherein
No nightly calm can be;
That droppeth never with the wind,
Nor drieth with the dew;
O calm it, God; thy calm is broad
To cover spirits too.
The river floweth on.

Mrs. Browning.*

CARLISLE STREET RUNS WESTWARD from the centre of Johnstown, across a great black bridge, down a hill and up again, by little shops and meat-markets, past single-storied homes, until suddenly it stops against a wide green lawn. It is a broad, restful place, with two large buildings outlined against the west. When at evening the winds come swelling from the east, and the great pall of the city's smoke hangs wearily above the valley, then the red west glows like a dreamland down Carlisle Street, and, at the

---

*From "A Romance of the Ganges" (1838), by Elizabeth Barrett Browning.
†From "I'll Hear the Trumpet Sound."

tolling of the supper-bell, throws the passing forms of students in dark silhouette against the sky. Tall and black, they move slowly by, and seem in the sinister light to flit before the city like dim warning ghosts. Perhaps they are; for this is Wells Institute, and these black students have few dealings with the white city below.

And if you will notice, night after night, there is one dark form that ever hurries last and late toward the twinkling lights of Swain Hall,—for Jones is never on time. A long, straggling fellow he is, brown and hard-haired, who seems to be growing straight out of his clothes, and walks with a half-apologetic roll. He used perpetually to set the quiet dining-room into waves of merriment, as he stole to his place after the bell had tapped for prayers; he seemed so perfectly awkward. And yet one glance at his face made one forgive him much,—that broad, good-natured smile in which lay no bit of art or artifice, but seemed just bubbling good-nature and genuine satisfaction with the world.

He came to us from Altamaha, away down there beneath the gnarled oaks of Southeastern Georgia, where the sea croons to the sands and the sands listen till they sink half drowned beneath the waters, rising only here and there in long, low islands. The white folk of Altamaha voted John a good boy,—fine plough-hand, good in the rice-fields, handy everywhere, and always good-natured and respectful. But they shook their heads when his mother wanted to send him off to school. "It'll spoil him,—ruin him," they said; and they talked as though they knew. But full half the black folk followed him proudly to the station, and carried his queer little trunk and many bundles. And there they shook and shook hands, and the girls kissed him shyly and the boys clapped him on the back. So the train came, and he pinched his little sister lovingly, and put his great arms about his mother's neck, and then was away with a puff and a roar into the great yellow world that flamed and flared about the doubtful pilgrim. Up the coast they hurried, past the squares and palmettos of Savannah, through the cotton-fields and through the weary night, to Millville, and came with the morning to the noise and bustle of Johnstown.

And they that stood behind, that morning in Altamaha, and watched the train as it noisily bore playmate and brother and son away to the world, had thereafter one ever-recurring word,— "When John comes." Then what parties were to be, and what speakings in the churches; what new furniture in the front room,—perhaps even a new front room; and there would be a new schoolhouse, with John as teacher; and then perhaps a big wedding; all this and more—when John comes. But the white people shook their heads.

At first he was coming at Christmas-time,—but the vacation proved too short; and then, the next summer,—but times were hard and schooling costly, and so, instead, he worked in Johnstown. And so it drifted to the next summer, and the next,—till playmates scattered, and mother grew gray, and sister went up to the Judge's kitchen to work. And still the legend lingered,—"When John comes."

Up at the Judge's they rather liked this refrain; for they too had a John—a fair-haired, smooth-faced boy, who had played many a long summer's day to its close with his darker namesake. "Yes, sir! John is at Princeton, sir," said the broad-shouldered gray-haired Judge every morning as he marched down to the post-office. "Showing the Yankees what a Southern gentleman can do," he added; and strode home again with his letters and papers. Up at the great pillared house they lingered long over the Princeton letter,—the Judge and his frail wife, his sister and growing daughters. "It'll make a man of him," said the Judge, "college is the place." And then he asked the shy little waitress, "Well, Jennie, how's your John?" and added reflectively, "Too bad, too bad your mother sent him off,—it will spoil him." And the waitress wondered.

Thus in the far-away Southern village the world lay waiting, half consciously, the coming of two young men, and dreamed in an inarticulate way of new things that would be done and new thoughts that all would think. And yet it was singular that few thought of two Johns,—for the black folk thought of one John, and he was black; and the white folk thought of another John, and he was white. And neither world thought the other world's thought, save with a vague unrest.

Up in Johnstown, at the Institute, we were long puzzled at the case of John Jones. For a long time the clay seemed unfit for any sort of moulding. He was loud and boisterous, always laughing and singing, and never able to work consecutively at anything. He did not know how to study; he had no idea of thoroughness; and with his tardiness, carelessness, and appalling good-humor, we were sore perplexed. One night we sat in faculty-meeting, worried and serious; for Jones was in trouble again. This last escapade was too much, and so we solemnly voted "that Jones, on account of re-peated disorder and inattention to work, be suspended for the rest of the term."

It seemed to us that the first time life ever struck Jones as a really serious thing was when the Dean told him he must leave school. He stared at the gray-haired man blankly, with great eyes. "Why,—why," he faltered, "but—I haven't graduated!" Then the Dean slowly and clearly explained, reminding him of the tardiness and the carelessness, of the poor lessons and neglected work, of the noise and disorder, until the fellow hung his head in confusion. Then he said quickly, "But you won't tell mammy and sister,—you won't write mammy, now will you? For if you won't I'll go out into the city and work, and come back next term and show you some-thing." So the Dean promised faithfully, and John shouldered his little trunk, giving neither word nor look to the giggling boys, and walked down Carlisle Street to the great city, with sober eyes and a set and serious face.

Perhaps we imagined it, but someway it seemed to us that the serious look that crept over his boyish face that afternoon never left it again. When he came back to us he went to work with all his rugged strength. It was a hard struggle, for things did not come easily to him,—few crowding memories of early life and teaching came to help him on his new way; but all the world toward which he strove was of his own building, and he builded slow and hard. As the light dawned lingeringly on his new creations, he sat rapt and silent before the vision, or wandered alone over the green campus peering through and beyond the world of men into a world of thought. And the thoughts at times puzzled him sorely; he could not see just why the circle was not square, and carried it out fifty-six decimal places one midnight,—would have gone fur-ther, indeed, had not the matron rapped for lights out. He caught terrible colds lying on his back in the meadows of nights, trying to think out the solar system; he had grave doubts as to the ethics of the Fall of Rome, and strongly suspected the Germans of being thieves and rascals, despite his text-books; he pondered long over every new Greek word, and wondered why this meant that and why it could n't mean something else, and how it must have felt to think all things in Greek. So he thought and puzzled along for himself,—pausing perplexed where others skipped merrily, and walking steadily through the difficulties where the rest stopped and surrendered.

Thus he grew in body and soul, and with him his clothes seemed to grow and arrange themselves; coat sleeves got longer, cuffs appeared, and collars got less soiled. Now and then his boots shone, and a new dignity crept into his walk. And we who saw daily a new thoughtfulness growing in his eyes began to expect something of this plodding boy. Thus he passed out of the preparatory school into college, and we who watched him felt four more years of change, which almost transformed the tall, grave man who bowed to us commencement morning. He had left his queer thought-world and come back to a world of motion and of men. He looked now for the first time sharply about him, and wondered he had seen so little before. He grew slowly to feel almost for the first time the Veil that lay between him and the white world; he first noticed now the oppression that had not seemed oppression before, differences that erstwhile seemed natural, restraints and slights that in his boyhood days had gone unnoticed or been greeted with a laugh. He felt angry now when men did not call him "Mister," he clenched his hands at the "Jim Crow" cars, and chafed at the color-line that hemmed in him and his. A tinge of sarcasm crept into his speech, and a vague bitterness into his life; and he sat long hours wondering and planning a way around these crooked things. Daily he found himself shrinking from the choked and narrow life of his native town. And yet he always planned to go back to Altamaha,—always planned to work there. Still, more and more as the day approached he hesitated with a nameless dread; and even the day after graduation he seized with eagerness the offer of the Dean to send him North with the quartette during the summer vacation, to sing for the Institute. A breath of air before the plunge, he said to himself in half apology.

It was a bright September afternoon, and the streets of New York were brilliant with moving men. They reminded John of the sea, as he sat in the square and watched them, so changelessly changing, so bright and dark, so grave and gay. He scanned their rich and faultless clothes, the way they carried their hands, the shape of their hats; he peered into the hurrying carriages. Then, leaning back with a sigh, he said, "This is the World." The notion suddenly seized him to see where the world was going; since many of the richer and brighter seemed hurrying all one way. So when a tall, light-haired young man and a little talkative lady came by, he rose half hesitatingly and followed them. Up the street they went, past stores and gay shops, across a broad square, until with a hundred others they entered the high portal of a great building.

He was pushed toward the ticket-office with the others, and felt in his pocket for the new five-dollar bill he had hoarded. There seemed really no time for hesitation, so he drew it bravely out, passed it to the busy clerk, and, received simply a ticket but no change. When at last he realized that he had paid five dollars to enter he knew not what, he stood stock-still amazed. "Be careful," said a low voice behind him; "you must not lynch the colored gentleman simply because he's in your way," and a girl looked up roguishly into the eyes of her fair-haired escort. A shade of annoyance passed over the escort's face. "You *will* not understand us at the South," he said half impatiently, as if continuing an argument. "With all your professions, one never sees in the North so cordial and intimate relations between white and black as are everyday occurrences with us. Why, I remember my closest playfellow in boyhood was a little Negro named after me, and surely no two,—*well!*" The man stopped short and flushed to the roots of his hair, for there directly beside his reserved orchestra chairs sat the Negro he had stumbled over in the hallway. He hesitated and grew pale with anger, called the usher and gave him his card, with a few peremptory words, and slowly sat down. The lady deftly changed the subject.

All this John did not see, for he sat in a half-maze minding the scene about him; the delicate beauty of the hall, the faint perfume, the moving myriad of men, the rich clothing and low hum of talking seemed all a part of a world so different from his, so strangely more beautiful than anything he had known, that he sat in dreamland, and started when, after a hush, rose high and clear the music of Lohengrin's swan. The infinite beauty of the wail lingered and swept through every muscle of his frame, and put it all a-tune. He closed his eyes and grasped the elbows of the chair, touching unwittingly the lady's arm. And the lady drew away. A deep longing swelled in all his heart to rise with that clear music out of the dirt and dust of that low life that held him prisoned and befouled. If he could only live up in the free air where birds sang and setting suns had no touch of blood! Who had called him to be the slave and butt of all? And if he had called, what right had he to call when a world like this lay open before men?

Then the movement changed, and fuller, mightier harmony swelled away. He looked thoughtfully across the hall, and wondered why the beautiful gray-haired woman looked so listless, and what the little man could be whispering about. He would not like to be listless and idle, he thought, for he felt with the music the movement of power within him. If he but had some master-work, some life-service, hard,—aye, bitter hard, but without the cringing and sickening servility, without the cruel hurt that hardened his heart and soul. When at last a soft sorrow crept across the violins, there came to him the vision of a far-off home,—the great eyes of his sister, and the dark drawn face of his mother. And his heart sank below the waters, even as the sea-sand sinks by the shores of Altamaha, only to be lifted aloft again with that last ethereal wail of the swan that quivered and faded away into the sky.

It left John sitting so silent and rapt that he did not for some time notice the usher tapping him lightly on the shoulder and saying politely, "Will you step this way, please, sir?" A little surprised, he arose quickly at the last tap, and, turning to leave his seat, looked full into the face of the fair-haired young man. For the first time the young man recognized his dark boyhood playmate, and John knew that it was the Judge's son. The white John started, lifted his hand, and then froze into his chair; the black John smiled lightly, then grimly, and followed the usher down the aisle. The manager was sorry, very, very sorry,—but he explained that some mistake had been made in selling the gentleman a seat already disposed of; he would refund the money, of course,—and indeed felt the matter keenly, and so forth, and—before he had finished John was gone, walking hurriedly across the square and down the broad streets, and as he passed the park he buttoned his coat and said, "John Jones, you're a natural-born fool." Then he went to his lodgings and wrote a letter, and tore it up; he wrote another, and threw it in the fire. Then he seized a scrap of paper and wrote: "Dear Mother and Sister—I am coming—John."

"Perhaps," said John, as he settled himself on the train, "perhaps I am to blame myself in struggling against my manifest destiny simply because it looks hard and unpleasant. Here is my duty to Altamaha plain before me; perhaps they'll let me help settle the Negro problems there,—perhaps they won't. 'I will go in to the King, which is not according to the law; and if I perish, I perish.'"* And then he mused and dreamed, and planned a life-work, and the train flew south.

Down in Altamaha, after seven long years, all the world knew John was coming. The homes were scrubbed and scoured,—above all, one; the gardens and yards had an unwonted trimness, and Jennie bought a new gingham. With some finesse and negotiation, all the dark Methodists and Presbyterians were induced to join in a monster welcome at the Baptist Church; and as the day drew near, warm discussions arose on every corner as to the exact extent and nature of John's accomplishments. It was noontide on a gray and cloudy day when he came. The black town flocked to the depot, with a little of the white at the edges,—a happy throng, with "Good-mawnings" and "Howdys" and laughing and joking and jostling. Mother sat yonder in the window watching; but sister Jennie stood on the platform, nervously fingering her dress,—tall and lithe, with soft brown skin and loving eyes peering from out a tangled wilderness of hair. John rose gloomily as the train stopped, for he was thinking of the "Jim Crow" car; he stepped to the platform, and paused: a little dingy station, a black crowd gaudy and dirty, a half-mile of dilapidated shanties along a straggling ditch of mud. An overwhelming sense of the sordidness and narrowness of it all seized him; he looked in vain for his mother, kissed coldly the tall, strange girl who called him brother, spoke a short, dry word here and there; then, lingering neither for handshaking nor gossip, started silently up the street, raising his hat merely to the last eager old aunty, to her open-mouthed astonishment. The people were distinctly bewildered. This silent, cold man,—was this John? Where was his smile and hearty handgrasp? "'Peared kind o' down in the mouf," said the Methodist preacher

---

*See the Bible, Esther 4:16. Esther pledges to save her people from Haman: ". . . and so will I go in unto the king, which is not according to the law: and if I perish, I perish" (KJV).

thoughtfully. "Seemed monstus stuck up," complained a Baptist sister. But the white postmaster from the edge of the crowd expressed the opinion of his folks plainly. "That damn Nigger," said he, as he shouldered the mail and arranged his tobacco, "has gone North and got plum full o' fool notions; but they won't work in Altamaha." And the crowd melted away.

The meeting of welcome at the Baptist Church was a failure. Rain spoiled the barbecue, and thunder turned the milk in the ice-cream. When the speaking came at night, the house was crowded to overflowing. The three preachers had especially prepared themselves, but somehow John's manner seemed to throw a blanket over everything,—he seemed so cold and preoccupied, and had so strange an air of restraint that the Methodist brother could not warm up to his theme and elicited not a single "Amen"; the Presbyterian prayer was but feebly responded to, and even the Baptist preacher, though he wakened faint enthusiasm, got so mixed up in his favorite sentence that he had to close it by stopping fully fifteen minutes sooner than he meant. The people moved uneasily in their seats as John rose to reply. He spoke slowly and methodically. The age, he said, demanded new ideas; we were far different from those men of the seventeenth and eighteenth centuries,—with broader ideas of human brotherhood and destiny. Then he spoke of the rise of charity and popular education, and particularly of the spread of wealth and work. The question was, then, he added reflectively, looking at the low discolored ceiling, what part the Negroes of this land would take in the striving of the new century. He sketched in vague outline the new Industrial School that might rise among these pines, he spoke in detail of the charitable and philanthropic work that might be organized, of money that might be saved for banks and business. Finally he urged unity, and deprecated especially religious and denominational bickering. "To-day," he said, with a smile, "the world cares little whether a man be Baptist or Methodist, or indeed a churchman at all, so long as he is good and true. What difference does it make whether a man be baptized in river or wash-bowl, or not at all? Let's leave all that littleness, and look higher." Then, thinking of nothing else, he slowly sat down. A painful hush seized that crowded mass. Little had they understood of what he said, for he spoke an unknown tongue, save the last

word about baptism; that they knew, and they sat very still while
the clock ticked. Then at last a low suppressed snarl came from
the Amen corner; and an old bent man arose, walked over the
seats, and climbed straight up into the pulpit. He was wrinkled
and black, with scant gray and tufted hair; his voice and hands
shook as with palsy; but on his face lay the intense rapt look of the
religious fanatic. He seized the Bible with his rough, huge hands;
twice he raised it inarticulate, and then fairly burst into the words,
with rude and awful eloquence. He quivered, swayed, and bent;
then rose aloft in perfect majesty, till the people moaned and
wept, wailed and shouted, and a wild shrieking arose from the corners where all the pent-up feeling of the hour gathered itself and
rushed into the air; John never knew clearly what the old man
said; he only felt himself held up to scorn and scathing denunciation for trampling on the true Religion, and he realized with
amazement that all unknowingly he had put rough, rude hands on
something this little world held sacred. He arose silently, and
passed out into the night. Down toward the sea he went, in the fit-
ful starlight, half conscious of the girl who followed timidly after
him. When at last he stood upon the bluff, he turned to his little
sister and looked upon her sorrowfully, remembering with sudden
pain how little thought he had given her. He put his arm about her
and let her passion of tears spend itself on his shoulder.

Long they stood together, peering over the gray unresting
water.

"John," she said, "does it make every one—unhappy when they
study and learn lots of things?"

He paused and smiled. "I am afraid it does," he said.

"And, John, are you glad you studied?"

"Yes," came the answer, slowly but positively.

She watched the flickering lights upon the sea, and said
thoughtfully, "I wish I was unhappy,—and—and," putting both
arms about his neck, "I think I am, a little, John."

It was several days later that John walked up to the Judge's
house to ask for the privilege of teaching the Negro school. The
Judge himself met him at the front door, stared a little hard at him,
and said brusquely, "Go 'round to the kitchen door, John, and
wait." Sitting on the kitchen steps, John stared at the corn, thoroughly perplexed. What on earth had come over him? Every step

he made offended some one. He had come to save his people, and before he left the depot he had hurt them. He sought to teach them at the church, and had outraged their deepest feelings. He had schooled himself to be respectful to the Judge, and then blundered into his front door. And all the time he had meant right,—and yet, and yet, somehow he found it so hard and strange to fit his old surroundings again, to find his place in the world about him. He could not remember that he used to have any difficulty in the past, when life was glad and gay. The world seemed smooth and easy then. Perhaps,—but his sister came to the kitchen door just then and said the Judge awaited him.

The Judge sat in the dining-room amid his morning's mail, and he did not ask John to sit down. He plunged squarely into the business. "You've come for the school, I suppose. Well, John, I want to speak to you plainly. You know I'm a friend to your people. I've helped you and your family, and would have done more if you had n't got the notion of going off. Now I like the colored people, and sympathize with all their reasonable aspirations; but you and I both know, John, that in this country the Negro must remain subordinate, and can never expect to be the equal of white men. In their place, your people can be honest and respectful; and God knows, I'll do what I can to help them. But when they want to reverse nature, and rule white men, and marry white women, and sit in my parlor, then, by God! we'll hold them under if we have to lynch every Nigger in the land. Now, John, the question is, are you, with your education and Northern notions, going to accept the situation and teach the darkies to be faithful servants and laborers as your fathers were,—I knew your father, John, he belonged to my brother, and he was a good Nigger. Well—well, are you going to be like him, or are you going to try to put fool ideas of rising and equality into these folks' heads, and make them discontented and unhappy?"

"I am going to accept the situation, Judge Henderson," answered John, with a brevity that did not escape the keen old man. He hesitated a moment, and then said shortly, "Very well,—we'll try you awhile. Good-morning."

It was a full month after the opening of the Negro school that the other John came home, tall, gay, and headstrong. The mother wept, the sisters sang. The whole white town was glad. A proud man was the Judge, and it was a goodly sight to see the two swing-ing down Main Street together. And yet all did not go smoothly between them, for the younger man could not and did not veil his contempt for the little town, and plainly had his heart set on New York. Now the one cherished ambition of the Judge was to see his son mayor of Altamaha, representative to the legislature, and—who could say?—governor of Georgia. So the argument often waxed hot between them. "Good heavens, father," the younger man would say after dinner, as he lighted a cigar and stood by the fireplace, "you surely don't expect a young fellow like me to settle down permanently in this—this God-forgotten town with nothing but mud and Negroes?" "*I* did," the Judge would answer laconi-cally; and on this particular day it seemed from the gathering scowl that he was about to add something more emphatic, but neighbors had already begun to drop in to admire his son, and the conversation drifted.

"Heah that John is livenin' things up at the darky school," vol-unteered the postmaster, after a pause.

"What now?" asked the Judge, sharply.

"Oh, nothin' in particulah,—just his almighty air and uppish ways. B'lieve I did heah somethin' about his givin' talks on the French Revolution, equality, and such like. He's what I call a dan-gerous Nigger."

"Have you heard him say anything out of the way?"

"Why, no,—but Sally, our girl, told my wife a lot of rot. Then, too, I don't need to heah: a Nigger what won't say 'sir' to a white man, or—"

"Who is this John?" interrupted the son.

"Why, it's little black John, Peggy's son,—your old play-fellow."

The young man's face flushed angrily, and then he laughed.

"Oh," said he, "it's the darky that tried to force himself into a seat beside the lady I was escorting—"

But Judge Henderson waited to hear no more. He had been nettled all day, and now at this he rose with a half-smothered oath, took his hat and cane, and walked straight to the schoolhouse.

For John, it had been a long, hard pull to get things started in the rickety old shanty that sheltered his school. The Negroes were rent into factions for and against him, the parents were careless, the children irregular and dirty, and books, pencils, and slates largely missing. Nevertheless, he struggled hopefully on, and seemed to see at last some glimmering of dawn. The attendance was larger and the children were a shade cleaner this week. Even the booby class in reading showed a little comforting progress. So John settled himself with renewed patience this afternoon.

"Now, Mandy," he said cheerfully, "that's better; but you must n't chop your words up so: 'If—the—man—goes.' Why, your little brother even would n't tell a story that way, now would he?"

"Naw, suh, he cain't talk."

"All right; now let's try again: 'If the man—'"

"John!"

The whole school started in surprise, and the teacher half arose, as the red, angry face of the Judge appeared in the open doorway.

"John, this school is closed. You children can go home and get to work. The white people of Altamaha are not spending their money on black folks to have their heads crammed with impudence and lies. Clear out! I'll lock the door myself."

Up at the great pillared house the tall young son wandered aimlessly about after his father's abrupt departure. In the house there was little to interest him; the books were old and stale, the local newspaper flat, and the women had retired with headaches and sewing. He tried a nap, but it was too warm. So he sauntered out into the fields, complaining disconsolately, "Good Lord! how long will this imprisonment last!" He was not a bad fellow,—just a little spoiled and self-indulgent, and as headstrong as his proud father. He seemed a young man pleasant to look upon, as he sat on the great black stump at the edge of the pines idly swinging his legs and smoking. "Why, there is n't even a girl worth getting up a respectable flirtation with," he growled. Just then his eye caught a tall, willowy figure hurrying toward him on the narrow path. He looked with interest at first, and then burst into a laugh as he said, "Well, I declare, if it is n't Jennie, the little brown kitchen-maid! Why, I never noticed before what a trim little body she is. Hello, Jennie! Why, you have n't kissed me since I came home," he said gaily. The young girl stared at him in surprise and confusion,—faltered something inarticulate, and attempted to pass. But a wilful mood had seized the young idler, and he caught at her arm.

Frightened, she slipped by; and half mischievously he turned and ran after her through the tall pines.

Yonder, toward the sea, at the end of the path, came John slowly, with his head down. He had turned wearily homeward from the schoolhouse; then, thinking to shield his mother from the blow, started to meet his sister as she came from work and break the news of his dismissal to her. "I'll go away," he said slowly; "I'll go away and find work, and send for them. I cannot live here longer." And then the fierce, buried anger surged up into his throat. He waved his arms and hurried wildly up the path.

The great brown sea lay silent. The air scarce breathed. The dying day bathed the twisted oaks and mighty pines in black and gold. There came from the wind no warning, not a whisper from the cloudless sky. There was only a black man hurrying on with an ache in his heart, seeing neither sun nor sea, but starting as from a dream at the frightened cry that woke the pines, to see his dark sister struggling in the arms of a tall and fair-haired man.

He said not a word, but, seizing a fallen limb, struck him with all the pent-up hatred of his great black arm; and the body lay white and still beneath the pines, all bathed in sunshine and in blood. John looked at it dreamily, then walked back to the house briskly, and said in a soft voice, "Mammy, I'm going away,—I'm going to be free."

She gazed at him dimly and faltered, "No'th, honey, is yo' gwine No'th agin?"

He looked out where the North Star glistened pale above the waters, and said, "Yes, mammy, I'm going—North."

Then, without another word, he went out into the narrow lane, up by the straight pines, to the same winding path, and seated himself on the great black stump, looking at the blood where the body had lain. Yonder in the gray past he had played with that dead boy, romping together under the solemn trees. The night deepened; he thought of the boys at Johnstown. He wondered how Brown had turned out, and Carey? And Jones,—Jones? Why, *he* was Jones, and he wondered what they would all say when they knew, when they knew, in that great long dining-room with its hundreds of merry eyes. Then as the sheen of the starlight stole over him, he thought of the gilded ceiling of that vast concert hall, and heard stealing toward him the faint sweet music of the swan.

Hark! was it music, or the hurry and shouting of men? Yes, surely! Clear and high the faint sweet melody rose and fluttered like a living thing, so that the very earth trembled as with the tramp of horses and murmur of angry men.

He leaned back and smiled toward the sea, whence rose the strange melody, away from the dark shadows where lay the noise of horses galloping, galloping on. With an effort he roused himself, bent forward, and looked steadily down the pathway, softly humming the "Song of the Bride,"—

"Freudig geführt, ziehet dahin." *

Amid the trees in the dim morning twilight he watched their shadows dancing and heard their horses thundering toward him, until at last they came sweeping like a storm, and he saw in front that haggard white-haired man, whose eyes flashed red with fury. Oh, how he pitied him,—pitied him,—and wondered if he had the coiling twisted rope. Then, as the storm burst round him, he rose slowly to his feet and turned his closed eyes toward the Sea.

And the world whistled in his ears.

---

*Joyfully guided, draw near (German). Du Bois has altered a line from act 3, scene 1 of *Lohengrin* (1848), by Richard Wagner. The original line is "Treulich [faithfully] geführt, ziehet dahin." The line that follows translates as "to where the blessing of love shall preserve you."

XIV

The Sorrow Songs

I walk through the churchyard
*   To lay this body down;*
I know moon-rise, I know star-rise;
I walk in the moonlight, I walk in the starlight;
I 'll lie in the grave and stretch out my arms,
I 'll go to judgment in the evening of the day,
And my soul and thy soul shall meet that day,
*   When I lay this body down.*

                                        Negro Song.*

THEY THAT WALKED IN DARKNESS sang songs in the olden days—
Sorrow Songs—for they were weary at heart. And so before each
thought that I have written in this book I have set a phrase, a
haunting echo of these weird old songs in which the soul of the
black slave spoke to men. Ever since I was a child these songs have
stirred me strangely. They came out of the South unknown to me,
one by one, and yet at once I knew them as of me and of mine.
Then in after years when I came to Nashville I saw the great temple builded of these songs towering over the pale city. To me Jubilee Hall† seemed ever made of the songs themselves, and its
bricks were red with the blood and dust of toil. Out of them rose

---

*From "Lay This Body Down."
†From "Wrestling Jacob."
‡See footnote on p. 48.

177

for me morning, noon, and night, bursts of wonderful melody, full of the voices of my brothers and sisters, full of the voices of the past.

Little of beauty has America given the world save the rude grandeur God himself stamped on her bosom; the human spirit in this new world has expressed itself in vigor and ingenuity rather than in beauty. And so by fateful chance the Negro folk-song—the rhythmic cry of the slave—stands to-day not simply as the sole American music, but as the most beautiful expression of human experience born this side the seas. It has been neglected, it has been, and is, half despised, and above all it has been persistently mistaken and misunderstood; but notwithstanding, it still remains as the singular spiritual heritage of the nation and the greatest gift of the Negro people.

Away back in the thirties the melody of these slave songs stirred the nation, but the songs were soon half forgotten. Some, like "Near the lake where drooped the willow," passed into current airs and their source was forgotten; others were caricatured on the "minstrel"* stage and their memory died away. Then in war-time came the singular Port Royal experiment after the capture of Hilton Head, and perhaps for the first time the North met the Southern slave face to face and heart to heart with no third witness. The Sea Islands of the Carolinas, where they met, were filled with a black folk of primitive type, touched and moulded less by the world about them than any others outside the Black Belt. Their appearance was uncouth, their language funny, but their hearts were human and their singing stirred men with a mighty power. Thomas Wentworth Higginson hastened to tell of these songs, and Miss McKim and others urged upon the world their rare beauty. But the world listened only half credulously until the Fisk Jubilee Singers sang the slave songs so deeply into the world's heart that it can never wholly forget them again.

There was once a blacksmith's son born at Cadiz, New York, who in the changes of time taught school in Ohio and helped defend Cincinnati from Kirby Smith. Then he fought at Chancellorsville and Gettysburg and finally served in the Freedman's

---

*Performances in which white actors in blackface presented stereotypes of black speech and song.

Bureau at Nashville. Here he formed a Sunday-school class of black children in 1866, and sang with them and taught them to sing. And then they taught him to sing, and when once the glory of the Jubilee songs passed into the soul of George L. White, he knew his life-work was to let those Negroes sing to the world as they had sung to him. So in 1871 the pilgrimage of the Fisk Jubilee Singers began. North to Cincinnati they rode,—four half-clothed black boys and five girl-women,—led by a man with a cause and a purpose. They stopped at Wilberforce, the oldest of Negro schools, where a black bishop blessed them. Then they went, fighting cold and starvation, shut out of hotels, and cheerfully sneered at, ever northward; and ever the magic of their song kept thrilling hearts, until a burst of applause in the Congregational Council at Oberlin revealed them to the world. They came to New York and Henry Ward Beecher dared to welcome them, even though the metropolitan dailies sneered at his "Nigger Minstrels." So their songs conquered till they sang across the land and across the sea, before Queen and Kaiser, in Scotland and Ireland, Holland and Switzerland. Seven years they sang, and brought back a hundred and fifty thousand dollars to found Fisk University.

Since their day they have been imitated—sometimes well, by the singers of Hampton and Atlanta, sometimes ill, by straggling quartettes. Caricature has sought again to spoil the quaint beauty of the music, and has filled the air with many debased melodies which vulgar ears scarce know from the real. But the true Negro folk-song still lives in the hearts of those who have heard them truly sung and in the hearts of the Negro people.

What are these songs, and what do they mean? I know little of music and can say nothing in technical phrase, but I know something of men, and knowing them, I know that these songs are the articulate message of the slave to the world. They tell us in these eager days that life was joyous to the black slave, careless and happy. I can easily believe this of some, of many. But not all the past South, though it rose from the dead, can gainsay the heart-touching witness of these songs. They are the music of an unhappy people, of the children of disappointment; they tell of death and suffering and unvoiced longing toward a truer world, of misty wanderings and hidden ways.

The songs are indeed the siftings of centuries; the music is far more ancient than the words, and in it we can trace here and there signs of development. My grandfather's grandmother was seized by an evil Dutch trader two centuries ago; and coming to the valleys of the Hudson and Housatonic, black, little, and lithe, she shivered and shrank in the harsh north winds, looked longingly at the hills, and often crooned a heathen melody to the child between her knees, thus:

Do ba - na co - ba, ge - ne me, ge - ne me!

Do ba - na co - ba, ge - ne me, ge - ne me!

Ben d' nu - li, nu - li, nu - li, nu - li, ben d' le.

The child sang it to his children and they to their children's children, and so two hundred years it has travelled down to us and we sing it to our children, knowing as little as our fathers what its words may mean,[1] but knowing well the meaning of its music.

This was primitive African music; it may be seen in larger form in the strange chant which heralds "The Coming of John":

> *"You may bury me in the East,*
> *You may bury me in the West,*
> *But I 'll hear the trumpet sound in that morning,"* *

—the voice of exile.

Ten master songs, more or less, one may pluck from this forest of melody—songs of undoubted Negro origin and wide popular currency, and songs peculiarly characteristic of the slave. One of these I have just mentioned. Another whose strains begin this

---

* "You May Bury Me in the East"; also known as "I'll Hear the Trumpet Sound."

book is "Nobody knows the trouble I 've seen." When, struck with
a sudden poverty, the United States refused to fulfil its promises
of land to the freedmen, a brigadier-general went down to the Sea
Islands to carry the news. An old woman on the outskirts of the
throng began singing this song; all the mass joined with her, swaying. And the soldier wept.

The third song is the cradle-song of death which all men
know,—"Swing low, sweet chariot,"—whose bars begin the life
story of "Alexander Crummell." Then there is the song of many
waters, "Roll, Jordan, roll," a mighty chorus with minor cadences.
There were many songs of the fugitive like that which opens "The
Wings of Atalanta," and the more familiar "Been a-listening." The
seventh is the song of the End and the Beginning—"My Lord,
what a mourning! when the stars begin to fall"; a strain of this is
placed before "The Dawn of Freedom." The song of groping—
"My way's cloudy"—begins "The Meaning of Progress"; the ninth
is the song of this chapter—"Wrestlin' Jacob, the day is a-break-
ing,"—a pæan of hopeful strife. The last master song is the song
of songs—"Steal away,"—sprung from "The Faith of the Fathers."

There are many others of the Negro folk-songs as striking and
characteristic as these, as, for instance, the three strains in the third,
eighth, and ninth chapters; and others I am sure could easily make
a selection on more scientific principles. There are, too, songs that
seem to me a step removed from the more primitive types: there is
the maze-like medley, "Bright sparkles," one phrase of which heads
"The Black Belt"; the Easter carol, "Dust, dust and ashes"; the
dirge, "My mother's took her flight and gone home"; and that burst
of melody hovering over "The Passing of the First-Born"—"I hope
my mother will be there in that beautiful world on high."

These represent a third step in the development of the slave
song, of which "You may bury me in the East" is the first, and songs
like "March on" (chapter six) and "Steal away" are the second. The
first is African music, the second Afro-American, while the third is
a blending of Negro music with the music heard in the foster land.
The result is still distinctively Negro and the method of blending
original, but the elements are both Negro and Caucasian. One might
go further and find a fourth step in this development, where the
songs of white America have been distinctively influenced by the
slave songs or have incorporated whole phrases of Negro melody,

as "Swanee River" and "Old Black Joe."[*] Side by side, too, with
the growth has gone the debasements and imitations—the Negro
"minstrel" songs, many of the "gospel" hymns, and some of the
contemporary "coon" songs,—a mass of music in which the novice
may easily lose himself and never find the real Negro melodies.

In these songs, I have said, the slave spoke to the world. Such
a message is naturally veiled and half articulate. Words and music
have lost each other and new and cant phrases of a dimly understood theology have displaced the older sentiment. Once in a
while we catch a strange word of an unknown tongue, as the
"Mighty Myo," which figures as a river of death; more often slight
words or mere doggerel are joined to music of singular sweetness.
Purely secular songs are few in number, partly because many of
them were turned into hymns by a change of words, partly because the frolics were seldom heard by the stranger, and the music
less often caught. Of nearly all the songs, however, the music is
distinctly sorrowful. The ten master songs I have mentioned tell in
word and music of trouble and exile, of strife and hiding; they
grope toward some unseen power and sigh for rest in the End.

The words that are left to us are not without interest, and, cleared
of evident dross, they conceal much of real poetry and meaning beneath conventional theology and unmeaning rhapsody. Like all
primitive folk, the slave stood near to Nature's heart. Life was a
"rough and rolling sea" like the brown Atlantic of the Sea Islands; the
"Wilderness" was the home of God, and the "lonesome valley" led to
the way of life. "Winter'll soon be over," was the picture of life and
death to a tropical imagination. The sudden wild thunderstorms of
the South awed and impressed the Negroes,—at times the rumbling
seemed to them "mournful," at times imperious:

> *"My Lord calls me,*
> *He calls me by the thunder,*
> *The trumpet sounds it in my soul."* [†]

The monotonous toil and exposure is painted in many words.
One sees the ploughmen in the hot, moist furrow, singing:

---

[*]Stephen Foster (1826–1864) wrote both of these popular songs.
[†]From "Steal Away."

"Dere 's no rain to wet you,
Dere 's no sun to burn you,
Oh, push along, believer,
I want to go home." *

The bowed and bent old man cries, with thrice-repeated wail:

"O Lord, keep me from sinking down,"

and he rebukes the devil of doubt who can whisper:

"Jesus is dead and God's gone away." †

Yet the soul-hunger is there, the restlessness of the savage, the wail of the wanderer, and the plaint is put in one little phrase:

My soul wants some thing that's new, that's new

Over the inner thoughts of the slaves and their relations one with another the shadow of fear ever hung, so that we get but glimpses here and there, and also with them, eloquent omissions and silences. Mother and child are sung, but seldom father; fugitive and weary wanderer call for pity and affection, but there is little of wooing and wedding; the rocks and the mountains are well known, but home is unknown. Strange blending of love and helplessness sings through the refrain:

---

*From "There's No Rain to Wet You."
†From "Keep Me from Sinking Down."
‡From "My Soul Wants Something New."

> *"Yonder 's my ole mudder,*
> *Been waggin' at de hill so long;*
> *'Bout time she cross over,*
> *Git home bime-by."* °

Elsewhere comes the cry of the "motherless" and the "Farewell, farewell, my only child."

Love-songs are scarce and fall into two categories—the frivolous and light, and the sad. Of deep successful love there is ominous silence, and in one of the oldest of these songs there is a depth of history and meaning:

Poor Ro - sy, poor gal; Poor Ro - sy,

poor gal; Ro - sy break my poor heart.

Heav'n shall - a - be my home.

A black woman said of the song, "It can't be sung without a full heart and a troubled sperrit." The same voice sings here that sings in the German folk-song:

> *"Jetz Geh i' an's brunele, trink' aber net."* †

Of death the Negro showed little fear, but talked of it familiarly and even fondly as simply a crossing of the waters, perhaps—who knows?—back to his ancient forests again. Later days transfigured his fatalism, and amid the dust and dirt the toiler sang:

° From "O'er the Crossing."
† From "Poor Rosy."
‡ "Now I go to the little well, but I don't drink."

"Dust, dust and ashes, fly over my grave,
But the Lord shall bear my spirit home." *

The things evidently borrowed from the surrounding world undergo characteristic change when they enter the mouth of the slave. Especially is this true of Bible phrases. "Weep, O captive daughter of Zion," is quaintly turned into "Zion, weep-a-low," and the wheels of Ezekiel are turned every way in the mystic dreaming of the slave, till he says:

There's a little wheel a-turnin' in-a-my heart." †

As in olden time, the words of these hymns were improvised by some leading minstrel of the religious band. The circumstances of the gathering, however, the rhythm of the songs, and the limitations of allowable thought, confined the poetry for the most part to single or double lines, and they seldom were expanded to quatrains or longer tales, although there are some few examples of sustained efforts, chiefly paraphrases of the Bible.‡ Three short series of verses have always attracted me,—the one that heads this chapter, of one line of which Thomas Wentworth Higginson has fittingly said, "Never, it seems to me, since man first lived and suffered was his infinite longing for peace uttered more plaintively." The second and third are descriptions of the Last Judgment,—the one a late improvisation, with some traces of outside influence:

"Oh, the stars in the elements are falling,
And the moon drips away into blood,
And the ransomed of the Lord are returning unto God,
Blessed be the name of the Lord." §

And the other earlier and homelier picture from the low coast lands:

---

*From "Dust and Ashes."
†From "There's a Little Wheel a-Turnin'."
‡See the Bible, Ezekiel 1:15–21.
§From "My Lord, What a Mourning!"

"*Michael, haul the boat ashore,*
Then you 'll hear the horn they blow,
Then you 'll hear the trumpet sound,
Trumpet sound the world around,
Trumpet sound for rich and poor,
Trumpet sound the Jubilee,
Trumpet sound for you and me." *

Through all the sorrow of the Sorrow Songs there breathes a hope—a faith in the ultimate justice of things. The minor cadences of despair change often to triumph and calm confidence. Sometimes it is faith in life, sometimes a faith in death, sometimes assurance of boundless justice in some fair world beyond. But whichever it is, the meaning is always clear: that sometime, somewhere, men will judge men by their souls and not by their skins. Is such a hope justified? Do the Sorrow Songs sing true?

The silently growing assumption of this age is that the probation of races is past, and that the backward races of to-day are of proven inefficiency and not worth the saving. Such an assumption is the arrogance of peoples irreverent toward Time and ignorant of the deeds of men. A thousand years ago such an assumption, easily possible, would have made it difficult for the Teuton to prove his right to life. Two thousand years ago such dogmatism, readily welcome, would have scouted the idea of blond races ever leading civilization. So wofully unorganized is sociological knowledge that the meaning of progress, the meaning of "swift" and "slow" in human doing, and the limits of human perfectability, are veiled, unanswered sphinxes on the shores of science. Why should Æschylus have sung two thousand years before Shakespeare was born? Why has civilization flourished in Europe, and flickered, flamed, and died in Africa? So long as the world stands meekly dumb before such questions, shall this nation proclaim its ignorance and unhallowed prejudices by denying freedom of opportunity to those who brought the Sorrow Songs to the Seats of the Mighty?

---

*From "Michael, Row the Boat Ashore!"

Your country? How came it yours? Before the Pilgrims[2] landed we were here. Here we have brought our three gifts and mingled them with yours: a gift of story and song—soft, stirring melody in an ill-harmonized and unmelodious land; the gift of sweat and brawn to beat back the wilderness, conquer the soil, and lay the foundations of this vast economic empire two hundred years earlier than your weak hands could have done it; the third, a gift of the Spirit. Around us the history of the land has centred for thrice a hundred years; out of the nation's heart we have called all that was best to throttle and subdue all that was worst; fire and blood, prayer and sacrifice, have billowed over this people, and they have found peace only in the altars of the God of Right. Nor has our gift of the Spirit been merely passive. Actively we have woven ourselves with the very warp and woof of this nation,—we fought their battles, shared their sorrow, mingled our blood with theirs, and generation after generation have pleaded with a headstrong, careless people to despise not Justice, Mercy, and Truth, lest the nation be smitten with a curse. Our song, our toil, our cheer, and warning have been given to this nation in blood-brotherhood. Are not these gifts worth the giving? Is not this work and striving? Would America have been America without her Negro people?

Even so is the hope that sang in the songs of my fathers well sung. If somewhere in this whirl and chaos of things there dwells Eternal Good, pitiful yet masterful, then anon in His good time America shall rend the Veil and the prisoned shall go free. Free, free as the sunshine trickling down the morning into these high windows of mine, free as yonder fresh young voices welling up to me from the caverns of brick and mortar below—swelling with song, instinct with life, tremulous treble and darkening bass. My children, my little children, are singing to the sunshine, and thus they sing:

And the traveller girds himself, and sets his face toward the Morning, and goes his way.

THE AFTERTHOUGHT

Hear my cry, O God the Reader; vouchsafe that this my book fall not still-born into the world-wilderness. Let there spring, Gentle One, from out its leaves vigor of thought and thoughtful deed to reap the harvest wonderful. (Let the ears of a guilty people tingle with truth, and seventy millions sigh for the righteousness which exalteth nations, in this drear day when human brotherhood is mockery and a snare.) Thus in Thy good time may infinite reason turn the tangle straight, and these crooked marks on a fragile leaf be not indeed

The End

GLOSSARY OF NAMES

Aeschylus (525–456 B.C.). Greek tragic dramatist.

Armstrong, Samuel (1839–1893). Founded Hampton Institute in Hampton, Virginia, in 1868.

Attucks, Crispus (1723?–1770). The first man to fall in the Boston Massacre of 1770.

Aycock, Charles Brantley (1859–1912). Governor of North Carolina from 1901 to 1905; sought to increase literacy rates among blacks and poor whites in his state.

Balzac, Honoré de (1799–1850). French novelist.

Banneker, Benjamin (1731–1806). Free black; self-taught mathematician and astronomer.

Barbadoes, James G. (1796–1841). A founder of the American Antislavery Society, established in 1833.

Beecher, Henry Ward (1813–1887). Abolitionist brother of Harriet Beecher Stowe and pastor of Plymouth Congregational Church in Brooklyn, New York.

Belknap, William (1829–1890). U.S. secretary of war (1869–1876) under President Ulysses S. Grant.

Bowen, J. W. E. (1855–1933). Educator and Methodist minister; earned a Ph.D. in philosophy from Boston University and became the first fully appointed black professor at Gammon Theological Seminary.

Brodie, Benjamin (1783–1862). British surgeon.

Brown, John (1800–1859). Attempted to spark a slave insurrection with his raid at Harpers Ferry, Virginia, in October 1859.

Brown, William Wells (1816–1884). Abolitionist and author of *Clotel, or the President's Daughter* (1853).

Bruce, Blanche K. (1841–1898). Fugitive slave, educator, and the first and last black to serve a full term as U.S. senator from Mississippi (1875–1881).

191

Butler, Benjamin F. (1818 –1893). Civil War general from Massachusetts.

Cameron, Simon L. (1799–1889). U.S. secretary of War (1861–1862).

Carlyle, Thomas (1795–1881). Scottish philosopher and historian.

Cato. Leader of a slave insurrection in Stono, South Carolina, in 1739.

Chase, Salmon P. (1808–1873). U.S. secretary of the treasury (1861–1864).

Cravath, Erastus (1833–1900). Helped to start Fisk University in Nashville, Tennessee, in 1866.

Crummell, Alexander (1819–1898). Educated at Cambridge University in England; ordained in the Anglican Church and served as a missionary in Liberia; founding member of the American Negro Academy. See chapter XII for more information.

Cuffee, Paul (1759–1817). Wealthy merchant in New Bedford, Massachusetts; later attempted to establish a colony of African Americans in Sierra Leone.

Davis, Garret (1801–1872). U.S. senator from Kentucky (1861–1872).

Davis, Jefferson (1808–1889). President of the Confederacy during the Civil War.

Derham, James (1763–?). Black physician.

De Soto, Hernando (c.1500–1542). Spanish explorer who discovered the Mississippi River.

Douglass, Frederick (1817–1895). Best-known abolitionist and black leader of the nineteenth century; author of *Narrative of the Life of Frederick Douglass, an American Slave* (1845).

Du Bois, Alexander. William Du Bois's grandfather.

Dumas, Alexander (1802–1870). French playwright and novelist.

Elliot, Robert Brown (1841–1884). Thought to be a native of Liverpool, England; editor of one of the first Southern black newspapers, the *South Carolina Leader*; elected to the U.S. House of Representatives in 1870; later served as attorney general of South Carolina but was removed from office in 1877 when Democrats returned to power.

Fessenden, William Pitt (1806–1869). U.S. secretary of the treasury (1864–1865).

Forten, James (1766–1842). Philadelphia-based sail-maker, entrepreneur, and activist; one of the organizers of the Negro conventions.

Fremont, John C. (1813–1890). Civil War general and Republican candidate for president in 1856.

Froude, James Anthony (1818–1894). English historian.

Garrison, Lucy McKim (1842–1877). Daughter of abolitionist William Lloyd Garrison; transcribed spirituals she collected in South Carolina.

Green, Beriah (1795–1874). Founder of the Oneida Institute in Whitesboro, New York.

Grimke, Archibald H. (1849–1930). Author, lawyer, and activist based in Washington, D.C.

Grimke, Francis (1850–1937). Important minister.

Haleck, Henry H. (1815–1872). Union general.

Harris, William T. (1835–1909). U.S. commissioner of education (1889–1906).

Higginson, Thomas Wentworth (1823–1911). Union Army officer who wrote *The Spirituals*, one of the earliest studies of black music.

Hose, Sam (?–1899). Black farm laborer from Palmetto, Georgia, accused in 1899 of killing his employer and raping his employer's wife; confessed to the murder but maintained he did not rape the woman. Hose was lynched and mutilated, his body parts publicly displayed in shop windows; the lynching tree was cut down and pieces of it sold as souvenirs.

Howard, Oliver Otis (1830–1909). Commissioner of the Freedmen's Bureau (1865–1872); helped found Howard University (1867) and served as its president (1869–1874).

Ingles, John. Anglican bishop.

Jackson, Andrew (1767–1845). U.S. general from Tennessee who led the fight (1813–1814) against the Creek Indians; president of the United States (1829–1837).

Jay, John (1817–1894). Anti-slavery activist; son of William Jay, an abolitionist, and grandson of John Jay, Supreme Court justice.

Johnson, Samuel (1709–1784). English poet and critic; wrote *Dictionary of the English Language* (1755).

Kirby-Smith, Edmund (1824–1893). Confederate general.

Langston, John Mercer (1829–1897). Lawyer and founder of the law department at Howard University, where he was dean from 1869 to 1873; later was president of Virginia Normal and Collegiate Institute, served in the U.S. diplomatic and consular service (1877–1885), and was U.S. congressman from Virginia (1889–1891).

L'Ouverture, Toussaint. See, below, Toussaint-L'Ouverture, François Dominique.

Macaulay, Thomas (1800–1859). English historian and writer.

Miller, Kelly (1863–1939). Mathematician and sociologist who taught at Howard University (1890–1934).

Morgan, John Tyler (1824–1907). White supremacist; U.S. senator from Alabama (1877–1907).

Nell, William Cooper (1816–1874). In the 1840s sought to integrate schools in Boston; author of *The Colored Patriots of the American Revolution* (1855).

Oglethorpe, James Edward (1696–1785). Founder of the colony of Georgia in 1733.

Osceola (c.1800–1838). Seminole Indian/African-American leader who led the Seminole War against the United States (1835–1837); many fugitive slaves were adopted into his tribe in Florida.

Page, Thomas Nelson (1853–1922). Novelist who romanticized the Old South.

Payne, Daniel (1811–1893). Educator, historian, and bishop of the African Methodist Episcopal Church; one of the founders of Wilberforce University, where he served as president (1863–1876).

Pierce, Edward W. (1829–1897). Massachusetts abolitionist sent to South Carolina by U.S. secretary of the treasury Salmon P. Chase to oversee his Port Royal Experiment, which from 1862 to 1865 paid freed blacks to produce cotton.

Poor, Salem. Free black of Massachusetts who served in the Continental Army.

Price, Joseph C. (1854–1893). Minister of the A.M.E. Zion Church and president of Zion Wesley College, which later became Livingstone College, in Salisbury, North Carolina.

Prosser, Gabriel (c.1776–1800). Leader of an attempted slave revolt in 1800 in Richmond, Virginia; sometimes known simply as Gabriel.

Purvis, Sr., Robert (1810–1883). Philadelphia-based abolitionist; along with William Lloyd Garrison, one of the founders of the American Anti-Slavery Society in 1833.

Remond, Charles Lenox (1810–1873). Black abolitionist from Boston.

Salem, Peter (1750–1816). One of the Minutemen in the Battle of Concord on April 19, 1775; also fought at Bunker Hill, Saratoga, and Stony Point.

Shadd, Abraham (1801–1882). Black activist from Delaware.

Shadd, Mary Ann (1823–1893). Born in Delaware; lived as an expatriate in Canada, where she edited *The Provincial Freeman*; rumored to have been involved in planning John Brown's raid on Harpers Ferry in 1859.

Sherman, William T. (1820–1891). Union general who captured Atlanta and Savannah, Georgia.

Stanley. May be Arthur Penrhyn, author and clergyman, according to commentary in *The Souls of Black Folk: Authoritative Text, Contexts, Criticism*, edited by Henry Louis Gates, Jr., and Terri Hume Oliver, New York: W. W. Norton, 1999.

Sumner, Charles (1811–1874). U.S. senator from Massachusetts (1851–1874); aggressive abolitionist and leader in Congress among the opponents of slavery.

Thirwell, Connop (1797–1875). Anglican bishop and historian.

Tillman, Benjamin Ryan (1847–1918). White supremacist governor of South Carolina (1890–1894) and U.S. senator (1895–1918); advocated violence against blacks.

Toussaint-L'Ouverture, François Dominique (c.1744–1803). Haitian revolutionary and liberator.

Trumbull, Lyman (1813–1896). U.S. senator from Illinois (1855–1873).

Turner, Nat (1800–1831). Leader of an attempted slave revolt in 1831, in Southampton County, Virginia.

Vesey, Denmark (c.1767–1822). Leader of an attempted slave revolt in 1822, in Charleston, South Carolina.

Walker, David (1785–1830). Author of the militantly radical *Walker's Appeal in Four Articles; Together with a Preamble, to the Coloured Citizens of the World, but in Particular, and Very Expressly, to Those of the United States of America* (1829).

Ware, Edmund (1837–1885). Established Atlanta University (chartered 1867).

Washington, Booker T. (1856–1915). Educator, lecturer, and founder of the Tuskegee Institute (1881). In 1895, in a controversial speech in Atlanta, Georgia, he said blacks should achieve economic independence before agitating for social equality. In 1900 he organized the National Negro Business League, which worked for economic independence for African Americans.

Wheatley, Phillis (1753?–1784). Purchased as a slave at age seven or eight by John and Susannah Wheatley, who taught her to read and

write. The poet-prodigy became the first African American and
second American woman to publish a collection of poetry, *Poems
on Various Subjects, Religious and Moral* (1733).

White, George L. (1838–1895). Music teacher at Fisk and founder
(1871) of the Jubilee Singers.

Whitefield, George. Minister who defended slavery.

Wilberforce, Samuel (1805–1873). Anglican bishop and son of the
abolitionist Samuel Wilberforce (1759–1833).

Wood, Fernando (1812–1881). U.S. congressman from New York
(1841–1843, 1863–1865, 1867–1881).

Young, Arthur (1741–1820). British author of *Travels in France during the Years 1787, 1788, and 1789* (1792).

ENDNOTES

The Forethought

1. (p. 3) *the problem of the Twentieth Century:* Du Bois first made this statement in his address to the Pan-African Conference of July 1900 in London. The address was titled "To the Nations of the World."

2. (p. 4) *the Sorrow Songs:* This is Du Bois's term for the spirituals, a body of music created by enslaved African Americans who combined African song and nineteenth-century Christian hymns.

Chapter I: Of Our Spiritual Strivings

1. (p. 7) *Of Our Spiritual Strivings:* An earlier version of this chapter appeared as "Strivings of the Negro People," in *The Atlantic Monthly* (August 1897), pp. 194–198.

2. (p. 7) following the bar of music: Each chapter of *The Souls of Black Folk* opens with a selection of verse from the Western literary tradition and a bar of music from one of the "Negro spirituals"—religious songs communally composed by enslaved blacks. As with many folk songs, it is almost impossible to identify a single lyricist or composer for most of the spirituals. Passed down orally from one generation to the next, the songs borrow from and adapt the various forms of music the slaves heard in the New World as well as the musical traditions they brought with them from Africa. The spirituals were first gathered and published by the Reverend Richard Allen in 1801 and since then have been published in many versions. Du Bois seems to have relied on two popular volumes for his transcriptions: *The Story of the Jubilee Singers with Their Songs*, by J. B. T. Marsh, Boston: Houghton Mifflin, 1872, and *Hampton and Its Students*, by M. F. Armstrong and Helen W. Ludlow, arranged by Thomas P. Fenner (New York: G. P. Putnam's Sons, 1874).

3. (p. 9) *Seventh Son, born with a veil, and gifted with second-sight:* In African-American culture, children born with a caul (the remnants of the placenta covering the face) are thought to possess psychic abilities and the gift of prophecy. It is also believed that they have the ability to see and speak with the dead.

197

4. (p. 11) *revolution of 1876:* Three southern states—Louisiana, Florida, and South Carolina—disputed the results of the presidential election of 1876, in which Rutherford B. Hayes ran against Samuel J. Tilden, and threatened to secede from the Union. The dispute resulted in the Hayes-Tilden compromise, whereby the protesting states and southern Democrats accepted the election of Hayes and the North agreed to leave the fate of the freedmen to the southern states. The compromise marked the beginning of the end of Reconstruction.

Chapter II: Of the Dawn of Freedom

1. (p. 16) *Of the Dawn of Freedom:* An earlier version of this essay appeared as "The Freedmen's Bureau," in *The Atlantic Monthly* (March 1901), pp. 354–365.

2. (p. 17) *War Amendments:* The reference is to amendments made to the Constitution following the Civil War: The Thirteenth Amendment (1865) freed the slaves; the Fourteenth (1868) made them citizens and provided "equal protection under the law"; and the Fifteenth (1870) gave black males the right to vote.

3. (p. 17) *Freedmen's Bureau:* Founded in 1865, the U.S. Bureau of Refugees, Freedmen, and Abandoned Lands served as an advocate for the freedmen and helped to establish schools, hospitals, and courts to handle labor relations between the newly freed blacks and their former masters.

4. (p. 18) *Secretary Chase:* U.S. secretary of the treasury from 1861 to 1864, Salmon P. Chase sent Massachusetts abolitionist Edward W. Pierce to South Carolina to oversee the Port Royal Experiment, which from 1862 to 1865 paid freed blacks to produce cotton.

5. (p. 18) *the* Amistad: African captives took over the slave ship *Amistad* off the coast of Cuba in June 1839. The Africans demanded that the remaining crew members return the ship to Africa, but they sailed it to the United States instead. The Africans were imprisoned for two years in New Haven, Connecticut. With the assistance of abolitionists their case went to the Supreme Court, and they eventually were released and gained the right to return to Africa.

6. (p. 20) *"Field-order Number Fifteen":* This order, issued by Union General William T. Sherman in January 1865, allowed freed slaves to farm land from Charleston, South Carolina, to Jacksonville, Florida. In the fall of 1865, President Andrew Johnson overturned the order and returned the land to white landowners.

7. (p. 24) *women who dared . . . rhythm of the alphabet:* Du Bois here refers to women schoolteachers who traveled south to teach the freedmen.

Chapter III: Of Mr. Booker T. Washington and Others

1. (p. 35) *Of Mr. Booker T. Washington and Others:* An earlier version of this essay appeared as "The Evolution of Negro Leadership," in *The Dial* (July 16, 1901), pp. 53–55.

2. (p. 36) *"Atlanta Compromise":* Du Bois sarcastically refers to Washington's Atlanta Exposition Address, delivered on September 18, 1895, at the Cotton States Exposition in Atlanta.

3. (p. 36) *French grammar:* In his autobiography *Up from Slavery*, Washington writes critically of a poor young black boy surrounded by "filth" who spends time trying to learn French.

4. (p. 39) *the terrible Maroons, the Danish blacks, and Cato of Stono:* Here Du Bois cites instances of violent rebellion by enslaved blacks. The Maroons were communities of runaway, revolutionary blacks throughout the Caribbean and Latin America; in 1723 Danish blacks gained control for six months of the island of St. John in the Virgin Islands of the United States (before 1917 known as the Danish West Indies); Cato was the leader of a slave insurrection in Stono, South Carolina, in 1739.

Chapter IV: Of the Meaning of Progress

1. (p. 48) *Of the Meaning of Progress:* An earlier version of this essay appeared as "A Negro Schoolmaster in the New South," in *The Atlantic Monthly* (January 1899), pp. 99–104.

2. (p. 51) *worked Colonel Wheeler's farm on shares:* After the Civil War many southern blacks entered into arrangements with white slave owners. Under these arrangements the blacks were tenants who farmed land they did not own and paid the landowner in crops instead of rent. The vast majority of the yield went to the landowner, and the little that was left went to pay debts incurred for other necessities throughout the season.

Chapter VI: Of the Training of Black Men

1. (p. 67) *Of the Training of Black Men:* This is a revision of an essay of the same name first published in *Atlantic Monthly* (September 1902), pp. 287–297.

2. (p. 75) *Atlanta, Fisk, and Howard, Wilberforce and Lincoln, Biddle, Shaw:* The locations and dates of the origins of these universities are: Atlanta University, Atlanta, Georgia, chartered 1867; Fisk University, Nashville, Tennessee, opened 1866; Howard University, Washington, D.C., founded 1867; Wilberforce University, Wilberforce, Ohio, chartered 1856; Lincoln University, Oxford, Pennsylvania, chartered in 1854 as the Ashmun Institute, adopted new name in 1866; Biddle Memorial Institute, Charlotte, North Carolina, 1867, later became Biddle University, is now Johnson C. Smith University; Shaw University, Raleigh, North Carolina, founded 1865.

3. (p. 76) *Conference at Atlanta University:* While teaching at Atlanta University, Du Bois organized a series of conferences and published a series of monographs on black life. The fifth conference, "The College Bred Negro," took place in 1900.

4. (p. 77) *the energetic wife of the principal:* Du Bois refers to the important activist and intellectual Margaret Murray Washington, who was a former classmate of his at Fisk and the third wife of Booker T. Washington.

5. (p. 79) *Talented Tenth:* This term refers to Du Bois's theory of an educated black elite who would lead the masses. He later revised this thesis, finding the black elite too self-serving to lead.

6. (p. 81) *Pisgah, between Philistine and Amalekite:* Pisgah is the mountaintop from which Moses first saw the Promised Land. The Philistines and the Amalekites were enemies of the Israelites as they traveled to the Promised Land.

Chapter VII: Of the Black Belt

1. (p. 82) *Of the Black Belt:* This chapter and chapter VIII are revisions of "The Negro as He Really Is," published in *The World's Work* (June 1901), pp. 848–866.

2. (p. 83) *Delegal riots:* On August 23, 1899, blacks in Darien, Georgia, stopped a mob lynching. They were tried for insurrection, and twenty-one were sent to jail.

3. (p. 83) *Moravians of Ebenezea:* The Moravians were Scottish immigrants who came to Georgia in the eighteenth century; a Protestant denomination that opposed slavery, they founded two settlements near Savannah, Georgia.

4. (p. 83) *national statute of 1808:* This act of Congress, passed in 1807, sought "to Prohibit the Importation of Slaves into any Port or Place Within the Jurisdiction of the United States, From and After the First Day of January, in the Year of our Lord One Thousand Eight Hundred and Eight."

Chapter VIII: Of the Quest of the Golden Fleece

1. (p. 98) *Of the Quest of the Golden Fleece:* This chapter and chapter VII are revisions of "The Negro as He Really Is," published in *The World's Work* (June 1901), pp. 848–866.

2. (p. 98) *Jason and his Argonauts:* In Greek mythology, Chrysomallus was a flying ram known for his golden fleece. Jason, son of King Aeson, lost his birthright through trickery; in order to prove himself worthy of the throne, he set out to capture the golden fleece of Chrysomallus. The Argonauts were Jason's shipmates on the perilous journey.

Chapter IX: Of the Sons of Master and Man

1. (p. 117) *Of the Sons of Master and Man:* An earlier version of this chapter was published as "The Relation of the Negroes to the Whites in the South," in *An-*

nals of the American Academy of Political and Social Science (July–December 1901), pp. 121–140.

Chapter X: Of the Faith of the Fathers

1. (p. 134) *Of the Faith of the Fathers:* This chapter is a revision of "The Religion of the American Negro," which was published in *The New World: A Quarterly Review of Religious Ethics and Theology* (December 1900), pp. 614–625.

Chapter XI: Of the Passing of the First-Born

1. (p. 149) *the Shadow of Death:* Du Bois's son, Burghardt Du Bois, died on May 24, 1899, from diphtheria. He was not yet two years old. Du Bois could not find a black doctor to care for the child, and white doctors refused to treat black patients.

Chapter XII: Of Alexander Crummell

1. (p. 155) *dragged it into the middle of a swamp:* Before attending Oneida, Crummell attended Noyes Academy in New Hampshire; he was forced to leave when a white mob dragged one of the school's buildings into a swamp.

2. (p. 156) *cannot admit a Negro:* Benjamin T. Onderdonk, bishop of the Episcopal Church, turned Crummell away from the Episcopal General Theological Seminary in New York.

3. (p. 160) *sought a new heaven and a new earth:* Crummell moved to Liberia, where he lived and worked from 1853 to 1872.

Chapter XIV: The Sorrow Songs

1. (p. 180) *what its words may mean:* Du Bois's biographer David Levering Lewis notes that the lyrics are similar to a song from Senegambia, in the Wolof language, about confinement and captivity. Lewis translates the phrase "Gene me, gene me!" as "Get me out, get me out!"

2. (p. 187) *Before the Pilgrims:* The first Africans arrived in Jamestown, Virginia, in 1619. The Pilgrims landed at Plymouth Rock, Massachusetts, in 1620.

INSPIRED BY
THE SOULS OF BLACK FOLK

Politics

In 1905 W. E. B. Du Bois formed an organization of black intellectuals known as the Niagara Movement, which promoted an agenda that differed in its basic assumptions from that of Booker T. Washington, as exemplified in a speech he gave in 1895. Washington believed that blacks should first better themselves economically, then seek social equality. Du Bois's view was that blacks should strive immediately not only for economic equality but also for political and social rights on a par with those of whites.

In a political context, *The Souls of Black Folk* stands as a historical document that outlines Du Bois's incipient philosophy of political, civil, and social rights for black people, a philosophy he would later preach to the thirty chapters of the Niagara Movement. In 1908, with the Springfield Race Riot, the Niagara Movement became increasingly militant. Du Bois invited white liberals to join the organization, and in 1909 the National Association for the Advancement of Colored People (NAACP) eclipsed the Niagara Movement, which formally dissolved in 1910. For decades thereafter, the NAACP's Legal Defense and Education Fund served as the primary legal safeguard for the civil rights movement, helping to win landmark cases like *Brown v. Board of Education* (1954), which acknowledged and reversed the inherent inequality of enforced segregation in public schools.

Literature and the Arts

Along with James Weldon Johnson's *Autobiography of an Ex-Coloured Man* (1912), W. E. B. Du Bois's *The Souls of Black Folk* was a forerunner of the Harlem Renaissance, a primarily literary movement that gave voice to numerous talented black writers. Du Bois's tripartite demand for the right to vote, civic equality, and the education of youth according to ability catalyzed an artistic awakening among African Americans. In the introduction to the anthology *The New Negro* (1925)—which included works by Claude McKay, Jean Toomer, Countee Cullen, Zora Neale Hurston, and Langston Hughes—philosopher and intellectual Alain Locke called for a collective expression of this newly defined black person. In the literary community that emerged in the wake of this manifesto, those writers and many more produced poetry and prose that celebrated an African heritage and chronicled the American black experience. The literature of the Harlem Renaissance, along with closely related developments in African-American music, theater, and art, has inspired subsequent generations of black writers and artists.

COMMENTS & QUESTIONS

In this section, we aim to provide the reader with an array of perspectives on the text, as well as questions that challenge those perspectives. The commentary has been culled from sources as diverse as reviews contemporaneous with the work, letters written by the author, literary criticism of later generations, and appreciations written throughout history. Following the commentary, a series of questions seeks to filter W. E. B. Du Bois's The Souls of Black Folk *through a variety of points of view and bring about a richer understanding of this enduring work.*

Comment

NEW YORK TIMES
It is generally conceded that Booker T. Washington represents the best hope of the negro in America, and it is certain that of all the leaders of his people he has done the most for his fellows with the least friction with the whites who are most nearly concerned, those of the South. Here is another negro "educator," to use a current term, not brought up like Washington among the negroes of the South and to the manner of the Southern negro born, but one educated in New England—one who never saw a negro camp-meeting till he was grown to manhood and went among the people of his color as a teacher. Naturally he does not see everything as Booker Washington does; probably he does not understand his own people in their natural state as does the other; certainly he cannot understand the Southern white's point of view as the principal of Tuskegee does. Yet it is equally certain that "The Souls of Black Folk" throws much light upon the complexities of the negro problem, for it shows that the key note of at least some negro aspiration is still the abolition of the social color-line. For it is the Jim Crow car, and the fact that he may not smoke a cigar and drink

a cup of tea with the white man in the South, that most galls William E. Burghardt Du Bois of the Atlanta College for Negroes. That this social color-line must in time vanish like the mists of the morning is the firm belief of the writer, as the opposite is the equally firm belief of the Southern white man; but in the meantime he admits the "hard fact" that the color-line is, and for a long time must be.

The book is of curious warp and woof, and the poetical form of the title is the index to much of its content and phraseology. To a Southerner who knows the negro race as it exists in the South, it is plain that this negro of Northern education is, after all, as he says, "bone of the bone and flesh of the flesh" of the African race. Sentimental, poetical, picturesque, the acquired logic and the evident attempt to be critically fair-minded is strangely tangled with these racial characteristics and the racial rhetoric: After an eloquent appeal for a fair hearing in what he calls his "Forethought," he goes in some detail into the vexed history of the Freedman's Bureau and the work it did for good and ill; for he admits the ill as he insists upon the good. A review of such a work from the negro point of view, even the Northern negro's point of view, must have its value to any unprejudiced student—still more, perhaps, for the prejudiced who is yet willing to be a student. It is impossible here to give even a general idea of the impression that will be gained from reading the text, but the underlying idea seems to be that it was impossible for the negro to get justice in the Southern courts just after the war, and "almost equally" impossible for the white man to get justice in the extra judicial proceeding of the Freedman's Bureau officials which largely superseded the courts for a time. Much is remembered of these proceedings by older Southerners—much picturesque and sentimental fiction, with an ample basis of truth, has been written about them by Mr. Thomas Nelson Page and others. Here we have the other side.

When all is said, the writer of "The Souls of Black Folk" is sure that the only side interference of which the Freedman's Bureau was the chief instrument was necessary for the negro's protection from supposed attempts of his former masters to legislate him back into another form of slavery, yet he admits that "it failed to begin the establishment of good-will between ex-masters and freedmen." It is proper to place beside this, of course, the consensus of fair Southern opinion that the interference in question and the instrumentalities it employed were the cause of the establishment of an ill-will previously non-existent. Here is a point where Booker T. Washington, as a Southern negro, has the advantage of his present critic in this that he knows by inherited tradition what the actual antebellum feeling between the races was. Du Bois assumes hostility.

While the whole book is interesting, especially to a Southerner, and while the self-restraint and temperateness of the manner of stating even things which the Southerner regards as impossibilities, deserve much praise and disarm harsh criticism, the part of the book which is more immediately concerned with an arraignment of the present plans of Booker T. Washington is for the present the most important.

In this matter the writer, speaking, as he says, for many educated negroes, makes two chief objections—first, that Washington is the leader of his race not by the suffrage of that race, but rather by virtue of the support of the whites, and, second, that by yielding to the modern commercial spirit and confining the effort for uplifting the individual to practical education and the acquisition of property and decent ways, he is after all cutting off the negro from those higher aspirations which only, Du Bois says, make a people great. For instance, it is said that Booker Washington distinctly asks that black people give up, at least for the present, three things: first, political power; second, insistence on civil rights; third, higher education for negro youth, and concentrate all their energies on industrial education, the accumulation of wealth, and the conciliation of the South. This policy has been courageously and insistently advocated for over fifteen years, and has been triumphant for perhaps ten years. As a result of this tender of the palm branch what has been the return? In these years there have occurred: 1. The disenfranchisement of the negro. 2. The legal creation of a distinct status of civil inferiority for the negro. 3. The steady withdrawal of aid from institutions for the higher training of the negro.

These movements are not, to be sure, direct results of Washington's teachings, but his propaganda has, without a shadow of a doubt, helped their speedier accomplishment.

The writer admits to the great value of Booker Washington's work. However, he does not believe so much in the gospel of the lamb, and does think that a bolder attitude, one of standing firmly upon rights guaranteed by the war amendments, and alluded to in complementary fashion in the Declaration of Independence, is both more becoming to a race such as he conceives the negro race to be, and more likely to advance that race. "We feel in conscience bound," he says, "to ask three things: 1, The right to vote; 2, Civic equality; 3, The education of youth according to ability" and he is especially insistent on the higher education of the negro—going into some statistics to show what the negro can do in that way. The value of these arguments and the force of the statistics can best be judged after the book is read.

Many passages of the book will be very interesting to the student of the negro character who regards the race ethnologically and not politically, not as a dark cloud threatening the future of the United States, but as a peculiar people, and one, after all, but little understood by the best of its friends or the worst of its enemies outside of what the author of "The Souls of Black Folk" is fond of calling the "Awful Veil." Throughout it should be recalled that it is the thought of a negro of Northern education who has lived long among his brethren of the South yet who cannot fully feel the meaning of some things which these brethren know by instinct—and which the Southern-bred knows by a similar instinct; certain things which are—by both accepted as facts—not theories—fundamental attitudes of race to race which are the product of conditions extending over centuries, as are the somewhat parallel attitudes of the gentry to the peasantry in other countries.

—April 25, 1903

Questions

1. What do you think about the *Times'* constant reference to the perspective of the Southerner (both white and black)? Does this interpretation tend to narrow the scope of *The Souls of Black Folk?*

2. The article claims that Du Bois, because he is northern, does not have an empirical understanding of relations between the

races and therefore must "assume hostility." Does Du Bois have this attitude? If so, how would it affect his claim that *Souls* is a methodological study?

3. How does this review distinguish Du Bois from Booker T. Washington, and is this different from how Du Bois differentiates himself from Washington? Do you think the article is racist?

4. Does Du Bois have a prose style of his own? How would you describe it? Think about his choice of words, and his use of allusion, rhythm, and repetition.

5. Does Du Bois's argument in *The Souls of Black Folk* ring true? Are there places where he manipulates the evidence to make his point?

6. Do you think that relations today between blacks and whites are mostly the same or markedly different in the North and in the South?

FOR FURTHER READING

Autobiographies, Biographies, and Correspondence

Aptheker, Herbert. *The Correspondence of W. E. B. Du Bois*. Vol. 1, *Selections, 1877–1934*. Amherst: University of Massachusetts Press, 1997.

Du Bois, W. E. B. *The Autobiography of W. E. B. Du Bois: A Soliloquy on Viewing My Life from the Last Decade of Its First Century*. New York: International Publishers, 1968.

———. *Dusk of Dawn: An Essay Toward an Autobiography of a Race Concept*. 1940. Reprint: New York: Schocken Books, 1968.

Lewis, David Levering. *W. E. B. Du Bois*. Vol. 2, *The Fight for Equality and the American Century 1919–1963*. New York: Henry Holt, 2000.

———, ed. *W. E. B. Du Bois: A Reader*. New York: Henry Holt, 1995.

Marable, Manning. *W. E. B. Du Bois: Black Radical Democrat*. Boston: Twayne Publishers, 1986.

Sundquist, Eric J., ed. *The Oxford W. E. B. Du Bois Reader*. New York: Oxford University Press, 1996.

Secondary Critical Sources

Baker, Houston, Jr. "The Black Man of Culture: W. E. B. Du Bois and *The Souls of Black Folk*." In his *Long Black Song*. Charlottesville: University of Virginia Press, 1972.

Gates, Henry Louis, Jr. "Preface." In *The Souls of Black Folk: Authoritative Text, Contexts, Criticism*, edited by Henry Louis Gates, Jr., and Terri Hume Oliver. New York: W. W. Norton, 1999.

James, Joy. *Transcending the Talented Tenth: Black Leaders and American Intellectuals.* New York: Routledge, 1997.

Rampersad, Arnold. *The Art and Imagination of W. E. B. Du Bois.* Cambridge, MA: Harvard University Press, 1976.

Stepto, Robert B. "The Quest for the Weary Traveler: W. E. B. Du Bois." In his *From Behind the Veil: A Study of Afro-American Narrative.* Urbana: University of Illinois Press, 1979.

Sundquist, Eric J. "Swing Low: *The Souls of Black Folk.*" In his *To Wake the Nations: Race in the Making of American Literature.* Cambridge, MA: Harvard University Press, 1993.

West, Cornel. "W. E. B. Du Bois: The Jamesian Organic Intellectual." In his *The American Evasion of Philosophy: A Genealogy of Pragmatism.* Madison: University of Wisconsin Press, 1989.

Zamir, Shamoon. *Dark Voices: W. E. B. Du Bois and American Thought, 1888–1903.* Chicago: University of Chicago Press, 1995.

Additional Works Cited in the Introduction

Carby, Hazel V. *Race Men.* Cambridge, MA: Harvard University Press, 1998.

Du Bois, W. E. B. "The Study of Negro Problems." *The Annals of the American Academy of Political and Social Science* (Summer 2000). Originally published in *The Annals of the American Academy of Political and Social Science* (January 1898).

Lewis, David Levering. *W. E. B. Du Bois.* Vol. 1, *Biography of a Race, 1868–1919.* New York: Henry Holt, 1993.

Monteiro, Anthony. "Being an African in the World: The Du Boisian Epistemology." *The Annals of the American Academy of Political and Social Science* (March 2000), pp. 236–249.

Savage, Barbara. "W. E. B. Du Bois and 'The Negro Church.'" *The Annals of the American Academy of Political and Social Science* (March 2000), pp. 235–249.